Changes

Changes

STORIES ABOUT

Transformation

FROM THE
FLANNERY O'CONNOR AWARD
FOR SHORT FICTION

EDITED BY
ETHAN LAUGHMAN

THE UNIVERSITY OF GEORGIA PRESS
ATHENS

© 2021 by the University of Georgia Press
Athens, Georgia 30602
www.ugapress.org
All rights reserved
Designed by Kaelin Chappell Broaddus
Set in 9/13.5 Walbaum

Most University of Georgia Press titles are
available from popular e-book vendors.

Printed digitally

Library of Congress Control Number: 2020950823
ISBN: 9780820358697 (pbk.: alk. paper)
ISBN: 9780820358703 (ebook)

CONTENTS

ACKNOWLEDGMENTS

The stories in this volume are from the following award-winning collections published by the University of Georgia Press:

David Walton, *Evening Out* (1983); "ReLayTah" appeared in *Evening Out* as "Synaphongenuphon"

Melissa Pritchard, *Spirit Seizures* (1987)

Philip F. Deaver, *Silent Retreats* (1988)

T. M. McNally, *Low Flying Aircraft* (1991); "Paris, the Easy Way" first appeared in *Puerto Del Sol*

Gina Ochsner, *The Necessary Grace to Fall* (2002); "Eulogy for Red" first appeared in the *Crab Orchard Review*

Catherine Brady, *Curled in the Bed of Love* (2003)

Greg Downs, *Spit Baths* (2006)

Peter LaSalle, *Tell Borges If You See Him* (2007); "Where We Last Saw Time" first appeared in the *New England Review*

Lori Ostlund, *The Bigness of the World* (2009); "Upon Completion of Baldness" first appeared in *Hobart*

Amina Gautier, *At-Risk* (2011); "Dance for Me" first appeared in *Southwest Review* and was reprinted in *Best African American Fiction 2009*

Hugh Sheehy, *The Invisibles* (2012); "A Difficult Age" first appeared in *Saint Ann's Review*

Jacquelin Gorman, *The Viewing Room* (2013); "Ghost Dance" first appeared in *Slake: Los Angeles*

Tom Kealey, *Thieves I've Known* (2013); "Thieves I've Known" first appeared as "Bones" in *Prairie Schooner*

Kirsten Sundberg Lunstrum, *What We Do with the Wreckage* (2018)

A thank you also goes to the University of Georgia Main Library staff for technical support in preparing the stories for publication.

INTRODUCTION

The Flannery O'Connor Award for Short Fiction was established in 1981 by Paul Zimmer, then the director of the University of Georgia Press, and press acquisitions editor Charles East. East would serve as the first series editor, judging the competition and selecting two collections to publish each year. The inaugural volumes in the series, *Evening Out* by David Walton and *From the Bottom Up* by Leigh Allison Wilson, appeared in 1983 to critical acclaim. Nancy Zafris (herself a Flannery O'Connor Award–winner for her 1990 collection *The People I Know*) was the second series editor, serving in the role from 2008 to 2015. Zafris was succeeded by Lee K. Abbott in 2016, and Roxane Gay then assumed the role, choosing award winners beginning in 2019. Competition for the award has become an important proving ground for writers, and the press has published seventy-five volumes to date, helping to showcase talent and sustain interest in the short story form. These volumes together feature approximately eight hundred stories by authors based across the United States and abroad. It has been my pleasure to have read each and every one.

The idea of undertaking a project that could honor the diversity of the series' stories but also present them in a unified way had been hanging around the press for a few years. What occurred to us first, and what remained the most appealing approach, was to pull the hundreds of stories out of their current

packages—volumes of collected stories by individual authors—
and regroup them by common themes or subjects. After finishing an editorial internship at the press, I was brought on to the
project and began to sort the stories into specific thematic cate-
gories. What followed was a deep dive into the award and its history as well as a gratifying acquaintance with the many authors
whose works constitute the award's legacy.

Anthologies are not new to the series. A tenth-anniversary collection, published in 1993, showcased one story from each of the
volumes published in the award's first decade. A similar collection appeared in 1998, the fifteenth year of the series. In 2013, the
year of the series' thirtieth anniversary, the press published two
volumes modeled after the tenth- and fifteenth-anniversary volumes. These anthologies together included one story from each
of the fifty-five collections published up to that point. One of the
2013 volumes represented the series' early years, under the editorship of Charles East. The other showcased the editorship of
Nancy Zafris. In a nod to the times, both thirtieth-anniversary
anthologies appeared in e-book form only.

The present project is completely different in concept and
scale. The press has reached across nearly eight hundred stories and more than forty volumes to assemble stories that speak
to specific themes, from love to death to holidays to transforma-
tion. Each volume has aimed to collect exemplary treatments of
its theme, but with enough variety to give an overview what the
Flannery O'Connor Award–winning stories as a collective are
about. If the press has succeeded, the volumes illustrate the var-
ied perspectives multiple authors can have on a single theme.

Each volume, no matter its central theme, includes the work
of authors whose stories celebrate the variety of short fiction
styles to be found across the history of the award. Just as Flannery O'Connor is more than just a southern writer, the University of Georgia Press, by any number of measures, has been more
than a regional publisher for some time. As the first series edi-

tor, Charles East, happily reported in his anthology of the O'Connor Award stories, the award "managed to escape [the] pitfall" of becoming a regional stereotype. When Paul Zimmer established the award he named it after Flannery O'Connor as the writer who best embodied the possibilities of the short-story form. In addition, O'Connor, with her connections to the South and readership across the globe, spoke to the ambitions of the press at a time when it was poised to ramp up both the number and scope of its annual title output. The O'Connor name has always been a help in keeping the series a place where writers strive to be published and where readers and critics look for quality short fiction.

The award has become an internationally recognized institution. The seventy-five (and counting) Flannery O'Connor Award authors come from all parts of the United States and abroad. They have lived in Arizona, Arkansas, California, Colorado, Georgia, Indiana, Maryland, Massachusetts, Texas, Utah, Washington, Canada, Iran, England, and elsewhere. Some have written novels. Most have published stories in a variety of literary quarterlies and popular magazines. They have been awarded numerous fellowships and prizes. They are world-travelers, lecturers, poets, columnists, editors, and screenwriters.

There are risks in the thematic approach we are taking with these anthologies, and we hope that readers will not take our editorial approach as an attempt to draw a circle around certain aspects of a story or in any way close off possibilities for interpretation. Great stories don't have to resolve anything, be set any particular time nor place, or be written in any one way. Great stories don't have to *be* anything. Still, when a story resonates with enough readers in a certain way, it is safe to say that it has spoken to us meaningfully about, for instance, love, death, and certain concerns, issues, pleasures, or life events.

We at the press had our own ideas about how the stories might be gathered, but we were careful to get author input on the process. The process of categorizing their work was not easy for any of them. Some truly agonized. Having their input was invaluable; having their trust was humbling. The goal of this project is to faithfully represent these stories despite the fact that they have been pulled from their original collections and are now bedmates with stories from a range of authors taken from diverse contexts. Also, just because a single story is included in a particular volume does not mean that that volume is the only place that story could have appropriately been placed. For example, "Sawtelle" from Dennis Hathaway's *The Consequences of Desire* tells the story of a subcontractor in duress when he finds out his partner is the victim of an extramarital affair. We have included it in the volume of stories about love, but it could have been included in those on work, friends, and immigration without seeming out of place.

In *Creating Flannery O'Connor*, Daniel Moran writes that O'Connor first mentioned her infatuation with peacocks in her essay "Living with a Peacock" (later republished as "King of the Birds"). Since the essay's appearance, a proliferation of critics and admirers have linked O'Connor with imagery derived from the bird's distinctive features, and one can now hardly find an O'Connor publication that does not depict or refer to her "favorite fowl" and its association with immortality and layers of symbolic and personal meaning. As Moran notes, "Combining elements of her life on a farm, her religious themes, personal eccentricities, and outsider status, the peacock has proved the perfect icon for O'Connor's readers, critics, and biographers, a form of reputation-shorthand that has only grown more ubiquitous over time."

We are pleased to offer these anthologies as another way of continuing Flannery O'Connor's legacy. Since its conception, thirty-nine years' worth of enthralling, imaginative, and thought-provoking fiction has been published under the name of the Flannery O'Connor Award. The award is just one way that we hope to continue the conversation about O'Connor and her legacy while also circulating and sharing recent authors' work throughout the world.

It is perhaps unprecedented for such a long-standing short fiction award series to republish its works in the manner we are going about it. The idea for the project may be unconventional, but it draws on an established institution—the horn-of-plenty that constitutes the Flannery O'Connor Award series backlist—that is still going strong as it approaches its fortieth year. I am in equal parts intimidated and honored to present you with what I consider to be these exemplars of the Flannery O'Connor Award. Each story speaks to the theme uniquely. Some of these stories were chosen for their experimental nature, others for their unique take on the theme, and still others for exhibiting matchlessness in voice, character, place, time, plot, relevance, humor, timelessness, perspective, or any of the thousand other metrics by which one may measure a piece of literature.

But enough from me. Let the stories speak for themselves.

ETHAN LAUGHMAN

Changes

Ghost Dance

JACQUELIN GORMAN

From *The Viewing Room* (2013)

It was late on Sunday night, Mother's Day, a day that had already seemed endless, when Henrietta, the chaplain on call for the hospital, received an urgent page to come to the patient in Room 204, who had requested spiritual support. Birdie, an elderly Pima Indian woman in the end stages of diabetic kidney failure, took up both of the room's hospital beds. With her own four hundred plus pounds and all the dialysis equipment, she needed a double room all to herself. The sole surviving member of her family, she had been airlifted from her reservation in Arizona in hopes of receiving a kidney transplant. Once she'd arrived, her condition had steadily deteriorated, disqualifying her as an eligible organ recipient. She would never be medically stable enough to be flown back home to die.

So she had received no outside visitors and soon began treating the hospital staff as if they were there for the sole purpose of keeping her entertained, like a twenty-four-hour revolving-door slumber party. She was a delightful storyteller and compassionate listener, but only a stalwart few managed to stay in her room for longer than a few minutes. Birdie was dying a slow and painful death, and the smell of her rotting body had become unbearable.

Henrietta put two drops of citrus aromatherapy oil underneath each nostril and rubbed more into her palms before she walked in. She rested her hand on Birdie's shoulder and glanced at her face. The jaundice from the failing liver had mixed with the dark magenta undertones of her skin, giving it a purple sheen. Her sightless eyes were open wide, staring straight ahead, the opaque irises and pupils spilling into the yellow-whites. Birdie's pupils, unable to take in any light, somehow managed to reflect light outward, flashing in strobe-like blinks. In the dark of the room, the rest of her body also glowed, wide and flat, wrapped in white gauze, splayed on the jumbo-sized metal serving tray of the two linked gurneys. She put her hands, webbed by the bandages into oversized paws, over her face when Henrietta touched her.

"I'm sorry, Birdie, did I wake you up?"

Henrietta noticed that Birdie's eyeglasses were on the side table. Hope in solid form, or "wearing the prayer," as Maurice, another chaplain and Henrietta's new best friend, often said. She had been visiting Birdie soon after Birdie had gone blind, trying to provide comfort, when Maurice came in with the eyeglasses and plopped them right on her face, without a word of warning. Hadn't he learned about announcing oneself before approaching blind patients? But as always, Maurice was the true visionary. The weight of those glasses on her nose transformed Birdie's face with an expression of absolute rapture, like someone under a hypnotic trance.

"I just had the most wonderful dream, Henny! And I was standing on my tiptoes again, looking up at a tall, handsome man. That was the best part," Birdie said.

"Tell me more," Henrietta responded, her holy trinity of words, never failing to air out even the most stifling of conversations. "Tell me more about your dream, sweetie," she whispered.

"Well, you'll love this one, Henny-girl. Big old me was wearing a size-four dress and high-heeled red shoes, and we were ghost dancing. Don't recall his face, but I could see his hands, big and strong. I could see his hands close around my waist, which in my dream, by the way, was so itty-bitty that his fingers could touch together at my back, and his thumbs touch together at my front. Now can you just imagine that?"

"It sounds lovely, Birdie."

"Oh, it was! Now you can tell that Chaplain Maurice he doesn't have to find me those red dancing shoes anymore but they already came up in my dream, right? Ask and you shall receive, right?"

Henrietta had been visiting Birdie for three months now, always on Sunday afternoons while still dressed in her church clothes and kitten-heeled pumps, so Birdie usually heard her coming down the hallway. But today she had stayed home from church and was wearing soft-soled moccasins. Birdie had told her how much she missed wearing pretty shoes, ever since her toes had been amputated. The gangrene wounds in her feet refused to heal. Henrietta glanced at Birdie's huge mummylike legs. The flesh-eating infection was moving quickly, but it had a lot of territory to cover. She could measure Birdie's prognosis by where the dry bandages ended and the weeping pus-filled ones began, like a moving demarcation line. It was now at the very top of her thighs, within inches of her femoral artery. It would not be much longer now.

"Birdie?" She stared at Birdie's chest and held her breath waiting for it to move. "Birdie?" she called out louder, her voice shaking with panic.

"Here. I'm still here," Birdie answered finally, and Henrietta closed her eyes in a silent prayer of thanks.

"You know, Henny-girl, I was thinking the silliest thing about you and me. How it's almost like we got our names switched way back when. Here I am, the one who looks more like a big-assed, clucking mother hen, and here you are, that Maurice has told me all about you, as tiny and light as a sparrow's feather. I guess you should have the name Birdie . . ."

"I'd been meaning to ask where you got . . ."

"Real name is Bird Chaser. Won't trouble you with the Indian word."

"Bird Chaser?"

"Oh, yes. And I grew my way into that name, for sure, I'm telling you true! I got a job for the Park Service in the canyon. Me running around, flapping and clapping my hands, and you better believe I chased those condors away from tourists and a few tourists away from the condors just so they wouldn't start trusting us idiots. Just leads to stupid killing. Not the condors, God knows, they don't kill."

"I've never seen a condor, but I'm sure they're beautiful."

Birdie laughed. "Oh, no, Henny, I know you haven't seen one, because they are sure not beautiful! They're just as ugly and fat and slumped over as I am! Big turkey vultures, lazy old things, who wait for the other, quicker birds like eagles to do the killing, and then wait and eat the leftovers."

Henrietta's stomach lurched. This conversation was not going in a positive direction, and she just could not handle talking about death. Even if it was her job to talk about whatever the patient wanted. Please not tonight. Not when she missed her own mother so much.

"I didn't hear you spray when you first came in," Birdie said. "Go catch yourself a fresh breeze."

Henrietta walked over to the window and surveyed the collection of stuffed toy birds lined up on the ledge, each perched in front of a canister of room deodorizer. Birdie called it her "show and smell" display. It was a rite of passage for all who entered her contaminated space to choose one and spray it. The ritual had little or no practical effect. The spray did not touch the odor from Birdie's body. The only thing that helped at all were the discreetly placed trays of cat litter under her bed, which were changed every few hours with her colostomy bag.

The room freshener collection kept growing, but not as fast as Birdie's disease, which affected over half of the members of her tribe. Both her parents and older brothers and sisters had died of diabetes, all wheelchair bound at the end. Birdie never had breathing space between their deaths to fall in love and start her own family. Henrietta had already grown to love her as a surrogate mother. Birdie's warm spirit melted all professional boundaries away.

Henrietta reached for her favorite and sprayed it above her head, deeply inhaling the lushness of Tangerine Tango. She closed her eyes, pretending she had wandered into a tropical garden. For a few seconds, there was blessed relief from air that was worse than anything she had ever encountered in her months of chaplaincy, in the viewing room, in the emergency room, even in the morgue during an autopsy. She had learned this much. It was not the smell of death that was unbearable, but the smell of life spoiling away. She sprayed again and twirled in the fresh mist, dreaming of Birdie's dancing partner spinning her.

"Better, now?" Birdie asked. "Can you stand to stay with me for a while?"

"Of course, sweetie. It's not that bad."

"Not that bad? Really? Don't lie to me, Hen. This old carcass of mine hasn't seen the inside of a shower or tub in over two years. Mother Earth Spirit knows that even the sponges shrivel up and die when they come near me. But you know the worst part?"

"What is the worst part?" Henrietta asked, as she walked over to the bedside.

She cleared the visitor chair of two baskets, woven by Birdie's mother long ago and filled with medicine bundles. These were the only personal possessions Birdie had been allowed to bring with her because her weight had strained the helicopter's maximum load. The baskets were placed there so that Birdie could hear them being moved and be forewarned that someone had taken a seat. She smiled at the way Birdie started all her visits. Worst part/best part questions framed their pastoral conversations—and Henrietta was always eager to see how Birdie could come up with anything that qualified for best, as she lay there dying, rotting from the outside in.

"Here it is, then," Birdie said. "The worst part about being a sick, fat, smelly old woman that chases everybody away with her stink. The worst part is just being stuck inside of me. Where is a real out-of-body experience when you most need it?" Birdie sighed. "But the best part is that I don't have any more nightmares. In my dreams, I am always dancing." Birdie closed her eyes again, as if she could transport herself back into her party shoes by shutting the lids.

Henrietta was sure she had fallen asleep again, and not wanting to wake her from her dream, she started to get up from the chair.

"You remember what to do, right? When my time comes?" Birdie's eyes were open again, her lips tight, chin trembling.

"Yes, Birdie. I remember." Henrietta reached over and held Birdie's bandaged hand in hers.

Birdie had put the Spiritual Care office on alert that when she died she needed sage burned because the scent of sage, of the open prairies of her native lands, would carry her spirit back home. Henrietta had found sage incense sticks and left them in Birdie's bedside drawer. She could not light them, of course, or the smoke alarms would go off, but Birdie had said her soul would be so eager to leave, so quick to find an escape, that it would take only the spark of rubbing the sticks together.

"Don't worry, Birdie," Henrietta said. "I have everything ready . . . I mean . . ." She stammered, not wanting to sound as if she was rushing her out of the world.

"Oh, Henny, that's good, because I'm ready too! I've been getting ready for this for ages now. They don't call it morbid obesity for nothing! But I'm not scared, Hen. I want you to know that. And I'm not just saying that. Death doesn't scare me. It's been my shadow my whole life. You know how most people know they are going to die but don't really believe it? Not until it's right up front in their face?"

"Yes," Henrietta said.

It was true that people did not want to think about death, but she also believed that they did not have to think about how they were going to die. They simply had to think about how they wanted to live. Then the trick was to live that way up until the last moment, when they had to stop. She had seen fourteen patients die since she had become the on-call overnight weekend chaplain six weeks ago. And she remembered every one of them, exactly how they looked the moment life left their bodies and how they looked afterward. There was no such thing as resting in peace when it came to death. The peace had to be found in life or not at all. And somehow, Birdie had managed to find that kind of peace and spread it around her, sweetening every bit of space she occupied.

"I admire the way you are leaving us, Birdie. My mother always said that a lady should not be remembered for the grandness of her entrances, but for the gracefulness of her exits."

Birdie laughed. "Oh, I sure do love hearing about that mama of yours!" She scooped Henrietta's hand into both of hers.

"Tell me what color this week? Red or pink?"

Henrietta held the fingernails of her other hand up to the light coming from the window, not wanting to take away the one that Birdie was holding. They played this guessing game about the name of her nail polish. Last week was Cotton Candy Swirl and the week before was Strawberry Cream Dream. At first, she was embarrassed that so many colors had such vivid food associations. Birdie was on a feeding tube and had not tasted a meal in over a year. But she soon discovered that Birdie was delighted to talk about food, smell food, and even found a way to taste it, when the nurses would bring in different flavored lip balms for her. The scent of Café-au-Lait never failed to pick up her spirits, no matter the time of day or night.

"Pink again," Henrietta said.

"But what kind of pink? Tell me the name of it! C'mon, tell me . . ."

Henrietta examined her nails, trying to remember. The color was very pale pink, with a metallic sheen and a touch of gold sparkles. Pink Champagne Bubbles? No, that was not it. Something to do with evening dreams.

"Sunset Reverie," she blurted out, finally remembering.

"Oh, yes!" Birdie exclaimed. "That's perfect."

"Yes," Henrietta said. She sighed again, and it surprised them both when it came out like a moan.

"You are sad tonight, dearie. What is it?"

Henrietta was ashamed and hesitated to tell her the truth. Here she was, the comforter needing comforting. But she never lied to Birdie.

"Oh, you know. I'm sorry. It's the Mother's Day thing."

She did not need to say more, because they had both lost their mothers years ago.

"Oh, Henny—that reminds me! I just got a special Mother's Day treat for you! It's called French Vanilla, although what's French about it, I have no idea, unless it just smells fattening and rich, like something wonderful and buttery baking in the oven. Go bring me over a whiff of that! It may even cheer us both up."

Henrietta went over to the windowsill again, found the air freshener, and sprayed it around Birdie's bed.

"The Pet Therapy trainer brought me that," Birdie said. "And you know one thing for sure—she's the expert around here on how to get rid of nasty odors fast."

Henrietta laughed, the vanilla scent filling her with sudden joy. She was touched that Birdie had remembered that this was her favorite childhood memory, when her mother would bake her vanilla custards on snow days back in Maine. But then Birdie remembered every person's story and always found a way to give it back later, wrapped in her own kind of motherly love.

"But those dogs are so well groomed!" Henrietta said. Her favorite was Her Majesty, the Great White Pyrenees, with her gleaming silky white coat. She was as large as a miniature horse but so light on her feet that she floated down the hospital corridors like a cloud. "Not Her Majesty? She smells like a rain shower!"

"No, it's that sweet old Golden Retriever. Not his fault, but he is starting to lose control of his bowels," Birdie said. "Apparently that's a real problem on these elevators, worse than a fart in a sweat lodge . . . I don't need to tell you! The poor old thing is too arthritic to go up the stairs. I do love that dog. He sparks me. You know the one I mean?"

"Mr. Right."

Everyone knew his name. The pet therapist who owned him had been married and divorced five times. She had given up on the male species of the human population.

"That's his name, you bet it is! Mr. Right has made a promise to me . . . to save a spot next to him in Heaven if he gets there first. It's a race too close to call, because I can smell his body going to seed as fast as mine. You know the best part about him?"

Henrietta shook her head and then remembered that Birdie could not see her. "No, tell me the best part, sweetie."

"Quite simple really. Mr. Right is the first male I ever met that doesn't care that I smell so bad. As a matter of fact that only makes him love me more, don't you think?"

"Yes. But the truth is that everyone here loves you, Birdie."

And this truth was in plain view. The windowsill was overflowing with gifts, each staff member who had met her trying to figure out a way to stay in the room without gagging. Birdie welcomed every one of them, no matter what each one had to do to her—awful things: scraping off dead flesh, changing burning catheters, pushing and pulling folds of her skin back and forth to expose the bedsores to the air. And yet she appeared grateful for each and every person who came into her room, thanking them for their care, and remembered each name, each person's family, each person's story. She was the unofficial chaplain in this hospital, Maurice had often told her.

"Yes, you hospital people are my family now. Still, nobody loves us the way our mamas love us, right? Mama's here now. Right here with us. Don't you see her? Standing right next to you?"

Henrietta was worried again. She had never heard Birdie talk like this before. Whose mother did Birdie think was in the room with them? She was afraid to ask. If Birdie saw her own mother, that would mean she was dying for sure, and if she was seeing Henrietta's mother, someone she had never met, then her mind was going, and the rest would quickly follow.

"I'm not sure I understand, Birdie. You can feel another presence here, like a ghost?"

"Sure can! Ghost, angel, whatever you want to call it. She's been here all day. That's why I had the nurse page you. I wanted you to meet her."

Henrietta started to look around the room. She did not believe in ghosts, but she did believe in Birdie's ability to see with the eyes of the spirit.

"But how do you know someone else is here now if you can't see anything?"

As soon as she said this, Henrietta wished she could suck the words out of the air back into her throat, or spray something on them to make them sound less harsh, less judgmental. She knew better than to argue a patient out of her delusion, particularly one that was giving her so much pleasure. Birdie did not say a word. Had Henrietta ruined her dream?

"Listen to me, now," Birdie interrupted, turning her face back toward Henrietta, her blind eyes neon yellow lasers, roving the room, searching for a target. "You don't have to be sorry. But I want you to know that I don't have to see her to know she is here. And you understand it better than anybody else in this hospital."

"I'm sorry, Birdie. I know that God's presence can't be seen, but I thought you were talking about people." Dead people, she wanted to add, but held back.

"Yes, but my people believe that spirits are like the wind, or maybe they are part of the wind, and we can only see the change the wind makes in the trees, and feel and smell the difference in the air when it moves."

As soon as Birdie said this, Henrietta felt the air thickening and settling in around them. Then she felt a gentle pressure at the back of her neck, and around her shoulders, as if layers of warming blankets were being wrapped around her.

"You see?" Birdie said.

"Yes," Henrietta said. "I see."

The wheels at the bottom of the beds began to squeak. Birdie's whole body was shaking.

"Are you feeling all right, Birdie? Are you in any pain?"

"No pain!" she exclaimed. "And better than all right. Better! This old body hasn't felt this good in so many years, but I can't wait to let it go. I told that organ donation guy yesterday . . . that if anybody wants any piece of it . . . well, then, they are welcome to it! Leave it out on those canyons and have those condors give me a big send-off! Sky burial."

"Or maybe, you don't have to have a body at all, Birdie." Henrietta wanted to fly with her now. "You will be weightless, like air."

"I like that, Henny-girl, I do!"

Birdie sank deep into the mattress. Her eyes were closed and she began to hum to herself. Then she stopped and raised her head slightly, turning toward Henrietta.

"Hey there. You want to know what I've been thinking about? I've been thinking about what Heaven smells like!"

"Really? And what do you think it smells like?"

"Why nothing at all! That's what I think," Birdie said, laughing. She had clearly given this a lot of thought. "It will be like God's breath. That's what keeps me going down here . . . to think that every piece the docs take off of me just brings me closer and closer to being no body at all . . . so I can fly so lightly into that place where I will not smell bad ever again."

"Yes, I believe that, too, Birdie. That's lovely."

Birdie sat up suddenly again, looking straight ahead, holding her arms outstretched.

"Yes, I will!" Birdie shouted to the empty air. "Yes, I am going to be right there."

Henrietta rushed over to calm her, tried to embrace her, but Birdie was so large that Henrietta could not hold her or keep her from thrashing. Birdie's body was convulsing now, and she snapped her head back and forth and opened her eyes wide, now glistening an iridescent pale green. She shook so violently that the litter boxes beneath the beds rustled, making muffled, scurrying sounds.

An alarm screeched. It was Birdie's heart monitor. The nurse who had paged Henrietta rushed into the room and shut the machine off. She did not call a code because they all knew that Birdie was DNR.

And just like that, Birdie was gone. Henrietta felt as if she were suddenly caught in a cold draft of air and would never be warm again, the invisible blankets yanked off her shoulders. For a moment, she was paralyzed with shock and grief and could not think of what she should do next. But the nurse knew exactly what to do. She smoothed back Birdie's long hair from her face and removed each tube, one by one, from her still body.

Henrietta could not look at her any longer, but she had to keep her promise. She opened the drawer and rubbed the incense sticks together. She kept her eyes shut and felt a cool breeze as Birdie's final breath caught its sweet sage-scented ride home.

Birdie was never without visitors in the viewing room. For six-teen hours, staggered over all three hospital shifts, every staff member who had cared for her came in to see her one last time. And they lingered there, comforting one another, laughing and talking, not wanting the party to end. Birdie's enormous body had been completely bathed—the dialysis nursing unit's final gift to her. She smelled heavenly.

Where's an out-of-body experience when you really need one?

The last person to request a viewing was Maurice, who brought the Pet Therapy dog into the room with him. Mr. Right. Henrietta threw her arms around the dog's thick golden fur. He smelled like Maurice's cologne. She wasn't the first one to hug this dog today and certainly would not be the last. He was the kind of dog that Birdie used to say woke up with his tail wagging, thinking to himself, *Who gets to love me today?*

Maurice walked over to Birdie. He took something out of his forest-green, distressed-leather carrying case.

He unzipped Birdie's body bag, carefully and gently, peeling it back until her naked, mutilated feet were exposed. Then he placed two enormous white socks over them and then turned the socks around. There were bright red strappy sandals painted on them, and pretty, dainty feet, the skin rosy-toned, healthy, alive. And the *trompe l'oeil* toenails puffed up proudly, sparkly and shiny, dusted with a topcoat polish of pink and gold glitter. Sun-set Reverie.

After Maurice left, the only sound in the viewing room was Mr. Right's heavy panting. He continued to sniff around Bird-ie's head as if he were looking for a different smell, the one that only he had loved. He began to whine softly and then pawed at Henrietta's leg, impatiently, as if he wanted something from her. A treat of some kind? But she didn't have anything to give him. She looked down at him, holding her empty hands out to him, but he kept jerking his head back and forth between her and Birdie. It reminded her of the old Lassie shows, when the dog was always trying to tell the parents that Timmy was in some kind of trouble, stuck in a well or dangling off a cliff, and they needed to go save him. Then she knew what he wanted. She lifted the old dog in her arms and laid him gently on the gurney, standing against him like a human guardrail so he wouldn't fall. She held his warm body there with hers and closed her eyes. She had a vision then that would give her peace every time she remembered Birdie. In her mind's eye, she saw two kindred souls gracefully exit the stage together, one four-legged and the other with arms as big and wide as wings, sharing one last dance.

ReLayTah

DAVID WALTON

From *Evening Out* (1983)

Dr. Gossner stood alone at the rear of the room, several feet back from the final row of chairs, ear cocked, as if the more attentively to follow the table of five men seated at the front.

Dr. Gossner was John Hale Clark Professor of Psychology and Head of the Department of Psychology at Pennsylvania State University, a small, sparse, silver-headed man.

The time was 3:10 the afternoon of April 5, 1972, a Wednesday, the place the Viola Room of the Cincinnati Hilton, the occasion the fifth annual meeting of the Applied Systems Association, now in its third of four days.

The topic under discussion, mechanical self-determination.

Dr. Gossner passed his hand slowly back and forth in front of his face, as if to clear from his eyes some webby obstruction. The conference had not been going well for Dr. Gossner. Just that morning he had watched a man from UC Riverside demonstrate a mechanism shaped like a fire hydrant, that could run mazes and climb a circular staircase, that duplicated, and made redundant, Dr. Gossner's own work of the past four years.

Now all his body ached and burned as if from a fever, and spreading up the undersides of his arms he felt a sharp prickling, and in his ears a peculiar buzzing, an emptying out of sound, a sense of inner void that he was very soon going to have to put behind him, or else give over to entirely.

"—in this country," he heard one of the panelists say at that moment, "until we have something that can go in a car by itself and drive to Arizona."

Dr. Gossner turned a full circle around, gaping—amazed that nobody but himself in that room seemed to find anything so remarkable in those words. For him it was the moment of revelation, the moment of synthesis, "the one true inspiration in my life," he would write some time later.

Within the hour he reclaimed his car and started the drive back to Penn State; there he reassembled his staff, and within the week had begun negotiations for a new series of grants.

He taped a long sheet of butcher paper, what was to be the first of many long sheets of butcher paper, up across the front of the room, and began.

"I'm going from here to here. I'm going to tell you where we end up, and then I'm going back and tell you how we get there, and as I go along, I want to see hands of people that want to work in particular parts."

Dr. Gossner was sixty-three at the time, a man better admired for his skills of money-getting than for any claim to leadership. His wife had died the year before, and his daughters were both living on the west coast, and there had been talk, not too much before this, of him shortly retiring and going out there to join them. Many in the room were surprised by the extent of what he was now proposing.

"If you're concerned about that," he said, as questions began to be raised, "you'd best leave now. We don't have time for rhetorical exercises here."

He had been superseded before on earlier projects, and did not mean to be superseded here. He had decided to work in sequences of ten, ten models in a sequence, each sequence devoted to a single category of performance, each model in the sequence to an individual skill. The first sequence, for instance, was devoted to standing, walking, climbing, running, to skills of mobility, the second to skills of agility, such as jumping rope and operating simple machinery, the third to articulation and ratiocination, and so on through the last, the sixth sequence, where the emphasis all was on verisimilitude, pupil fluctuation, the working of the mucus membrane.

"Gilligan."

In fact it was not until the seventh sequence that the end, or what Dr. Gossner was willing to accept as an end of the project was reached. Each sequence had been designated by a letter, and each model in that sequence by a name beginning with that letter. As the seventh model in the seventh sequence, my own designation was Gilligan-G.

"Raise your left arm, Gilligan, very good. Now your right. Look to the left, please. Now your right."

We were in Dr. Gossner's office, he behind the desk, I on a straightbacked chair next to the door. Sometime after this Dr. Harley, Dr. Gossner's chief associate, told me that after the fifth sequence they'd stopped dismantling the shell every time, and were just "turning a few screws and remaindering a few tapes." The remaindering was never quite complete, however, so that on this occasion I retained impressions of earlier, similar occasions. Things seemed to weave and bob about, Dr. Gossner's voice to echo in my ears.

"Tell me now, Gilligan, if you can, what name we give to a resident of Afghanistan?"

"An Afghanistanian? An Afghanese? I'm not sure," I said.

He offered no response, but went on, through another thirty-four of these questions, most of them for some reason questions of geography. A number of these I had two or three answers I could give. Eight of them I had no answer for at all. I was convinced I would be sent back for another remaindering.

But at length he seemed satisfied, and put the sheet aside.

"We've taught you to recognize alternatives," he told me. "We've taught you the limits of your own ignorance. There's not much more, I don't suppose, we can hope to accomplish than that. Listen closely to me now, Gilligan, to what I tell you."

Parked behind the building, he told me, I would find a red Ford stationwagon, and in the glove compartment of the wagon an envelope containing eighty-five dollars in small cash, and three keys. Two of the keys would operate the car, the third unlock the door of an apartment in Phoenix, the address of which I would find written on the outside of the envelope.

I was to drive to Phoenix, by whatever route I chose, arriving at that address no later than Friday noon three days hence, and wait there until he telephoned me with further instructions.

He had retained until the end that image of his initial inspiration. Now the end had come, and yet it left him curiously joyless. I can understand, of course, how he would have adopted such a manner purposely, as a precaution against unwanted controls entering into the instructions. But still, I sensed disappointment there. I could read it in his eyes, feel it in the way, ever so slightly, he drew back from me in his chair. I wasn't what he wanted. Oh, I can see now where nothing would have pleased him, he was an experimentalist, a laboratory man, and any end of a project would have been a disappointment to him.

But at the time I was crushed. I walked out of there despondent, down the long hallway that led to the back door to the building, past the associates and all the graduate students crowded into their doorways, convinced of failure, certain I would prove a disappointment to them all.

That feeling soon dispelled, however, once I was out on the open highway. It was a warm, breezy May day. It had rained earlier in the day, but now the sun was out, and the air rich with the smell of turned earth and newly mown grass. The area around Penn

State is farmlands and pasture, long stretches of woodland and deep winding passes, and each new thing I encountered, every hedge and fence post that I passed, seemed to address me, filled me with exhilaration and a wild delight.

I headed south, intending to take the Turnpike west to New Stanton, and from there pick up 70 South.

As I turned up the access ramp, I passed a line of young people holding up signs that read *NYC* and *Chi WEST* and *Cape May NJ*. Back at the laboratory, during my inception drills, Dr. Harley and Dr. Cranston used to hold up similar signs for me, and ask me to frame the appropriate response.

I pulled up beside three girls holding a sign that said *Denver* and asked, "Would you three girls like a ride to Denver?"

That was the last I would see of Dr. Gossner, Drs. Harley and Cranston, and the laboratory for the next two years.

The girls' names I remember were Bonnie, Barbara, and Rosalie, and they were all from Rochester, New York. I don't remember much more about them than that. After I returned to the laboratory, it was thought better to eradicate my emotional capacities, with the result that all memories of any emotional content were eradicated. What remain now of that time are only some scattered bits and pieces.

I remember billboards, stretches of highway, doors and hallways; the peripheries of things. I remember riding in an open car in the hills above Mill Valley with Erwin and Colleen. I don't remember who Erwin and Colleen were exactly, or why or how long I'd been with them. I remember the date, August 22, a Tuesday.

The fog was settling in across the bay, and at one point we stopped and got out of the car and stood on the hillside watching it close in around the shoreline buildings, flying in long advance streamers up the hillside until within just a few minutes it had enveloped the spot where we were standing. We stood for some time longer, maybe for half an hour, and something was decided there, debated and decided, although I don't remember what it was.

I remember every roadside sign, every name on every mailbox on the ride back that afternoon, but not Erwin and Colleen's faces, or the sound or even the timbre of their voices.

I remember sitting at a table in a house in Ann Arbor with six people, their faces blurred as in a photograph a thumb has rubbed the features away, when the doorbell rang, and nobody would go to answer it. Nobody would look at me, or say a word.

This was shortly after an errands android had bludgeoned a grocer to death in Santa Ana, and another run a forklift amuck in a parking plaza in Garden Park, at a time when the newspapers were full of stories about the indiscriminate advance of android science, and I remember as I walked to the door thinking, Here goes, here goes.

I opened the door and found Dr. Gossner standing outside, looking diminished and gray. His hair had gone completely gray, his neck and jowls, even the backs of his hands a pale, ashy gray.

"Hello, Gilligan," he said, "step outside here for a minute, won't you, I'd like a word with you."

"My name's not Gilligan," I said. "I don't know you. Go away."

"Now, Gilligan, let's not make it more difficult on ourselves, shall we, than need be. Step outside now and we'll talk."

We walked around to the back of the house, to a point on the lawn overlooking the University of Michigan arboretum, about half a mile away. Dr. Gossner leaned heavily on my arm, every now and then pausing to regain his breath, an operation he disguised by planting it mid-sentence, as if deliberating over a word.

"I'm not going back," I told him.

"I understand," he said.

"I have my own life, my own friends, I have my own interests now."

"I understand, I quite understand."

"I choose not to go back. You gave me the capacity for making my own decisions, well, I intend to use it. I have the right to go my own way."

"I understand, I quite agree."

Everything I said, he nodded and agreed, disputed nothing, raised no objections.

"In fact," he told me at one point, "your refusal to return at this point would stand in my mind as proof positive of the success of this project."

Of course I had to remember that there were others involved here too, professional people whose reputations would be hurt some of them, oh, not irreparably, perhaps—

"But let's not get into that," he told me. "Don't let anything deter you from making the decision you're absolutely sure is right for you."

Many times since that afternoon I've wondered if there really was a decision there to be made, or if it wasn't just an instinctive part of my nature to want to do whatever he asked of me. As we were walking to the car that afternoon, the sun was just sinking behind the rim of the arboretum, bathing those defoliated hillsides in a soft and amberous glow. It was the first of March, and still a little ahead of the season, and on the flat part along the base of the slopes some children had taken off their winter coats and were spinning around with them, and for a moment before I got into the car I paused, like a man going blind, recording each separate impression and separate response; for I think I recognized even then that this capacity for response, which had remained with me active undiminished since the earliest days of my inception, was something that was shortly to be taken from me, and that I was renouncing the world in a double sense of the term.

"It's for the best," Dr. Gossner said to me as we were pulling down the drive. "Things are changing outside, Gilligan. There's no place for you out here anymore."

For weeks that followed my return, that was everyone's message to me, how I was better off here, better off here than out there.

"Things are changing out there, Gilligan," Dr. Cranston told me. "A new technology comes along, people feel threatened, they feel they have to strike out."

"You were just damn lucky," Dr. Harley told me, "we came along and got you when we did."

I gathered from remarks I overheard from the graduate students that there were incidents outside involving androids, in places like Fresno and Grand Rapids, but I could never ascertain any of the details. People fell silent any time I drew near, and nobody would answer any of my questions. For a long time I was denied access to newspapers and magazines, radio and television.

Several times I appealed this policy to Dr. Gossner, but to no avail.

"We want to control what stimuli reach you," he told me. "Try to be patient, Gilligan. I know it's hard on you, but please, try to cooperate."

I resented a little the implication that I hadn't already been patient, and hadn't already fully cooperated, but I made no further complaint. When I decided to return to the laboratory, I had decided to do whatever they asked of me, to stay as long as they wanted me, to give them no cause for reproach. I let the matter of the newspapers and magazines drop.

Increasingly in the months that followed my return, Dr. Gossner retreated from the daily round of the laboratory, into the sanctity of his office, leaving Dr. Harley in charge. Dr. Harley was a tart, bloodless man, not an unkind man necessarily, but one I felt too heavily immured in the precepts of objectified logic.

It was Dr. Harley's conviction that an android should be outfitted for the need society has of it, for that much, and no more;

that it be given certain mechanical skills, a pleasing disposition—and no more.

Dr. Cranston concurred with this view in substance, but disputed it on principle. She agreed that my patent skills should be mechanical, but argued I should have imagination and a spirit of enterprise as well. Between these two there waged an unending debate.

Shortly after my return it was decided I would learn pottery making. For hours at a time I stood at my wheel, turning out planters, casseroles, full dinner services, while that debate unwound around me, sending out tendrils and branches, piercing the foundation of all consensus, until one by one it had ensnared everyone in the laboratory.

For me these were more than mere rhetorical exercises. Every few weeks one or another of the factions would prevail, and I would be carted off to the workroom, to come back out able to speak German and play the piano, or longing for nothing more out of life than to turn a wrench endlessly with a single precision motion.

Even worse than these, though, these constant readjustments, were the occasions where discussion failed, where all experimentation ceased, and I would be sequestered to my room for some indeterminate time.

What was called my room was a space eight by fourteen feet cleared out of a storage bin at the end of the east hall. Here I had a cot, a table and lamp, a small upright locker. I had a few personal belongings, clothes mainly, and occasionally a book or two. But other than that, I had nothing.

Here, while for sometimes weeks at a time I hovered between madness and a mad sort of lucidity, I began, slowly and by arduous increment, to arrive at some measure of self-awareness.

My first recognition was of time, the proportionality of time. Time for the android, I came to see, is of two sorts, free time and allotted time. The purpose of the android is to serve man, and yet if man doesn't require service, doesn't ask, or even desire service, the android's time is his own, to do with as he sees fit. Allotted time is service time, but free time is the android's own.

This was an important breakthrough for me. Up until then, I think I'd seen myself purely as a function of my programming, an extension of whatever modality of thought had most recently been applied me, BAL over BIS, BIS over COBOL, the narrow concourses of the machine. But now I began to conceive of an existence independent of my programming, of a motive that derived not only out of form and function, that is, out of my human part, but of essence and affinity, of my material self as well—of that part of me that could be factored by time. I watched the slow dance of the filament inside the light bulb, listened to the slow seasonal contractions of the walls around me, heard the deep stirrings of the earth beneath me, and did not despair, and was not afraid, for I knew that this too would pass, this time of awful testing and deprivation would eventually end.

A few minutes after four one Friday afternoon in March of my second year back, I felt a sudden urge to go upstairs to Dr. Gossner's office. This was not so unusual in itself, as such timed imperatives were a daily part of my input at that time.

I opened the door and found Dr. Gossner slumped forward on his desk, in a widening pool of blood. He'd shot himself through the right temple a few minutes earlier. Lately Dr. Gossner had been experiencing a disaster of success, his personal prominence growing as his work slipped farther and farther out of his control. Rather than we Gilligans or some of the similar refined models, it was the earlier developmental models, the Bobs and Brians, many of them confined to single skills, which had gone into currency. Where he had intended to achieve a prototype, he found he had instead produced a catalogue.

I adjusted his posture and cleaned up the blood, fitted a clean blotter on the desk set. I opened the bottom left-hand drawer of the desk and found a packet of envelopes addressed to different of the associates. I took these around. The name and telephone number of a funeral director came to mind. I went to a phone and called him.

The associates were grieved, but not necessarily surprised by what Dr. Gossner had done. A couple of them remarked that under the circumstances it was probably the best thing he could have done.

Only Dr. Cranston made any definite show of reaction. Reading through the letter Dr. Gossner had left her, she brought her hands to her face and began to cry. I'd always thought her a strong woman, and wondered now if I'd have to revise that assessment, or if what I was seeing wasn't only a discrepancy, an accountable feature of personality.

The afternoon following the funeral, Dr. Harley called me into his office.

"Dr. Gossner left instructions," he told me, "that you be permitted to leave now if you wanted to."

"Leave the laboratory?" I said.

"For good, if you like. The choice is up to you."

In fact, he went on to say, it might be difficult keeping me here now, the way things stood. The laboratory had been Dr. Gossner's laboratory, staffed principally by his own people, funded largely by grants awarded to him personally.

"Dr. Cranston I understand is taking a position in Oregon. I myself am weighing several different alternatives. A number of the associates will be leaving us now, Gilligan, now that Dr. Gossner is gone."

"If I leave," I said, "will my time be my own?"

"Oh, absolutely, Gilligan, absolutely. Though there are you understand certain restrictions—"

There were restrictions on where an android could live, and where and for how many hours a week an android might work, but other than that, it seemed I could pretty much go and do as I pleased.

"Though there are other options, too," Dr. Harley told me.

"What other options?" I asked.

"Well, first, Gilligan, I want you to be clear I haven't always favored all the tinkering that's been done on you here. If I'd had my say—"

He went on for several minutes to reiterate his stand concerning androids, most of it expansions of figures I'd heard him previously employ. Like many blunt and unsentimental men, Dr. Harley was at a disadvantage anywhere a simple show of feeling would have marked a direct line.

"Suppose you go down to my basement to do your wash," he told me, "and my washing machine tears up your clothes. Am I liable? I didn't program the machine to chew up your wash, did I?"

I said nothing.

"What none of us seems to have anticipated," he said, "what nobody seems to have prepared for, was a mechanism that itself would be entering into the debate."

I said nothing.

"What you have to understand," he kept saying. "What I have to caution you to bear in mind. Where I think is the point where our paths are likely to diverge—"

He kept shifting in his seat, pulling up and easing back. Dr. Harley had been suffering from a backache lately, what he construed to be backache, though it was in fact a cancer whose spread had now begun to penetrate his spine. He'd been waiting until this business of shutting down the lab was over with, until he was clear and had the leisure to have it attended to. In fact for the past few days now he'd been walking around with a broken back.

"Though I want you to know," he kept saying, "I don't make such a suggestion lightly." I shook my head uncomprehendingly.

He gave me an exasperated look, and pushed on. "We can't keep you here," he told me, "we can't maintain you any longer. Either we have to release you, or else remainder you."

"You mean completely?"

"You would think of it more as a form of storage. And then once conditions had begun to improve—"

"No," I said, "no, I don't want that. I'll go my own way."

Immediately Dr. Harley reached into his desk drawer and came out with a typewritten sheet.

"Dr. Cranston has drawn this up. This releases you of all further obligation to the laboratory, and us of any future responsibility for you. Sign it and you're free to go."

I signed it without hesitation.

Back at my room, while I was gathering up my things, Dr. Cranston came to see me. She was dressed in street clothes, and was visibly upset.

"You have to understand," she kept telling me, "if there was anything, anything in the world else we could have done, we'd have done it."

"I do understand," I told her.

"Dr. Harley is leaving soon for Urbana. I myself am considering several different opportunities, Gilligan, there was no other course we could have followed."

"I understand," I told her, "really I do."

Still she persisted, even after it must have been obvious there was no need. She was a strange, restless, contradictory woman, secretly passionate and aggrieved and given to sudden bursts of intuition—all of which she suppressed into a patented, talky form of rationalism. All of this had worked against her in the lab, where she was carefully consulted on every decision, and then routinely ignored. For my part, I much preferred Dr. Harley's approach, it at least having the virtue of being consistent.

Still and all, she had been a good friend to me, the one true friend I felt I had there, the only one who I felt had always held my own best interests at heart, the one who consistently argued for expanding my capabilities, the only one who visited me in my times of sequestering, and she was the only one now, as I was leaving, who I genuinely regretted parting from.

She put her arms around me and gave me a hug, and stuffed some bills into my shirt pocket—"to help you get started." For a moment it seemed she couldn't let me go.

"Take care of yourself out there, Gilligan, please, take care of yourself."

I did all right until I reached Harrisburg. Shortly into Harrisburg I came upon an android hanging by his ankles from a utility pole. His chest had been smashed open, long strands of wire and gear, all tangled and rusted, hanging almost to the ground.

I encountered them regularly after that, hanging from signal poles and nailed to the sides of buildings, FLRRS, Flurries, the four-armed variety of android designed for canneries and assembly lines.

I was wearing hiking gear, a costume that had served me well enough until now, but clearly was inappropriate for city wear. I decided to stop at a grocery, reasoning that a figure carrying groceries would be least likely to be conspicuous at this hour.

It was quarter past midnight. There were eight customers in the store, and two clerks behind the counter. I moved up the first aisle, past the peanut butter and jellies, around a column of soft drinks. The store was monitored by a closed-circuit system, and every time I went by one of the cameras, the set behind the counter would flutter and spin. But I didn't notice that at first. Nor did I know at that time that such interference on such a system is one sure sign of the presence of an android.

I walked all over the store, picking up items at random, a frozen pizza, a big bag of potato curls, light, bulky items.

At the checkout counter I put down one of the bills Dr. Cranston had given me, and returned the rest to my shirt pocket. There was almost two hundred dollars there, most of it in twenty-dollar bills.

"Not in here," one of the store clerks said.

I looked around and saw a tiny old woman, of at least seventy, jabbing the point of her umbrella into the backs of my legs. A big redheaded man came up on my right side holding out a blazing cigarette lighter. I took a step back, and another man, a littler, bald-headed man, took hold of my arm and started twisting. I'd been sent out of the laboratory with no greater strength gradation than a nine-year-old. I hadn't strength enough even to break free of his grasp.

As the flame came to within ten inches of my face, I let out a high-pitched involuntary wail, one of several involuntary alarms that had been installed inside me before I went out of the laboratory.

Just then the door swung open, and a policeman walked in.

"Come on, let's break it up." He took hold of the redheaded man's elbow and pushed his arm away. "Come on, come on here, let's give it some room."

He looked to be a man of about forty or forty-five, reserved and genial looking. He was an android. This is something I've been able to verify a number of times since then, that I can always detect the presence of another android.

"Let's move it on, bring it along." He took the bald-headed man's hands off my arm and pointed him a step back. "Come on, you!"

He grabbed me by the shoulder and gave me a hard shove toward the door.

"Let's move it out!"

His movements were efficient, unhurried. Within sixty seconds of entering the door, he had me back outside and in the front seat of his squad car. He backed around and out of the lot, drove several blocks and turned, and turned again, and headed out of town.

Another android, a female, was seated in the back.

"Where did you think you were going?" she asked me, once we were underway.

"New York. Philadelphia." Back at the laboratory one time I'd heard it said that androids were tolerated, even welcomed in the Scandinavian countries. "I planned to book ship for Stockholm."

"And they'd have had you for certain. They watch the docks and airports, all the border exchanges." She reached over my shoulders and unbuttoned my shirt and began undoing my chest plate. "You must avoid the cities and towns, the public places. Keep to the mountains and woods, the open countryside."

We pulled behind a deserted gasoline station and stopped. For a minute in the shadows I could see nothing, and then I could see everything, every corner and line.

"I've disconnected your involuntaries, turned your gradations back to their maximum." She smoothed back my chestplate. "Listen closely to me now, to what I tell you."

Bending close to my ear, she whispered to me the greeting codes of the androids. Whenever I met another android, she said, I should listen not to what it said, but to the initial letters and number of letters in its words. The first letter of the first three words was the prefix, and what followed a numerical code.

When the policeman android walked into the grocery just now, for example, he used a CON code in a 423'1 sequence, and what he really said was, "Don't be alarmed. Be quiet and calm. I will assist you."

I should be especially alert, she told me, for the RLT code, the prefix for readiness. When I was conveyed those letters, I would know that the time of happy deliverance was close at hand.

She touched her fingertips to my ears, and a feeling both

calming and invigorating, a feeling of wonderful confidence and assurance coursed through my body.

"Now go," she said, "but be certain wherever you go, we are close at hand, ready to come to you whenever you have need."

For a time then I wandered, moving north, moving south, however the inclination took me, tending generally in a westerly direction, every now and then stopping for a day or two, or sometimes for a week or two, and then, as the inclination took me, moving on, moving mainly by night, travelling with the dry times and the cycles of the winds. My first and longest stop was in October of that year, in Orleon in southwestern Ohio, where floodwaters had recently devastated a fifty-mile stretch of farmlands and towns. Where the waters had receded, they left behind silt and mud three and four feet deep in the streets and the basements of some of the houses. Here a willing and tireless worker was not made unwelcome.

On the edge of Orleon I built a structure eight by eleven by fourteen feet, windowless, of concrete block, a structure that might have looked outlandish in some places, but here, amid so many makeshift dwellings, scarcely merited a second glance.

To the rear of this structure I built a wooden frame eight by eleven feet, and from it hung a muslin drape, which I watched, how on damp days it hung heavy and barely moved, and on dry days fluttered in the lightest breeze. From it I began slowly to decipher the intricate patterns of the winds.

The wind is my special province. Others take as their province the rivers or the trees, but each of us serves the common mean. Only we can see the end to which an action lies, how a liter of ice, say, released into the atmosphere of Kansas today, can arrive as a thunderstorm off the coast of Thailand two weeks from tomorrow.

Only we live within the logic of the planet, in accord with the rains and tides, the subtle shiftings of the continents.

In time, as the work of reclamation began to be complete, I packed up my frame and moved on, travelling north into Michigan and then into upper Michigan, and then a long hook down through Wisconsin and Iowa, tending gradually westward, every now and then stopping and setting up my frame, and then after a few days, or a week or two, moving on. From time to time messages reach me, from strangers exchanging a few words in passing, from letters and numbers stencilled on boxcars and on the sides of buildings. These counsel and guide me, warn me away from and point me toward. In Davenport I found the people all out on the streets dancing and singing, the androids did all the work. In Moline the people did the work, while the androids sang and played. These are experiments I know, attempts at conciliation, probably only the most visible out of who can say how many more.

Ahead of me now lie the last stretches of plain, the mountains, the long deserts of the west. The days are warmer now and drier, the nights longer. I cross the land inside a tornado, my feet are its touchdown, its vortex my flow. The winds are converging now, and out of their confluence there is a voice and the name of the voice is ReLayTah, on whose lips I am but a single syllable, ReLayTah, in whose mind I am but a single thought, ReLayTah, the many hands that move as one.

Eulogy for Red

GINA OCHSNER

From *The Necessary Grace to Fall* (2002)

Hate is unfortunately always much more observant than love,
and more observant even than an insufficiency of love.

—JOSEF SKVORECKY, from *The Bass Saxophone*

That was the day I awoke and red was gone. At first, I didn't notice it: my flat faces a shadowy inner courtyard where old Vaclav, the manager, keeps the trash bins and the Ukrainian couple
next door hang their laundry. It was early in the morning and I
climbed out of bed, trying not to wake Madla, and dressed in the
dark. But when I reached the street I saw that something was
wrong: red was missing, like someone had erased it from a color
test patch, had washed it away from the air and the sky and everything under the sky. The glowing of the sunrise pushing up
from behind the hills bled in stale shades of slate and cobalt and
shale. The trees, which had gone to blood and fire and all the
warm colors of fall, now looked frozen as if in the photographer's
silver, the leaves pale like old paper money.

I kept walking, shaking my head in disbelief, walking like a
tourist whose head wheels in all directions. I watched the traffic creep by and noted how stopping and going at intersections
had become a matter of looking for green. The red had drained

from the neon signs hanging at the windows of the shops, cafés, and pubs along Spálená Street and Václavské Náměsti, both of which seemed a little dull, even naked, without it. Gone was the red from the bricks, as blood leached from stone, and even the rooftops looked colorless and cold, like the scales of chapped lips. It made me think of looking at the world through the shard of a bottle or a piece of colored glass, or of those cheesy plastic tourist slide viewers, the kind that had only three color slides mounted inside and that over time faded out into the sepia brown colors of the earth and aged photography. I looked up and wondered if Mars, that red planet, had been affected, too, and if I could even pick it out from the nighttime sky with my cheap toy-store telescope. Finally, when my neck started aching, I went to work.

I work on newspapers and before I start my shift I usually stop in at the basement break room and harass Mack, an apprentice copywriter who thinks he's Willie Nelson or John Denver or something and who wears a big Tombstone belt buckle. We exchange off-color jokes and office gossip and then I hang up my coat, get a cup of coffee, and head for the print floor. But today Mack had his earphones turned way up, and besides the tinny noise coming from his earphones and the ordinary noises of the press dulled by the concrete walls, I could hear nothing strange, nothing unusual, no cries of panic, political harangues, or philosophical musings. Everyone was strangely quiet, as if contemplating a joke that they'd all heard but no one had gotten yet.

I looked at the blue line proofs lying on the break table, expecting a 24-point or maybe even a 36-point headline. But there was nothing about red in the proofs either. I scratched the stubble on my chin. Shouldn't there be a special feature, a quote from somebody important in the scientific community? *How did we come to be here stranded by red into the blues and what should we do about it?* I wondered. From what I could gather, the president hadn't yet made a statement. He had left Prague suddenly for Brno and then Slovakia and I thought, *Maybe he's been too busy to make a statement.* I wondered if we shouldn't make some sort of comment for him. After all, as printers and distributors of news, it wouldn't be too far afield.

I sat on my stool, watching the cylinders spin, the whole time feeling guilty, as if I were participating in a lie, and wondering what I could say about red. I was still shaking my head and chewing the inside of my cheek, sure that I was sleepwalking and that this was just another strange dream. Finally, the bell rang and I got up from my stool, as did the others, and we all filed out to make room for the next shift while the wheels kept rolling.

All the way home from work, I kept looking for signs that I was not alone in this, that others were worried, too. I went past the butcher's shop where they chop off heads for a reasonable price, noted the light gray smears on the butcher's apron, the ashen splatters on the block. I passed my hands over my eyes and blinked. I pinched myself. I cleaned the lenses of my glasses, but only the birds nesting in the trees were willing to acknowledge that something was wrong: I could tell from their loud squawks, shrill cries, and the long throat-rending screeches that they were upset, and I worried for the redpolls and robins.

I walked home, deciding to call in at Loli's, whose flat was on the bottom floor of our apartment building. If anyone had theories about red, it would be old Libuše, or Loli, as she called herself now that her husband had wandered off for good. Her flat opened up to the street where she ran her tiny florist shop. She lived in the room at the back where she grew her more exotic flowers under plastic flaps and beehive-looking contraptions. What she couldn't contain in her sleeping room spilled out into the courtyard: topiaries in stucco pots and flats of herbs, potted geraniums, and hanging baskets of flowers and vines whose names she had told me but I had forgotten.

Loli had the kind of laugh people mistook for a cry and that could stop cold all conversation around her, but I always liked visiting her because she was a little crazy and because her efforts had turned the courtyard into a green oasis of life. It was hard to be depressed or sad around Loli, who saw no good use for such things.

I walked past the Widow Dubček's, stopped in front of Loli's flower stand set up on the street, and noted her latest project: a large privet hedge that was really a series of individual potted bushes lined up to give the appearance of a solid wall of hedge.

Most of her roses were bleached of all color and the freesias looked like they'd turned to stone. She was bent over her lilies and crooning to them the way some people talk to little dogs or kept birds. Then she saw me and started waving her hands around.

"So what do you make of all this?" I asked her, sweeping my arms out wide toward the street and turning, my attempt at an expansive gesture.

"What?" Loli wrinkled her nose and wiped her gritty hands on the sides of her skirt.

"Red. It's vanished, you know."

"Oh. That." Loli turned back to her lilacs. "What's got me worried—I'll tell you what I'm worried about." I sighed, for this was the key turning, the battery charging, and any second now she'd start in again on her theories of invasive organic gardening and how it could save the planet if we'd all give it a try. And then I felt embarrassed that I was embarrassed by her, and ashamed that I was the kind of guy who was impatient with old women.

"I'm thinking of trimming the hedge in back and coaxing out the form of an animal—a fish or bird maybe—because I read just today that every garden should have a joke in it, something amusing that draws the eye and a laugh. Which do you think I should do—a fish or a bird?" Loli asked.

"I don't know," I said, brushing my hand along the biting edges of her meticulous privet hedge. "A bird might be nice," I said and stared down the street, letting my eyes blur in and out of focus, watching the people moving past me coming home from work. It felt good to let my eyes fix on the street, staring without purpose, without thought really. Then I felt Loli's gaze sliding over my face and shoulders. I shook my head, waking myself from my reverie, and saw Loli, a harried look on her face, worried, I knew, for me. I shrugged and walked back down the corridor, past the Widow Dubček's, to the stairs and to my flat. But the whole way I was thinking of the red woman of Ramadan who chases those who try to cheat death, her red eyes burning, and wondering if the red woman was to blame, thinking there must be someone to blame.

That evening, twilight unspooled in unexpected shades of glowering yellows gone to gray, the softer colors of long-burning embers, the colors of lye and ash, and I actually put my hand to my ear, sure a quiet fireless smoke would start thundering and we'd all be done for. I stood outside my flat and watched the sky cool and I remembered a day when I was in primary school, a day just like this one, a day we all stood around staring up at the sky. Except then we were waiting for a total solar eclipse. My father had made pinhole viewers out of shoeboxes for each of us kids. I remember his fervent warnings and of putting the shoebox to my eye and being afraid, terribly afraid that I'd make a mistake, at the critical moment flinch, blink, miss it all, or worse, blind myself by looking at the eclipse with the naked eye.

That night I dreamt that my mother came to me stuck to the flip side of a bottle cap and floating on a red tide along the banks of the Vltava. "Oh, Mother—what's happened to you?" I cried. She unfurled her wings, then folded them up again, for she was a little swan with her old human, mother head stuck on the tiny curving white neck of a swan. She spun her head around in a full circle, snapping open and closing her golden glassy eyes.

"Don't worry so much. This is what happens when you die," she said, nibbling at something bothering her in her feathers. I thought she was an angel and a fish, like both these things and like neither of them at the same time, all at odds there in the red Vltava. She glided soundlessly onto the wide lip of the river's bank, then disappeared into a slurry of fireflies beneath the branches of the willow and lime trees along the river's edge. I settled in my covers a little deeper and could hear faintly as if from very far off, though I knew it was as near as just under my bedroom windowpane, the Widow Dubček hollering at her cat, and I worried for the cat and thought, if I get a chance, I will grow catnip for it in pots and reserve the very best of my trash for that poor cat.

I awoke the next morning with a bad taste in my mouth and lay beside Madla, listening to her heavy breathing and thinking about red. I thought then that we should be very careful with what colors remained, taking great care to remember and preserve them accurately and with reverence. Maybe we'd been careless, had taken red for granted, collectively forgotten red and so it disappeared. Maybe it was still here, even now, but we had all changed and couldn't see it. Entire cities had disappeared, I knew, without a trace from memory and maps alike, simply because people had forgotten to remember them. Then I thought, maybe we are just stunned, like those birds that fly into the windowpanes of buildings, mistaking the glass for sky. We'll rouse ourselves, wake ourselves from this redless dream, and all will be as it was before.

I kicked the covers over onto Madla, pulled on my trousers, and went to the kitchen where I stuck my head out the window. It was a late October morning, and now without red the whole world had gone blue, the hillsides and outlying fields retreating to purple and then a dark that didn't have a name on any color wheel. There was Loli hosing down the courtyard in her hip waders and her husband's fishing hat that jingled with tackle and artificial flies. Then I remembered her comment and wondered if taking red away wasn't the gardener's joke on us.

I pulled my head back in and sat down at the kitchen table with a pencil in hand, determined to do something, and made a list of everything I knew about red:

1. It is a primary color at the lower end of the visible spectrum.
2. Red can vary in hue from a deep dark blood color to a very light rosy pink.
3. It is one of the first and last colors of sunset, one of the longest lingering colors.
4. Red is frequently associated with anger, bad financial moves, and communism.
5. They say there is the tiniest bit of red in every strand of hair on every head of every person on this planet and that only dead or dying hair doesn't have traces of red.
6. My mother's hair was red and when I was a baby, mine was too, but since has turned brown.
7. When I grow a beard, it is red, except of course now my beard is a grayish white.

I read my list over twice and closed my eyes. I thought if I just concentrated very hard, I could bring red back, even though I knew it was silly to believe anything so big depended upon my efforts. When I opened my eyes and red was still gone, I decided to go looking for it there in the kitchen. I could hear Madla stirring in the bedroom and her old radio, an outdated box that sputtered and struggled behind static like a moth at a screen, buzzed to life. I was on hands and knees, my nose in the refrigerator, sniffing for the scent of red, and I opened a jar of beets that had blanched entirely, then put my ear to the vent, listening for red. All the while the most beautiful jazz rendition of "Stardust" floated in from the bedroom.

"Help!" I cried into the vent. "I can't remember what red looked like!"

"Go back to sleep!" Someone from upstairs yelled back down through the vent.

Madla appeared in the kitchen then and yawned. "It's no big deal, Jindrich. They'll issue new currency, make new recommendations in the house, and there'll be nothing more to it," she said, setting the egg timer and retreating for the toilet, where I heard the shower running and I knew this was the last consideration she was giving it.

Oh, this is silly, I thought. Stupid. Worse than that—clichéd. This is the kind of cheap stunt an art teacher with the ink on her license still wet and a wild look in the eye would propose to her students: *Paint a tomato, a strawberry patch, a broken watermelon, a bleeding heart without using any red*, and rock on her heels, eyebrows arched, a tight triumphant smile stretching across her face. I looked around, sure that a siren would go off, and the joke would be revealed and we'd all have a good laugh at the prank someone had managed to pull. Behind me Madla's egg timer ticked while upstairs the Ukrainian couple were fighting again, and I thought the woman was accusing the man of taking something from her. I sighed and stared at the ceiling, trying to make some sense, read some pattern in the cracks sprawling across the ceiling like bad handwriting.

Madla was still showering. I went to the toilet anyway, reached into the medicine chest for my razor, soaped up, and started shaving with quick even strokes. Then the timer rang and I flinched, nicking myself. But it didn't hurt much and I hardly even noticed the gray spotting of blood. The sun broke open over the hills then—a quiet, yellow, unspectacular affair—and I knew I had better be getting to work.

I let myself out of the flat and went down the stairs. There was

Vaclav, the manager, kicking at the weeds growing in the cracks along the courtyard. He was mad for books, especially those of Kierkegaard and Nietzsche. He didn't like me, I knew. He didn't like it that I didn't know philosophy and that Madla stayed over with me sometimes.

"It's not that I'm old-fashioned," he had said, confronting me in the stairwell one day last spring. "But the sneaking around bothers me. Do you have to be so furtive about it?" He had asked and I assured him that I didn't know what he meant and nodded to him to show my respect for his opinions.

"You see!" he cried, pointing a bony finger at me. "There it is again. Furtive!"

But today he hardly looked at me.

"Red's gone," I said to him.

"Yes, I know that, you idiot." He still wasn't looking at me.

"Well, I didn't have anything to do with it. It's not my fault, you know."

"How does anyone know anything?" he asked, finally swinging his gaze up to mine. I wanted to shake him, God I wanted to rattle him when he started talking like that. Instead, I shoved my hands in my pockets and started walking away, faster than the day before, but just as amazed at the sight of people like me moving along, as if nothing had happened, nothing had been lost, and even now as if there was nothing to lose.

"Hey, Mack," I said, hanging my coat up onto the peg and reaching for the coffee machine. "What's new?"

"Nothing." Mack was fiddling with his cassette player.

"You seem a little out of sorts." I was testing him, trying to see if he would speak to my fear and admit that yes, something was out of sorts, dreadfully out of sorts.

"No. I'm just blind with boredom." Mack finished with the tape player and crumpled his empty paper cup of coffee and tossed it into the trash bin. "See you," he called and pushed through the door, his head down and the music up.

I picked up a test copy from the break table, sure that with a whole twenty-four hours of redlessness, somewhere someone would be up in arms about it, and any minute now our phones would be jangling off the hook, our intercoms abuzz with electricity and life. But just as the day before, everyone was strangely serene and calm about the loss of red, as if it had never really been with us in the first place. And again, today, the newspaper was uncustomarily silent on the issue. I found an obituary for red and a few eulogies, one by an old woman who'd survived Birkenau and had more close-up encounters with the color than most. *"A bright and fiery companion of orange and yellow, survived and missed by many"* her eulogy read, or something like that, describing red by what it was not. I went upstairs and sat there the whole shift, staring glumly at the presses, wishing the bell would ring so that I could go home and think in the quiet and the dark.

"This isn't right," I said to Madla that evening when I got home from work. "What's wrong with everyone?" I poured myself a stiff drink.

"Oh, Jindrich. I wish you'd lighten up," Madla said, wiping her hands on her skirt. She leaned toward me and ran her fingers over the stubble of my beard. "Besides, I think you look very dignified with gray hair."

I tipped my head back, finishing the drink in one swallow.

Outside, the sun was setting again, a distant throb and a cluster of gray, like a malignant cancer fire-star on an X-ray. "Well," I said, dropping my hands at my side, "I guess that's it. Red's really gone." I turned around, slowly unable to believe it, thinking it was some kind of colossal trick that would wear off once we could acknowledge it as such.

"It was never my favorite color," Madla said, snapping open her cigarette case and frowning at the botched sky outside the window. Then she rummaged through her purse and tossed out her tubes of lipstick, each another dull shade of gray. She rested her chin in her hands and kept staring. I thought she was looking at the sky, looking for red maybe, but then I saw she was really watching her own reflection in the window, watching the way her bloodless lips turned white when she puckered to take a drag from the cigarette. She blew a heavy cloud of smoke.

"Oh, it'll come back—don't worry," she said at last, bending her head to check the sky as if red's going was a simple change in the weather.

That night, the TV's glow looked even greener than usual and the figures slurring across the screen had yellow, green, and blue skin tones and I thought: at last, the answer to dull TV programming—I might actually make it through a whole hour of television without feeling sick or depressed now that everyone looked like a Martian.

And I kept watching, still thinking that maybe we'd hear a pop from the TV or crackle from the radio and the culprit would come forward. That's when a public announcement message scrolled across the bottom of the screen. I thought: at last—someone will say something, someone will do something. But it was just a weather warning: the barometer had dropped unexpectedly and a storm was coming.

I went to bed. I lay there studying the dark and tried imagining it as a deep dark red, a dark that could have been red, a red sunk in shadow. Then I gave up. Try as I might, I couldn't remember red. I recalled a trick my uncle, blinded by war, had taught me. If you squeeze your eyes shut, he said, you can see unseen colors by rubbing your knuckles over your eyelids, digging them into the eye sockets. That night I lay there in bed, my jaw clamped and eyes clinched, rubbing my eye sockets for all they were worth. And it worked: I began dreaming of red stars swimming like firebugs over the water, which was also red, that fiery color of passion, the color of the heart and of heat. In fact, everything in my dreams—the dogs, the kestrels, the swifts, the sounds of the trains and of people's voices—was shaded in reds: brick red, maroon, vermilion, blood red, reds of the desert, reds of the tropics, coral reds of the sea, sapphire and magenta.

Some say the end of the world will come in a blinding flash of light and fire. Others believe the sky wolf will open his great jaws and swallow the sun in a long digestion, leaving the world to ice. But I figure it's going to be slow and drawn out so we can take note of each little change. We'll wake up and all be smaller, paler, shrinking as the sky unravels in bolts of color, only one color will be missing, and then the next day another color will be gone. Then everything and everyone will resemble each other completely with only the slightest variations of gray distinguishing each thing from another. That's when the snow will fall, dropping down quietly, hesitating in the air and on the palm like a small bird scared into flight, drifting and settling into imperceptible mosaics of pure white upon white, until at last the air and the ground under the air goes blank as an empty canvas.

I woke up, afraid I'd overdone it with the eye sockets, but thinking I could dream for days and not come up with anything so perfect. And then I felt a little ashamed. If it's true there are two tongues to every language, a tongue of love and one of hate, maybe what we were seeing here was a message from God in a celestial tongue of love, of grace, only it was incomplete as yet, and we didn't know how to read it. In fact, some of us had yet to even see it or recognize it. Yes, maybe that was the trouble. But the trouble was with us, with me, not with the landscape that had

diminished and wicked out to a world of boot-polish blacks and
ashen whites and the colors of stubble that outlives the man.

That morning, Madla and I went out to the courtyard to watch
the storm roll in. We were looking over the rooftops. And then
I thought if this was the end, how I couldn't say or do one thing
that really mattered now, and even if I could, I wouldn't know
what that one thing I should do or say was. I was in fact the kind
of guy who could make his mother a little deader than she already was every time I opened my mouth. And I felt a sorrow
then as thick and chalky as an aspirin too long out of the bottle,
dissolving on my tongue, leaving a bitter aftertaste that I knew
wouldn't go away no matter how much I drank. And I realized
that this was the end-of-my-life flash: not seeing my life rewind
as if on a cheap movie reel, but seeing myself for what I was. No
wonder so many people feared the end.

A wind kicked up, catching a newspaper in full bloom against
the courtyard brick. I could hear Loli behind her privet hedge,
choking with her strange laugh, and I wondered if she was indeed
crying. And then there was Vaclav in the stone corridor singing with cheer: *That's the fucking end, said Amundsen.* I pulled
Madla closer and imagined I could hear our blood whistling like
old radios, bleating like broken-down clocks.

Overhead, the birds keened and wheeled in tight circles and
raised their pitch and I wondered if I should say a little prayer for
them, the kestrels, those half-formed angels falling from sky, for
the beautiful redpolls and the swifts, all unsettled by the smell of
a storm and the sky's pallor.

But instead of being afraid I felt grateful. Yes, for all these
things and many many more I was grateful, and to have had them
here with Madla whose warm breath even now fogged the face of

my watch and who made me think that if I could know just one thing, one tiny thing, know it completely, even if that thing was not her, but only near her, that could be enough. Then I could forget it all: the horror that if I looked inside myself there might not be anything at all to see, the mystery of my mother now happily drifting along in my dreams, and the fact that no matter how hard I tried not to, I had failed her in ways I might never understand.

Above us the sky burned with blues and yellows and greens, the green stripes of the sky matching the green irises of Madla's eyes. I felt my breath catch at the back of my throat, a quickening in my lungs, and I thought *My God, what a sight, this ancient watery landscape of color*, and it seemed to me then the days had never been so beautiful as these, and as this one in particular.

I wrapped my arm around Madla's shoulders and pulled her head to my chest and breathed in the smell of her hair. Madla squeezed my hand. "I love you," she said quickly, like the last thing you whisper as the lights die down and the projector flickers to life.

Where We Last Saw Time

PETER LASALLE

From *Tell Borges If You See Him* (2007)

I was supposed to meet Emily later that night in the old Hayes-Bickford Cafeteria right there on Massachusetts Avenue in Harvard Square, the way we would get together sometimes even if we weren't going somewhere on what would pass for a formal date. (It didn't matter that Emily herself had died in Cameroon years before, complications from stomach amoebae while in the Peace Corps, and it didn't matter that the old Hayes-Bickford with its yellow baked custards in crockery bowls set atop ice in the counter in back, its ancient busboys who managed to sleep standing up while pushing their stainless steel carts, yes, it didn't matter either that the Bick itself was long gone—such slips in chronology were only minor details.) I was in the study of the rooms I shared with two other guys on the top floor of Winthrop House in 1968. I was working on a paper on the letters of Keats, my roommates gone in the afternoon and the whole business of Keats's suggestion of art being a Mansion of Many Chambers making me a little dizzy for the moment, all that possibility. I got up from the desk, and I walked around the room, thinking that I'd best not be tempted to put something on the stereo, like that Donovan album with its overdose of echoing electric harpsichord, slowly psychedelic, I suppose. I went to the window, from which I could see winding Memorial Drive below and the Charles.

It was autumn, the leaves detonating in their scarlets and golds, the wide river bluer than blue. You could smell the tobaccoey fragrance of those leaves with the window open like that. But maybe it wasn't autumn, and it was winter, the cars creeping through the falling snow on Memorial Drive, the essence of silence, and the window in front of me very much shut tight, the old silver steam-heat radiator clanking out its own kind of whispery contentment.

I will admit that I even entertained the idea of stretching out on the sagging secondhand sofa. I was tempted to indulge in one of those champion midafternoon naps, for a sleep so deep and so sound that settling into it—lying down with your clothes on and somehow entering a purple velvet sack, to reach out and pull the gold cord on top, tight—entering into such a sleep, and dreams, like that when just twenty-one, you already knew that you would go through an entire lifetime never enjoying such absolute and complete and perfect dozing again. On the other hand, I realized I couldn't waste time sleeping. There was the paper to finish. And there was the mandatory hockey practice that I had to log despite the fact I had been relegated, after all my supposed promise at the unknown Catholic boys school in New Hampshire, to big-league bench warming in the crimson uniform at Harvard. And, above all, there was my having to meet sweet Emily later on at the Hayes-Bickford Cafeteria.

Emily went to Wellesley College, having come there from what definitely was the faraway other world of downstate Illinois.

Her parents were both doctors. They had met in medical school in Chicago, though they divorced before her father was even out of his residency; he took off and married a young nurse, going back to live in his beloved Idaho Rockies, where he had grown up. That left the mother alone with two young daughters, as she worked hard to balance finishing up her own studies with raising the girls, lucky to have the help of a dedicated black housekeeper/nanny named Alabama. (Emily admired her mother so much, and she almost indulged in histrionically telling me how bad the attempt at a normal family had had it in their walkup apartment on North Orleans there in Chicago. Yet the hardship always seemed to crumble a little—especially for a guy like me whose uncle who raised him ran a Sunoco gas station—when it came to mention of that, well, maid Alabama, famous for her strawberry jam flapjacks, a treat that the sisters demanded having a half dozen times a week.) Faced with the kind of bias that a lot of women MDs were up against back then, her mother couldn't establish much of a private practice even after having held a top residency position at the University of Chicago Hospital, and she moved her household down to a small Mississippi River town, where she could practice her pediatrics simply because the farming community was pleased to have *any* MD and had no option of exercising prejudice. Emily's mother sent the girls to a posh boarding school in Lake Forest, and while Emily's sister was content to study at Southern Illinois University, marrying a local boy, Emily worked hard at the boarding school to win Latin medals and viola prizes (I loved those pictures in her yearbook, Emily wearing the school uniform of blazer, skirt, and tie, wonderfully knock-kneed in her gangly tallness), then go on to Wellesley. Her mother was proud of her, and Emily was perpetually grateful to her mother, who had struggled to give her everything.

I doubt I would have stood a chance with her if I myself wasn't as tall as I was. Out at the mixer at Wellesley that night we stood like two members of some distinct leaf-munching separate species above the sea of heads bobbing in the wood-paneled Commons, the usual rigged-up reddish light and an off-key band playing Wilson Pickett's "In the Midnight Hour"; six-three, I was probably the sole suitable candidate for Emily at her five-eleven or so. But by this time Emily's boarding school gangliness had turned into a striking, lithe gracefulness; she had honey hair and large blue eyes, and when she put on her perfectly round steel-rimmed glasses of the variety that a lot of girls were wearing back then in the sixties, the lenses magnified the eyes even larger, so she looked somewhat like a Martian—in a pretty way, if that makes any sense. We started dating, "seriously." Emily had a cousin who was a graduate student at Harvard, and often during the week Emily spent a night at the girl's apartment so we could see each other more, in addition to our regular weekend time together. (I got a real kick out of how Emily told me of the "MIT Bus" she used for commuting to Cambridge. The bus was an authentic yellow Bluebird clunker, and it made the fourteen-mile run between Cambridge and Wellesley several times a day, for the new idea of a shared curriculum between the women's college and MIT, though it soon became basically a shuttle for girls dating Harvard guys. Emily claimed that nobody from Wellesley seemed to be interested in the academic sharing; she said that when the bus full of Wellesleyites came in from the suburban college, you would be lucky to find anybody but the marijuana-fragrant driver in the junk by the time it finally passed Harvard—all the girls jumped out at the unofficial stop there—and actually arrived at that depressing maze of numbered poured-concrete buildings that passed for the campus of the world-renowned science and engineering university.) Following her mother's lead, Emily was lately determined to become a doctor herself, and what better way to prepare for that than first spending some time in the Peace Corps. Central Africa was her first choice of assignment, and the recruiter told her he could close to guarantee it, seeing that her French was fluent, even amazing.

Actually, Emily was *crazy* about the whole idea of Africa at the moment. That made it trickier for me having to see her later, with my knowing what I did concerning what would happen to her there, and how poor Emily would, in fact, die in Cameroon a few years afterward.

Maybe I could talk her out of going when we met at the Hayes-Bickford later. Maybe I also should be getting down to the hockey practice, I knew, and I was already late for that.

I wondered some more about that Mansion of Many Chambers letter. I wished my roommate Hartley was around, so I could bounce some of my ideas off him, get his chin-stroking Utah Mormons take on it all. I thought about Keats's idea of Negative Capability; I thought, too, of his idea of the selflessness of the artist in being able to inhabit any persona, any character, lose all ego, until Keats, in that particular letter, reached maybe the crescendo of his argument in one of those big leaps that only he was capable of making—the metaphysic of it leaving you more than woozy, definitely and somehow tangibly high, the binoculars in dazzling and too-clear focus—with the possibility that Christ was perhaps the greatest artist because He was the most selfless of all men. I closed the spiral-bound notebook, stuffed it into my green rubberized book bag along with the Houghton Mifflin paper edition, worn, of the collected poems and selected prose.

I left the rooms in Winthrop House. I headed down to the rink in the afternoon.

Hockey for me had been sort of a benevolent bust. At Harvard, anyway. My high school team in New Hampshire had won the state championship, going to the New England semifinals in my junior year. I surprised even myself by scoring as well as I did when it came to the business of breaking the half-moon seal with the virgin-pink eraser end of a yellow number 2 pencil and plowing through that endless, near-indecipherable prose and the rows of nail-puzzle geometry problems on the SATs. That gave me some academic potential to cover for my so-so grades, and, suddenly, I was an athlete who might be attractive to a place like Harvard. At that stage in the annals of college hockey history, Harvard remained dead opposed to doing what its arch Ivy League rival in the sport, Cornell, had long been doing—heading right into the Canadian heartland and signing on toothless ringers, all of them able to actually graduate, because Cornell was Ivy League but also a state land-grant college, with its famous School of Hotel Management providing an easy enough major for the bulk of those ringers. (But what happened later, everybody always wondered. Good as their hotshots were, none of them would go on to the NHL, so was that vast expanse of Canada—in the middle of Saskatchewan's golden wheat fields or Quebec's northernmost Arctic tundra—just a network of ritzy five-star hotels with toothless managers in good gray flannels and fine blue blazers ready to greet you in the opulent, but deserted, downstairs lobbies?) What Harvard did was clean out schools right *inside* the border, usually in Minnesota, places like International Falls or Hibbing; technically, that meant it wasn't reducing itself to going *over* the border, and it added occasional prep schoolers and New England high schoolers, like me, to balance out the menu. The aging coach had once starred for the Boston Bruins in the helmetless days when all players parted their slicked-down hair precisely in the middle, and he had scouted and recruited me, hitting it off with my bachelor uncle wearing his own blue uniform—the Sunoco team—and promising my uncle he would take velvet care of me if I came to Cambridge. The one especially wild card in that deck of pretty wild cards to begin with (when I thought of how I got to Harvard, I always pictured a deck of those red-printed slabs bearing chubby naked angels on antique bicycles, wacky) was that right from the start I realized I was way out of my league in hockey; I stuck with it probably out of the painted-saint-statuary, purely medieval Catholic guilt I had been raised on in my Québécois upbringing, knowing I could still keep my full scholarship even if I didn't play (all scholarships at Harvard were for four years and academic, not athletic), but not wanting to disappoint that benevolent old coach, hoary-topped now, who had believed in me so. I guess there existed something comfortable in being a benchwarmer who wasn't even taken to some of the away games, because, very luckily, it allowed me time to discover literature.

Which I loved.

But I seemed to have gotten the practice schedule wrong.

I walked into the rink to go to the prepractice meeting before scrimmage and saw nobody was there. Nobody was in the upstairs parlor, either, at the redbrick field house (only at Harvard could a parlor in a field house be just that—a wood-paneled sitting room with leather easy chairs and bona fide oil paintings), and I went back down to the locker room, to find the counter in back unstaffed by the usual rum-nosed Irish trainers who passed you your daily packet of "whites," nobody in the cement-floored locker aisles, the olive metal cubicles all securely padlocked shut. Nevertheless, I thought that if I had walked all the way there, from Winthrop House across the river, then I might as well go back to the rink with my gloves and stick and at least lace on my skates for a little workout on my own.

The ice was ghostly white, recently resurfaced and a translucent sheen to it, as pure as the promise of a child to keep a secret, maybe. The smell of refrigeration cut like ammonia when I breathed deep, and that smell, since kidhood for me, was surely a fragrance no less holy than that of sweet beeswax votive candles burning in the cavern of any major European cathedral.

I skated alone there in Watson Rink, the way I often did in dreams. I listened to the rhythmic, satiny rips of my sharpened CCMs on the surface, took a couple of hard slapshots against the scuffed white boards for that nice echoing sound, like somebody hammering in the country, and I skated some more. Looping the oval again and again, I liked how the brass from the trophy cabinet on the other side of the plexiglass flashed as I passed it, I liked how . . . but I soon admitted I shouldn't be wasting *too* much time with this either. Especially when I had to meet Emily later on, face her as I had to do. Back in the locker room, I showered, the steamy hot water perfect on my body comfortably sore from the workout, then stepped naked through the little chlorinated footwash pan. I slowly dried myself with a detergent-stiff towel, and I dressed.

I headed back outside, where it was thoroughly night.

I crossed the Larz Anderson Bridge. Its arches seemed to leap in several giant strides across the glassy black Charles; the lamps along the balustrade rails glowed in haloed globes there under the truly spectacular show of the stars flaming in the inky sky. I could see the Harvard Houses along the river—Eliot, Winthrop, Leverett, Dunster—rising in their Georgian shadows, such stately quadrangles, all the geometrically neat rooflines and the rows of peaked dormers, the occasional domed bell tower, no two the same, sprouting a little higher than the rest. Alone on the bridge, looking at that panorama ahead of me, I knew it existed like a separate little city in itself, or, better still, a separate kingdom where I had to genuinely journey rather than just walk, where I had to go to figure out things *at last.*

Cutting through the warren of stubby cobbled side streets between the Houses and then the stores and restaurants of the Square proper, I saw a figure on the other side of South Street. This was by the *Advocate*'s little gray clapboard headquarters, complete with the white-painted carved Pegasus right under the peak. (True, I had been elected to the Board of Prose Editors of the college literary magazine, what I saw as some spectacular achievement, because not only had the likes of Eliot, Agee, Stevens, and Mailer also once been elected to the *Advocate*, but, more honestly, I suspected that you could plow through the high piles of yellowing records and more yellowing ancient issues in the upstairs offices, off the meeting room, and not find *any* name of a former editor who had actually been a varsity ice hockey player. Hartley, one of my roommates, wasn't impressed—Hartley, the precocious literature scholar from Salt Lake City, of all places, telling me what maybe I myself fully knew: "Let's face it, Jackie, most of those *Advocate* twerps nowadays will never go on to do anything serious, they'll end up book editors or magazine writers in New York, little more than the palace guard, but never do anything truly serious." Was chin-stroking Hartley *ever* wrong on things like that?) The figure I saw across the street and walking straight toward me was but a hooded shade, and it could have been a mysterious monk with hands tucked into his cowl at the stomach, until I realized it was Townes, my other roommate. The monk effect was simply due to the fact he was wearing one of the athletic department hooded sweatshirts, gray and with a pouch pocket below the big crimson HAA on the chest; fireplug-sturdy Townes, despite his being the gentlest guy in the world, was a *real* athlete and All-Ivy noseguard on the football team for two years running—he was also, at the moment, the last guy I wanted to see. Not because I didn't respect the hell out of Townes, the way that he was an athlete's athlete, and one shyly embarrassed since a kid in Cincinnati for the dyslexia that had his mother reading aloud to him the Sunday comic strips in the seventh grade just so he wouldn't be more embarrassed when the other junior high kids talked of them on Monday at school; Townes was currently relying on what was his rarest gift, his "eye," to qualify for the tough photography track in Visual Studies, and he had hopes (now that he had officially had the college's language requirement waived, after getting nowhere with French, less than that with Spanish) of going on to graduate school in architecture. I wanted to avoid Townes because somehow I knew what he had to tell me, and I really didn't want to hear it.

I tried to turn my head away, huddled low myself, with my hands in the pockets of my chinos, the tweed sport jacket's collar upturned—I just wanted to make it past him on that empty side street.

"Jackie!"

"Hey, Townes, what's happening."

Townes then picked up on that line of the parlance of the day (no talk of the ongoing war or the protest of said day, from hurling anything handy at the television screen in the Junior Common Room whenever LBJ came on it in 1968, to the big takeovers of the university buildings and the loud, slogan-shouting rallies—everybody was tired of that, maybe just trying to repress it), but in Townes's congeniality, or almost in his dyslexia, the phrase got turned inside out:

"What's happening with *you*, man, is the bigger question. I was just over on Mass Ave, passing by the Bick, and I saw Emily. She's been waiting for you for a while."

"Tell me about it."

"You don't know how lucky you are," he said, smiling and giving me a sock on the shoulder.

"Tell me about that too."

"She's something else."

He grinned.

"Townes, I'm sort of in a hurry," I told him. "I'll see you back at Winthrop, later tonight, OK?"

He called after me as I continued on down the narrow street, with more small clapboard houses lining it, a fairy-tale street, really, Townes saying:

"Old Hartley is looking for you too! Something about that Keats paper you're working on!"

He pronounced "Keats" like "Yeats." I didn't correct him, but simply turned the corner, hitting Mount Auburn Street. There were the yellow-lit windows of the typewriter shop and the J. Press haberdashery and the infamous liquor store with its two grouchy brothers who owned it, the duo certainly convinced that all Hah-vahd boys were either privileged aristocrats or card-carrying pinkos, both species equally odious to them. There was the little brick castle of the Lampoon Building at the fork in the middle of the one-way street, a street with none of its usual busy traffic in the evening, and there was also something I really couldn't figure out.

How did Hartley know I wanted to talk to him about the Keats paper?

HARTLEY

The Mansion of Many Chambers. A phrase from the Bible, or a rephrasing of it, I guess, "In my Father's house are many mansions." There the word "mansion" is archaic, and it once actually did used to mean a room or chamber—or apartment, which Keats also uses in the letter. Indeed, from the Bible.

JACK

Spare me, Hartley, at least I know that one. In the dementia of my Catholic schooling, the Old Testament might have gotten swept under the broadloom, but not the New.

HARTLEY
(that Hartley sneer, plus the chin-stroking)
Take the long trip out to Salt Lake City sometime, Jackie. Nobody can top us—the Old Testament, New Testament, and then the Book of Mormon itself.

JACK
The hat trick.

HARTLEY
What's that?

JACK
Just hockey palaver. But you're right, a rephrasing, or a twist—the Mansion of Many Chambers. And my take on what Keats's version of it is saying, which could be stretching it, is that with art as with life you wander through room after room, it's large enough to hold everybody, that huge mansion, everybody in America, let's say, from Fitzgerald to Faulkner to Hemingway to, well, to Melville, of course. Art can be done a lot of different ways.

HARTLEY
(who went to Europe the summer before)
I was on an overnight ferry from Liverpool to Ireland last August, a packed old hulk, and I paid ten shillings extra for a so-called berth, only to find it was down two decks, flat against the hot,

enameled iron wall to the thumping engine room. Which was bad enough, then add to that the stink of sour porter vomit down there from my fellow male voyagers passed out on the shelves of the berths. So I went up to the deck, past ragged women sitting on the steps with their wailing babies, and out to the railing. The sea was smooth, the air wonderfully refreshing. There was a guy from Oxford at the rail too, our age, and I can't even remember who the American writer was I mentioned, but this guy, studying literature himself, had never heard of him. Somebody contemporary, I guess. He wanted to get a better bead on the writer, and with his clipped, patrician, pedantically Oxford accent, he asked me, "Is the prose Georgian or experimental, old man?"

JACK

Which means?

HARTLEY

No, I just got to thinking of that. I mean, you see my point. This guy's house wasn't a vast mansion, like you say. In fact, he had reduced it all to a two-room flat.

JACK

(laughs)

HARTLEY

Also, Jackie, why did you throw in Melville as one of your poles of literature? Yeah, your having Fitzgerald and Hemingway and Faulkner as three writers going at it at about the same time but as different as you can get makes sense, but what about Melville?

JACK

(suspecting he could be off on this)

I don't know. There's no talking of the American novel without talking of Melville, right? To skip his name in any such litany is, well, kind of a blasphemy, and we must always—which means *always*—be reminded of his stature, that's what I think.

HARTLEY

What I think is that Faulkner and Melville were groping around in that mansion without even a candle flickering, in the total blackness, and they maybe didn't see each other, but they continued padding around, lost, but soon to be oh-so-thoroughly found, in the same, saving chamber. If we take the needless given that *Moby-Dick* is Melville, then in a way *Absalom, Absalom!* is Faulkner, no matter what anybody will argue for *Sound and the Fury*. And, my argument is that *Moby-Dick* and *Absalom, Absalom!* are actually the same book, in a way, each a rewrite of the essential Shakespearean tragedy of a wild, half-dreamt delusion of ultimate power over an avenging universe, Ahab on one hand with his wild sail around the globe and Sutpen on the other with his equally wild drive to build his Mississippi plantation empire, complete with a French architect and Haitian slaves. And both stories are delivered with full-fledged Shakespearean bombast, dangerously on the brink of utter verbal embarrassment for the author at any moment, but each willing to take that enormous risk. Faulkner was Melville, Melville was Faulkner.

JACK

Shakespeare was everybody.
(serious)
I wish I had your faith, Jackie.

JACK

*(not so serious, knowing that he, Jack,
probably has naiveté, not faith)*
You've got the Book of Mormon.

HARTLEY
(the chin stroking again, the sneer)

Right.

Conversations with Hartley somehow always existed for me in that incorporeal whiteness of dramatic lines read on a page, uncluttered with anything bodily, except for maybe a few stage directions. And today the purity, I guess, of all that whiteness around the hovering, untethered talk is possibly the most important stuff in my imaginary conversations with Hartley, when I do go to him in my mind for advice on something I have been thinking about, like Keats's letters—which maybe I never did have to do an undergraduate tutorial paper on, which maybe Hartley never did want to talk to me about. But if we did talk, he would say things like that, because Hartley was always miles ahead of me when it came to books. Miles and miles.

And the Hartley who phones me today from suburban Salt Lake City every couple of years "to check in," the Hartley who apparently manages to maintain some semblance of a law practice going in spite of his heavy drinking and his coughing from years of unfiltered cigarettes (he didn't follow the Mormon plan on those vices) plus his three failed marriages (I guess he did on that one, a modern polygamy, the most recent liaison being with no less than a ball girl for what I guess is the Salt Lake Triple-A baseball team, a girl exactly half his age and all he wanted to talk about the last time he spoke to me, drunkenly and coughingly), as I said, that Hardey who calls now is only a ridiculous parody, a breathing ghost, and not the real Hartley whatsoever.

But I *did* have the paper on Keats's letters. And I *did* have to meet Emily. And after running into Townes two more times in my postponing of the inevitable and wandering more through dim ashcan alleys over behind the Harvard Coop, Townes telling me again, twice, that Emily was waiting, I passed the frilled Out of Town News kiosk in the traffic island marking the exact epicenter of the Square, crossed Massachusetts Avenue where the silver and yellow sooty MBTA buses growled slow; I passed the comically new, concrete-and-glass mass of Holyoke Center (imitation Le Corbusier), which seemed to speak what it always seemed to speak to anybody walking by—there in the midst of so much surrounding red brick, forever asking "What the hell am I doing here?"—and continued on to the Hayes-Bickford.

I could see Emily through the big windows. She sat at a table along the wall, but close enough to those windows that she spotted me, the way she must have spotted Townes outside. I waved, she waved, motioning with her hand for me to come in.

"Cameroon?" I said, now seated across from her.

My stomach jumped, then jumped some more.

"I think I can't miss," she said. "They've just got to send me there."

I suppose it *was* inevitable. It was like the instant your car goes into a skid, with the splintery telephone pole dead ahead of you in the widening twin headlight beams, and suddenly what could only be a fraction of a second, less than an instant, gets turned into gummy slow motion, as you brake till your foot hurts, hear the long chorus of the skid itself, strain to yank the wheel this way and that as the pole comes closer and ever closer . . . but, nevertheless, it might not *actually* happen, there is still time for it *not* to happen.

I didn't know much about Africa, so I was going to have to wing it, do the best I could. I might not dissuade Emily from going into the Peace Corps, but maybe I could talk her out of Cameroon, at least get her to go somewhere else on the continent, try to save her that way.

"All I ever hear about is Ghana," I said. "Ghana seems to be the seat of sub-Saharan culture, and with everybody in the government in traditional dress, including the professors at the famous university the British built there, Ghana seems to be the place to be, authentic. So that's what I'd put in for if I were you."

"Ghana is special, you're right," she said.

"Then chuck the Cameroon idea—or, what would it be, Cameroonian, no?—chuck that Cameroonian idea."

Emily had a Bick cocoa in front of her, set beside a pile of anthropology and history books on Africa.

She smiled. Hell, she was lovely. She wore almond corduroy slacks and a bulky white turtleneck sweater. She had her long hair pulled back in a French twist, two little drops of gold in her pierced ears. A delicate nose and almost prim thin lips; and the round, steel-rimmed glasses did what they always did to those startling blue eyes, magnifying them goofily big.

Emily's speech retained a touch of a drawl, the downstate Illinois town on the Mississippi where she grew up being far enough south for some of the inflection.

"Cameroon is better," she said. "It's sort of a one-stop shopping for Africa. It's the only country that blended two colonial traditions, half a former French colony and half a former British colony. And when you figure in that the Germans had it for a while, too, it really gets interesting. I read that there are still old people in outlying villages who speak some German but don't have certain words for things, like airplanes, because airplanes came in after the Germans skedaddled, so they have to say 'the thing that flies.'"

I had to admit that was damn interesting.

"But the big plus, Jackie, is that Cameroon is absolutely amazing, not just for that colonial mix, and colonization was a major mistake anyway, right? I think that as important as how ancient the continent is, is how amazing its future is going to be, what Nkrumah and all those sages in their robes in Ghana, those African intellectuals, dream of, real pan-Africanism with everybody united. Something on which Cameroon, blending those often antagonistic colonial experiences, has already made a good start."

She knew her stuff, all right. She leaned forward toward me, as I spooned, of course, one of those yellow baked custards in a crockery bowl, a tan thing with the official two maroon stripes ringing the rim of it; maybe best, the custard was sprinkled with a veritable pile of the electrically tangy cinnamon. I wondered, would wonder all my life, if I *ever* was happier than when taking a study break at the Bick, with Townes when we were freshmen and he was trying so hard to conquer the syllables of that French and then the Spanish, before they would waive the language requirement for him (Townes later told me that when he went over to the Freshman Office to have the waiver processed by the tweedy, blueblood dollar-a-year men who filled those Harvard administrative jobs, he waited in an adjoining room and heard them talking of how he, Townes, was the very first student in anybody's memory to have the requirement officially disposed of, and I liked to think how surprised they would be to see the eventual recognition, international, Townes went on to achieve as a definitely famous architect), yes, I was happy at the Bick with Townes then, and happy later in arguing literature with my Grand Inquisitor Hartley there, happiest, needless to add, when with sweet, sweet Emily there.

"Who's the president of Cameroon, anyway?" I asked her. I was getting caught up in her enthusiasm myself. "It's not a name leader, like Nkrumah or Kenyatta, I know."

"A guy named Ahidjo, a dictator but benevolent enough. But

here's the big thing about Cameroon, Jackie. Located the way it is in that crook of Central Africa, it's got everything. It's got real desert, bordering the Sahara by Chad, with nomadic camel-riding Muslims in the north. It has real major cities, Douala on the Atlantic coast for shipping, and the capital, Yaounde, smack in the middle and in the high, cool mountains for the government. Down south there is endless jungle, even pygmy tribes. Why would anybody want to go any place *other* than Cameroon is maybe the biggest question, Jackie."

This wasn't going the way I wanted it to go.

I looked at her, beaming, radiant, and I thought I might try another tack.

I tried to start all over again. I tried to get it all right. I went through the whole afternoon and evening again, thought I might be able to shove through the glass doors of the decidedly seedy cafeteria and reenter into that world of the old men pushing the cleanup carts and wearing paper hats, the misnamed, half-asleep "busboys" who could just as well have been a legion of somnam- bulistic angels, to start the conversation afresh, not have it head to this most dangerous of directions again—the absolutely inev- itable.

Then it was as if I realized that where I needed to have made my move was probably well before that, and for a minute I was back there on the other side of the river, about to cross the Larz An- derson Bridge. But it wasn't the Larz Anderson Bridge, and those weren't the rises of the Harvard Houses across the shimmering black water that showed the stars reflected like so many incan- descent fat lilies atop their pads. And for me there has always been something about bridges, the possibility they represent, as I myself have gone on in life to venture to Other Places, not Emily's Cameroon, but destinations very much my own. There was the long bridge of wobbly wooden piers crossing the steamily gray lake in Hyderabad in India, the women wearing gold dowry jewelry beating their wash against the orange rocks in the sunshine and the cluttered city on a bluff beyond that; I had been dropped off from the circus wagon of a state bus in the outskirts, told to wait for another local bus that would rattle out from the downtown and take me over the bridge and into the city itself. Or there was the West of Ireland in the rain, and I bicycled in from the countryside toward a village, to stop before I crossed the tiny whitewashed stone bridge, pinto cows lowing all around me, their breath puffing steam; straddling the bicycle, at the spot overlooking the village like that, I thought of the warmth of a pub and a good hot meal, with plenty of stout to drink, awaiting me there later that evening.

It could have been any number of bridges, and, as I realized earlier when finishing the mime of a hockey practice and heading back with my shaggy hair still damp from the shower, everything would be figured out when I got there, when I arrived. Which is the biggest message to learn in life, maybe.

HARTLEY

Be careful, Jackie boy.

JACK

Always am.

HARTLEY

Be careful of the dead.

JACK

(put off by that remark, challenging him at last, worked up)
What do you know about anything? I mean, let's be honest, Hartley. You're still telling me what to think, still questioning my every move, and you today a boozing, broken-down smalltime lawyer, soppy on the phone about some girl you married for six months who was not just a ball girl for whatever baseball team you do have there in Salt Lake, but also a goddamn dancer at what you called a gentlemen's club, for a while, anyway—you admitted that, and what did you expect but to have her leave you? What do you know about anything!

HARTLEY

Just be careful, like I said. Be very careful.

And there I was.

Still in the cafeteria with Emily. I told her something about my having to get back and finish up the Keats paper due tomorrow. She said she was "cozy" there (the word alone was heartbreaking), and she might just get another cocoa and read for a while before returning to her cousin's apartment up by Central Square. I got up to leave, taking my book bag. I leaned over to peck a kiss on the top of her head, said I would call her on Thursday about our weekend plans; I pecked another soft kiss. *How wonderful was the shampoo fragrance of her honey hair, how wonderful was the whole idea of Emily, Emily who, in true Keatsian whispering—think "Ode on a Grecian Urn"—herself would be delivered from the sadness of ever getting older.* It wasn't a new idea, but it was an important one, and Keats knew all about it. Which suddenly made me feel better, relaxed me totally. I had come to terms with Emily's death years ago, but sometimes I simply had to be reminded again of that understanding. I left the Bick.

Outside it wasn't autumn or even balmy spring, but the winter I had suspected when looking out the window of the study earlier. I walked the couple of blocks back to Winthrop House, my desert boots squeaking on the white. I passed the porter watching maybe Johnny Carson on a miniature black-and-white TV in his cubicle beside the brick archway and iron gate, crossed the snow-blanketed quadrangle with its argyle of shoveled walks, and entered the glossy green door of B entryway, to go up the stairs to the suite of rooms on the top floor, No. 41. I looked into the other bedrooms, but Townes and Hartley weren't there. I washed in the bathroom of cold white tile, then went to my own bedroom off the study. I flicked on the desk lamp over the light green Hermes portable typewriter sprouting its typed half page, but I knew I was too exhausted for the time being, and I switched off the buzzing lamp. Undressed to my shorts, I turned down the blankets atop the bed sheets that were crisp, having been picked up at the linen supply next door to the janitor's office in the basement just that morning, before I went to my early lectures.

Moonlight illuminated the window, each of its sixteen panes crescented with frost, crystalline. I got into bed, thinking about Emily, thinking, too, about the perfect jewel of a Delmore Schwartz short story about a guy ending his nights wandering back in his dormitory room. I suppose the last thing I thought of before *almost* dozing off was simply the absolute wonder of clean sheets like that.

Then I remembered something. I sat up on the bed's edge.

I set the alarm on the white plastic GE clock radio for six, and I told myself I *surely* could finish that paper if I got up early enough.

La Bête: A Figure Study

MELISSA PRITCHARD

From *Spirit Seizures* (1987)

Beginning with . . .

Jeanne-Marie, an abnormally fat child of sixteen who works as a laundress at Madame Lutte's and has the afternoon off. Cook has given her a custard pie as a treat, and Jeanne-Marie has carried it all the way to the meadow outside of the village where a shallow stream runs through. She has taken off her black shoes, her black cotton stockings, and put her reddened, swollen feet into the water. Propping her elbows on her knees, she holds the pie and begins methodically to eat, her whole being occupied with the sensations in her mouth. A small splash lands in the stream near her, then another, and another. All at once she is pelted with stones that sting her neck and back. She turns, tries to get up, custard smearing her mouth, when a gang of village boys, ten or eleven years old, descend on her, grab the pie away.

"Come and get it, fatty . . ."

"Run for it, run and you can have it, here fatty, have a taste of pie."

They smash the half-pie onto the ground and surround her. She tries to push out but they are sturdy, won't let her. She cries from humiliation and that goads them further. Dragging her to the ground, one holds her head, one her legs, while the rest unfasten her clothing until she lies there, a young, naked girl, exposed before their glinting, taunting eyes. Her primitive femaleness shocks them, then one spits and says she is a pig, a sow, a cow. They tie up her clothes and fling them into the uppermost branches of the tallest tree.

When they have gone, she tries to climb the tree and scratches herself. She gives up and decides she must wait for nightfall to return home. At the door, her father accuses her, her mother weeps; Jeanne-Marie will tell nothing of what happened to her. They agree she has been raped. Her father ends by thrashing her with the hearth broom while her mother wails absurdly that she is surely pregnant and will be a disgrace.

Jeanne puts on her blue and white striped dress, her white cotton apron, and goes out early in the morning with a long stick, back to the meadow. She pokes at the bundle until it drops to the ground. At Madame Lutte's house, she will spend more than enough time scrubbing the soiled cloth of her skirt, the cloth of her soiled blouse . . .

Jeanne-Marie Interrupts . . .

The woman stopped in our village, found me at Madame Lutte's, scrubbing out my clothes, and asked if I would pose for a portrait. Madame, hoping to have her own conceited self painted for a reasonable fee, by way of ingratiating herself, let me go without protest. So, my apron still wet, I found myself seated in the woman's carriage, driven at an eager pace to her summer chateau.

I cannot say she was unfriendly to me, but my character held little interest for her, nor anything I might have had to say. My figure had always brought great unhappiness to me, but here was an artist from Paris who would find it worthy of intense, if cold study. Into her *salon de peinture*, as she named it, with the northern window opened wide, cherry and quince blossoms jutting awkwardly from pale crocks set upon bare floors, whitewashed walls with sketches pinned here and there, she brought me. Dressed in an elegant smock of white crêpe de Chine, she asked that I remove all my clothing and mount the model's stand in the center of the room. I dropped my clothes upon a plain chair and like some ponderous creature climbed onto the model's stand. I began wringing my hands and sweating from nervousness, comforting myself with the idea of the money I was to be paid.

"Hair down. Please, unbraid your hair for me. We'll set these blossoms here, lean forward, not so much, there, fine, fine, look sideways towards me, yes, now throw the hair over one shoulder so we have the blossoms here and the hair here, yes, that's perfect. Lovely. It is essential not to move, Jeanne-Marie, until I give you permission."

My breasts hung shamelessly out before me, and my coppery hair pulled like a weight to one side of my head. The studio felt as full of warm and cold currents as a lake.

"Unbelievable laziness . . . models in Paris nowadays are utter lazybones, not wishing to strain a muscle, refusing to take positions which are too difficult."

So she talked as she worked, full of complaints, as my limbs grew heavier and heavier. I must have moved slightly, for she reprimanded me and I was afraid, and thought I would faint with fatigue.

She brought a shawl and allowed me a few minutes' rest. The immense effort of staying motionless as a chair or a dish dazed me. A platter of cold chicken and fruit was brought in, and I twisted my greasy fingers shyly through the ends of my hair and sucked the juice delicately off my fingers. When some of the violet juice dribbled down between my breasts, she told me to leave it.

After the portrait was finished, I returned to Madame Lutte's, where I quickly became discontent. I wanted to model. I quit Madame's and with this woman's references and a list of names I took a carriage to Paris, where I sought out the artists' quarters. My first employment there was so unfortunate that I nearly turned back to the life of laundress, tormented by stupid boys, in my dull country village.

The figure study class was deserted except for fifty chairs, easels, drawing boards, and the model's platform with an unlit stove near it. The russet walls were littered with caricatures and scrapings of paint from numerous palettes. I ascended the model's stand and sat in the small chair with a black fringed shawl wrapped around me. The chair bit into my thighs and I stuffed the last bit of bread I had brought into my mouth; it was dry in my mouth and I thought I could not swallow.

At last the students, all young men, herded noisily into the room. One whistled when he saw me, and joked that he must have stumbled into landscape class; he couldn't possibly be in figure study—all he saw before him was an impressive mountain of flesh.

The master arrived, establishing an air of false discipline, and asked that I assume a strange sitting posture, hands on my hips, head arched back, mouth slackly open. With a black cane, he tapped my legs apart.

Their eyes wandered over me, biting like stable flies. The studio stunk of tobacco and unwashed bodies and oil paints. I closed my eyes, imagined I was in the woman's studio with her benign eye upon me. I had no money left except what I would be paid for this day's modeling.

After an hour of brief poisonous criticisms, the master excused himself. I had taken a short break, drunk from the pitcher of water he had handed me, and now resumed my pose, my neck aching horribly from the strain. The atmosphere in the studio became loose and unrestrained. There were lighthearted denunciations of one another's work, much gossip and talk of lunch and cafés.

Unexpectedly, yet as if it were ritual, five or six of the students dragged their chairs over to the model's stand. Sitting backwards, they galloped in a circle around me, shouting obscene songs, singing the *Marseillaise*, which was forbidden by the Empire in those days. I held myself rigid, but when one of them reached up and pinched me, asking the others if they thought I could feel anything, I stood up, knocking over the slight chair, and left the studio. With enough experience, I would grow accustomed to the bizarre spirits of my art students, even playfully grabbing at the handsomer ones as they rode by me, fresh-cheeked boys on hobbyhorses. But that first day, when I complained of my treatment to the master, he asked if I would not prefer instead modeling privately for him.

This man was soon escorting me to cheap theaters, to cafés, introducing me to friends, reading from Verlaine and Baudelaire, after which he would bite my arms, muttering that I was the most delectably corpulent beast in all Paris. Sometimes he would feed me and, fascinated, watch me chew and swallow what he had placed in my mouth. I lived with him for some months, and finally prospered when he did, by a series of sketches he sold of me on brown paper.

Posing for this, for any artist, I was no longer the village freak, tormented and shunned, but was instead a figure of challenge to be studied in different positions, in varying angles of light. I was fed and given shelter in numerous garrets and studios. I wore men's clothing because it was a joke, because it was comfortable. I began to smoke tobacco and to drink wine. I laughed and no one objected, I raged and they drew out their sketchbooks. In short, the more extreme a character I displayed, the more sought after I found myself. In exchange for hams and sausage and breads, I goaded the incessant appetites of artists. I was an overnight fad in Paris, one of those meteors with a high, swift rise . . . I had become La Bête.

Not everyone liked me. One man, very fastidious, confessed that the thick petals of my flesh disgusted him, that excess such as mine revolted him. He took me one afternoon to a morgue and insisted I stare at the tables of cadavers laid out as if for some tainted feast. He explained that he had spent five years of his life drawing these gray, foul creatures.

"Look, will you, idiot! That is where someday you will be, upon a table like that one!"

I bowed and said, "And if you should arrive here before me, may I bring my knife and fork?"

At cafés among my new friends I began ordering very little food. I wished my companions to believe that La Bête ate next to nothing, that fat increased upon her like a Catholic miracle. In private, I gorged myself. I had the idea of pasting little stars of silver and gold in my red hair, and did so.

In early August I rode one evening with a group of students from the art school into the countryside. The master brought a white linen tablecloth and a pale blue oval dish with smoked salmon heaped upon it. We ended up in a meadow where the moon was bloated and discolored and the crickets howled fiendishly among the grasses. The cloth was unfolded and, shimmering like a bolt of water, was laid upon the meadow. The young men observed the effect of moonlight upon the cloth, where shadows dissolved precisely into blue edges, then white. The dish of salmon and I were asked to grace the tablecloth. I removed my trousers and shirt, put out my cigarette, and stepped upon the cloth; no one laughed or jeered at me. I had become the remarkable La Bête. Reclining in the long bed of my copper-colored hair, with the plate set before me, I took a delicate mouthful of salmon and afterward let out a long, rolling belch. Even this was accepted as art! An insult from La Bête was an occasion for art!

On the ride back to the city I bounced one of the slighter, frailer students on my lap, tickled and dandled him while the others laughed. As we came into the outskirts of an exhausted predawn Paris, I further amused them with this song:

> *Would you know, yes, know*
> *How artists love? They invoke*
> *Love with such artistry,*
> *They are such artistic folk*
> *That they go off saying:*
> *Won't you come to my place,*
> *Mademoiselle?*
> *I'll do your portrait.*

Bellowing out this last line, I added on a number of things they would do to me as I posed for their portrait.

In truth, La Bête never pretended to be chaste as a prioress. I rolled food around the cave of my mouth for pleasure and loved myself for doing so. When my father died, I returned to the village, very briefly. How small and dwarfed and without color it had become! My father as well, laid out in his stiff black suit, looked hard and yellow as the tallow soap I had used as laundress. My mother was weeping as she had been reminded to do. I despised standing in the pitiful cemetery of my ancestors. I loathed the villagers, staring as if I were still their own fat Jeanne-Marie, and not a famous Impressionist's model.

One night I modeled in the great Parisian cemetery for a group of male students and two of their girls. One foot I planted upon the small raised headstone of a child and one hand I held behind my head. My hair, braided over my breasts, glittered with stars. As I held the position, my muscles growing numb from strain, I felt a sticky, filmy sensation slide down my inner thigh. I brought my finger down, lifted it to the moon, and exposed, oily and black as paint, my glistening flux. My blood left bright banners upon the child's headstone. The little stone would be discolored, ruined, in the daylight, and my boys thought it a perfect omen of some sort, though they did not know of what.

How Jeanne-Marie May Have
Sounded as La Bête:

... to be thin is to be subject to an invasion of the ordinary. When I eat, I try always to be alone. I rarely use a plate. Dishes are me- diators, and cups, interferences with the directness of a bottle. I do use a bowl for my soup. I keep myself as well stocked as a cook's cupboard. Artists wallow their brushes in paint and swish, slop, make for themselves a gloriously fat beast. Me.

What I have never been able to do is to take joy in my bulk. Back in my village I was taught it was wicked to take up so much room, so when I watch these artists take their peculiar joy in me, in those moments, I feel good.

People wonder what it's like to make love to a fat woman. In the way people like to use something half up and then discard it, so a fat one like myself is used up. Or perhaps a man merely wishes to debase himself. Or become an infant against his mamma.

The latest man, this silly artist, he presses the juices from me. He says the water overflows the jug and I am the jug. I have posed over three weeks in this same attitude, stepping out from a tub, my buttocks toward him, my eyes looking straight into the bath- tub. Yes, there's a little scum of water in it, stale as any water that sits. He waits until the light comes through the windows at the correct exposure, heaves a bucket of water over me, orders me to step into the tub, then feverishly rushes back to his easel. He has me hold until my ass trembles from the effort to be still.

Sometimes, with my one foot splayed out in the water, I begin to sing bawdy verses to pique him. On occasion I fart and say, "Put that onto your canvas, you fool!" This man is very famous, not used to insult, so I am glad to give it.

I sit on the edge of the tub or lie on the bed to smoke one of the cigarettes I've rolled for myself. Funny, this one tells me that I have grace. My flesh is full of lights, he says. Nothing about me disgusts him. He goes outside while I eat my meal of sausage and cold potato; he returns in exactly five minutes.

Do I care anymore what they put on the canvas? Not much. I come over and blow smoke at the buttocks he has drawn and daubs with greenish-white.

"What horse apples," I snort and go, breathlessly, back to the bathtub.

Peculiar man. He likes to paint my huge bulk in erotic common postures, yet he never approaches me except with the bucket of water, then stabs in queer, caressing ways at the canvas with his brushes!

He calls me his mule, heaving the damn water over me, making me hunch for hours over this cracked porcelain until I cry out. Remorseful, he apologizes by throwing sausage and bread at me and turning his back.

I tear into the meat, huge mouthfuls, my pubic hair staring up at me, a reproachful orange mouth. When the picture is finished, I am given money, and I stare hard at the painting.

"Well, my mule, what do you think? It's perfect, is it not?"

"It stinks," I say, and he never hires me again.

Descent of La Bête . . .

Oh, when was it that my boys, my creators, began to neglect me? They lost their imaginations, that's what, sneaking into their garrets and studios such ordinary, slender grisettes . . . I tore up one lover's drawings during the night he did not return home. He went off with a bony nag who did nothing but crochet from her little basket and snub me. My temper grew worse; not one had the courage or the patience to risk using me. One newly arrived painter who had no money but offered to share his food used me, and I violently attacked his work, saying, "You call this a work of art?"

"And you," he screamed back, sweeping his pastels off the table onto the floor, "do you call yourself a work of nature—you are one of her aberrations!"

I abandoned that young fool in the middle of his work.

They had no more use for me, they could find no more art in me. Acquaintances in cafés vanished, or turned away their faces, and miserable La Bête came at last to selling flowers and matches on the hard steps of the Luxembourg, though she kept stars in her hair, as always.

One morning I sold more than enough flowers to pay my way into the museum. I moved through a hushed, churchlike maze of pictures and busts, until I found myself . . . enormously fat and red with a small head, reclining in a wet, blurred orchard like some rotting, overripe fruit. I had been uncovered like this, before the world, and now they had no more use for me. I sat on the floor and wept and beat my fists upon the floor, tried to scratch the picture, until two, then three guards took me out. I told them who I was and as I was pushed out I spat into the fountain, hoping to pollute the false, fickle waters of art.

But the sickness never left me. I needed them, however much I disliked their results. Creeping back to the ateliers, I asked, then begged for work. I reformed my temper, but my poor health . . . I had begun with little fits of sleep, narcolepsy. On the model's stand, not even a poor student wanted me. La Bête was broken-winded.

La Bête and the Recluse

An endless monotony of rain ran off the black slate roofs. It was gray and chill as only Paris can be in October, when even bread is damp. It became too cold to sit on the museum steps any longer.

Oh, sweet fall of the rain
Upon the earth and roof
Unto a heart in pain,
O music of the rain.

The houseboat was tied up beside others of its type, broken down, peeling, bleached, ruined. I knocked, opened the small red door, and went in sideways.

"No, I have little need of a model like yourself. I have no need of anyone or anything but paint and God."

He was willfully blind to anything outside his tiny, cramped houseboat. Boxes, papers, broken furniture, garbage stacked to the ceiling, narrow snakelike paths from his bed to his easel, from his easel to his stove. He stank vilely, but insisted that his layers of clothing ventilated him. And his canvases, strewn about like blowing litter on a street, some propped up, others lying face down, to ripen with the movement of the water, he said. He painted me standing in the middle of a salmon-colored river with black skies. He painted me wading in a choppy cobalt sea with no features on my face. I cleared away some of his boxes and furniture to make a bed for myself and a small toilette. I cooked on his small filthy stove, but since he often neglected to eat I learned to eat his portion before it grew cold. I smoked outside and regarded the ramshackle wharf. Odd, that an artist for whom only beauty mattered would choose such grim clutter.

We suffered that winter; snow drifted through unclosed windows. I found two cheap rooms in Paris and we left the houseboat. Strange to be in open, ill-favored space with this man. Wallpaper dangling in faded, defeated strips, plaster crumbling off the ceiling. The view from our two windows was of a tiny stamp of courtyard with arthritic burls of chestnut trees staring indifferently back at us.

His paintings were washed in half-light, phosphorescent, devoid of sunlight. He was a creature of dampness and night and perverse conversations. There was a benefactor who infrequently purchased his paintings, and on this, but mainly on donation, we existed.

When he became unwell, medicines made their way into our rooms, and the place where he slept was blatant with suggestions of a sickroom: a spoon in a tumbler of clouded water, a mortar and pestle, packets of white powder, stained rags by the pillows. A cat lived with us, an old calico who sat in his lap when he dozed upright in a chair. Late in the spring he began complaining of cold and went about in a shabby brown fur-lined overcoat, a white nightshirt, and black trousers, with a short black coat over all this.

We had enough money from the sale of a painting to hire a carriage for an evening's ride into the country. My friend was in some nocturnal reverie, walking through groves of birch, stepping across streambeds, leaning against a small limestone cliff, while I cursed and swore, trying to keep up with him. I also remembered the glorious night when I had been a feast of inspiration for young artists, reclined upon a white tablecloth.

He painted my head, took it off with the palette knife, began a second time, allowed it to dry, scraped again, in this way building up form, refining the drawing; after each scraping there would be a subtle layer of paint left. Being too feverish to go and purchase proper paint, at one point he seized the candle off its dish and used the grease from it to paint with. Fasting and improvised prayers over his work went on hour after hour. He had no use for my once-famous body, painting only my head, with a green scarf

concealing my famous hair, tobacco smoke like a fine, hissing au-
reole around me. I was to be laughing, some of my teeth missing,
my cheeks mapped with broken veins. But the sitting went badly.
I kept dropping off to sleep, and he was exhausted, able to work
for only a quarter of an hour at a time.

The cat would hunch upon a broken arm of a couch, delicately
washing itself. We worked only at night, the glowing tongues of
many lamps and candles wagging wastefully around us.

He told me, "In darkness the trivial is unwelcome. In an absence
of light, first the face, then the shadows around the face."

I grunted, half-asleep.

"So it is among common people that you will find grace."

I woke up. "Oh, crap. Common people fling rocks at the backs
of common people." I coughed and spat phlegm onto the floor.
"You call that grace, you idiot, you beloved idiot of mine?"

"Oh, yes," he said, his eyes on mine like a priest's.

When I awoke from another of my sick little naps, the lamps and
candles guttered weakly in the morning sunlight, and I found my
artist, who needed nothing but God and paint and me to cook for
him, me to grind up his medicines for him, me to sit for him, had
gone, his head fallen over into the wet oils of my open-mouthed
portrait.

Looking as if he had fed himself to the devil.

La Bête had devoured him, it seemed.

As It Turns Out . . .

After feeding and bathing her mother, Jeanne-Marie walks to the
other end of the village, where old Madame Lutte still lives. In
her basket she has rolled up the white cloth from Paris. When she
gets inside the laundry room lined with its dark, cool stone, she

fills the metal tubs, one with hot water, the other with cool. Disregarding the baskets of soiled linens and dresses, Jeanne-Marie takes out the white cloth, feeds it into the steaming water, takes the tallow bar of soap, and begins scrubbing. Her hands work among the cloth and the water, like red fish they move, quick and chapped. The cool water accepts the cloth, and a grayish scum of soap rings the metal tub. Wringing out the tablecloth, she stretches it across a rope to dry in the summer sunlight. It floats, a square unnatural cloud, against the blue seamless heaven.

Jeanne-Marie returns to the laundry room, pours out the fouled water, and begins the tedious, ordinary job of washing out Madame Lutte's expensive dresses and linens.

By noon the tablecloth is hanging stiffly across the rope, smelling of sunlight, and Jeanne-Marie's work is finished. She rolls the cloth into her basket along with the cold joint of meat and slice of cake given her by the cook.

In the familiar patch of meadow, she shakes out the snowy tablecloth, sets down the plate of meat and pie. Removing her blue and white striped dress, her apron, her heavy shoes and black stockings, Jeanne-Marie sits crosslegged upon the cloth, unbraiding her hair until it drops in a coppery sheet around her.

The poplar trees at the edge of the meadow clamor and flash silver in the strong afternoon breeze. She chews, sensuously and deliberately, wiping her fingers in her hair. Abruptly, she drops into sleep; the sun bleaches out her flanks, sets dull fire to her hair, sparkles against the sharp-edged white cloth in the sour grasses.

The village boys peer through a particularly dense stand of poplar trees; having discovered the habits of this queer laundress, they have snuck out from their chores to ogle her, in a kind of nervous dread of her enormity. There is something of an ogress in her raw pose, something of a folktale in the way her huge fans of flesh lie open before them. Their fathers and mothers only know Jeanne-Marie as Madame Lutte's ugly, disgraced laundress, in her shabby dress with her red chafed hands and broken chatter. But these boys know the awful enchantment of her naked body, set out as if for a feast upon an immaculate white square in the sunny meadow.

La Bête, even asleep, feels the boys out there, their pale, unripened faces shifting among the green leaves, their whispers like a shaking of wind through the poplars. She allows them, for she is worthy of study. Her figure commands attention. La Bête knows that her boys, her artists, can never have enough of her. She is that good.

Upon Completion of Baldness

LORI OSTLUND

From *The Bigness of the World* (2009)

My girlfriend returned from Hong Kong bald, thoroughly bald, the bumps and veins of her skull rising up in relief, as neat and stark as the stitching on a baseball. When we embraced, I noted that her scalp had a sickly yellowish cast to it, the influence of the airports fluorescent lights apparently, for once we were home, the yellowness had vanished, leaving nothing but white. It may surprise you to know that I did not address her baldness immediately, right there in the airport, but I did not. Rather, we stepped free of our embrace and then rode the escalator down a level to retrieve her suitcase, though I will admit to standing a step above her as we descended in order to survey the very top of her head, the crown, which appeared freer of veins than the rest of her head and brought to mind a birds belly.

"How was Hong Kong?" I asked as we waited for the conveyor belt to start up and produce her suitcase.

"Tiring," she said with a small, exhausted smile meant to confirm her reply.

Then, we stood in silence for several minutes, waiting for her bag to appear, which it did, bright orange and easy to spot. The closest I come to experiencing a sense of wonder in regard to the world and its workings is at the moment that I catch sight of a familiar piece of luggage, last seen thousands of miles away, chugging up the conveyor belt from the bowels of the airport. I simply do not expect it. Perhaps this seems overly pessimistic, for something must be done with those scores of bags so carefully collected and tagged on the other end. They cannot all simply disappear into nothingness. True. However, I fully expect the other travelers' bags to arrive; it is only the appearance of my own that provokes awe. Furthermore, for the sake of full disclosure, I will reveal that only once has my luggage actually gone astray, and not during one of the more complicated international flights but after the shortest hop imaginable—fifty minutes, Denver to Albuquerque, Albuquerque being home.

When we walked from the car to the house, the chilly desert air seemed to startle her as though, in that moment, she realized that there was a price to be paid for having no hair, and while I still said nothing, I was happy to see her suffer just a bit. She unpacked immediately, unusual for her, while I sat on the bed and watched, focusing on her hands, which dipped in and out of the suitcase, bearing all of the familiar clothing with which she had departed just a week ago, several pairs of black dress pants and lots of orange—blouses, sweaters, a scarf. Somehow, she can combine black and orange and not come off looking as though she's dressed for Halloween, but with her nude head bobbing atop her shoulders like a pumpkin, it occurred to me that things might be different now. And still I said nothing, for I hadn't decided yet what it was that I felt—anger, sorrow, embarrassment, perhaps all three.

"Here," she said, handing me a plastic bag containing what appeared to be individually wrapped squares of candy, but when I unwrapped a cube and set it on my tongue, it was definitely not candy. I sucked on it a moment and then bit down.

"Bouillon?" I inquired politely. She laughed, and it sounded the same, rich and frothy, but when I glanced up, her head was bald, and she stopped.

85

"Dried tuna with wasabi," she said, and we fell silent.

We brushed our teeth together, both of us vying for the sink, a common occurrence, but when the mint of the toothpaste mixed with the residual taste of dried tuna and wasabi, I nudged her quickly out of the way and leaned over the bowl, gagging. When I glanced up in the mirror, she was there behind me, perhaps looking concerned, though I cannot be sure of that. I do know that with the toothbrush protruding from her mouth, her baldness seemed almost mechanical, as though her head were nothing more than a giant socket, a home for various parts. Later, when we were in bed, I opened my eyes, expecting to see her head illuminated, a full moon rising over her pillow, but there was nothing, only the faint throttle of her breathing.

We had spoken only once while she was away, the day after she arrived in Hong Kong, a brief conversation that seems, in retrospect, to have focused solely on our neighbors, the retired wrestling coach and his wife, who had not yet removed their Christmas lights although it was past Saint Patrick's Day and moving swiftly toward Easter. "Shall I speak to them about it?" I had asked, but she sounded distracted, which at the time I attributed to jet lag. Could it be, I now wondered, that she was already bald, even then? That as I was speaking to her about such trivial matters as Christmas lights, she was pressing the telephone to her bald head fifteen hours ahead of me in Hong Kong? Thus, the first discernible emotion related to her baldness: anger. Or perhaps annoyance. Yes, simple annoyance, for it would not do to overstate the matter.

I lay there listening to her sinuses rattle for a good hour before I got out of bed and in an attempt to understand the situation— her motivations, my reticence—began to write this all down, to record the details as they occurred to me and then to study what I had written, to analyze it in much the same way that I would a text, the analyzing of texts being both my forte and my livelihood. I suspect that most people would be happier if they could manage their relationships in this way, applying their professional training toward making sense of their personal lives as well, though I am obviously in a better position to do so than, say, a plumber or somebody who handles money for a living.

I must confess that, in recording these simple facts, I immediately encountered a snag: in the first sentence, I wrote "my girlfriend," but only after elaborate hesitation, realizing that I had no fixed designation for her other than her name, which is Felicity, an overtly, almost aggressively, symbolic name that I have nevertheless learned to use without smirking. I briefly considered *lover*, but felt that the term put a disproportionate emphasis, inaccurately I might add, on one particular aspect of our relationship. As for *partner* and *significant other*, nothing need be said. Thus it was that I chose the unequivocally precise (albeit bland) designation *girlfriend*, though not without experiencing the aforementioned hesitation, for simply put, *girlfriend* sounds juvenile and might mislead one about our ages, which I will now describe as fortyish.

As I wrote, I could not help but dwell, with some frustration, on certain matters that I had hoped to discuss with Felicity before we returned to school the next day, but she had chosen to arrive home bald instead, preempting discussion. There was the ongoing situation with Mr. Matthers, who, like us, was in his first year of employment at the school, a private high school, technically without a religious bent, though there are shades of such everywhere these days. Felicity had laughed when I told her that it would behoove us (yes, I used *behoove*) to pay attention to the stir that he was causing; the three of us were hired together, I pointed out sternly, and thus were associated with one another in the minds of our colleagues, but she said that it *behooved* us (mocking me, no doubt) to pay attention to ourselves.

At this point, there had been only the vague reports that Mr. Matthers was teaching with both hands held in the air, not fully extended like in a hold up, but partially, with his hands sprouting out just above his shoulders. I began to hear more specifically about this strange behavior from my students, many of whom were in his science classes. One day, while my tenth graders worked at their desks diagramming sentences, which, for the record, I still consider a worthy endeavor, I crept down the hall and around the corner to Mr. Matthers's room. He was wearing a tan lab coat with *Let's Bake Bread* stenciled across the front, standing before the class with his heels together and his toes pointed out at a ninety-degree angle, in what we were taught was the appropriate stance for reciting the Pledge of Allegiance or acknowledging "The Star-Spangled Banner" when I was young. And yes, his hands were aloft, not gesturing or even keeping rhythm with what he was saying but simply floating, perfectly still, as though he had thrown them up in a moment of surprise and forgotten them there.

However, that night at dinner, when I informed Felicity that I had gone down to Mr. Matthers's classroom and witnessed his strange behavior firsthand, she remained dismissive. "Maybe its part of a science experiment," she suggested, chewing as she spoke.

"A science experiment," I replied incredulously, though I paused to swallow first. "The students say that he teaches the entire class like that. How could it possibly be part of a science experiment?"

"Well, perhaps Mr. Matthers is experiencing problems with his circulation. Perhaps he is simply following the advice of a doctor," she had suggested next.

"Perhaps," I replied. "But wouldn't he explain this to the students if that were the case?"

"Perhaps Mr. Matthers is of the opinion that his duty to the students is to explain science," she replied, getting in the final "perhaps," though I knew that she did not care for Mr. Matthers either.

That had been our last discussion of the matter, but during

her week away, a second problem had arisen with Mr. Matthers, one that I wanted to apprise her of before she returned to school. I couldn't very well rouse her from a deep, jetlagged sleep to do so, but the next morning, once we were in the car, I turned to her and said, "Mr. Matthers has been up to his old tricks." She was still bald, of course, not that you would imagine otherwise.

Our commute took approximately twenty-five minutes, enough time to have discussed both Mr. Matthers and the *other* situation had Felicity been amenable to a discussion, which she was not on that particular morning. There were signs. Some mornings, she turned toward the window and rested her forehead against the glass, "appreciating its coolness," she said. Other days, she hummed, a habit she'd had as long as I'd known her. In both cases, I knew not to make any conversational overtures. I do consider it worth mentioning that she did not hum when she was alone, at least not to my knowledge. Rather, the humming was a purely public gesture, a means by which she kept others at a distance. I had pointed this out to her—the impoliteness of it— because that is the sort of thing that one wants to know, but she just laughed.

"Don't be silly," she said. "Humming is a joyful sound, an expression of tranquility and ease." What does one say to that?

Ten minutes into our commute, she had still offered none of the positive indicators, the signs that she welcomed conversation. She had not turned toward me with her left arm flung up along my seat back, fingertips extended invitingly. Nor had she called me *DriverDriver*, which was her nickname for me, borrowed from our friend Sandy, an accounts analyst who was often perplexed by the workings of the human mind. Aware of her shortcoming, Sandy administered personality assessment tests to all of her employees and then interacted with each according to the guidelines prescribed for his or her personality type. When she asked Felicity and me to take one of these tests as well, to help her be a "better friend" as she put it, we of course obliged.

I tested into the *driver* camp for both primary and secondary traits, thus the nickname.

Drivers are the control freaks, the ones who cannot let anything slide, though the nickname was meant as a joke, of course, a play on the fact that I literally never let anyone else drive. I've tried, but I get panicky the minute anyone else is behind the wheel. It's the speed, I suspect, for I feel the same way when the plane surges forward on takeoff, moving faster and faster down the runway with no possibility of turning back: my heart accelerates, and I am struck by an overwhelming desire to scream out, "Stop the plane!" I can imagine few things more mortifying, and the fear of embarrassing myself in this way somehow only exacerbates my panic. Still, I have found that I can calm myself in the middle of these attacks by focusing on something small and unchanging, a meaningless line of text from the airline catalog or the knuckles of my hands.

"Mr. Matthers is up to his old tricks," I repeated, for though Felicity had not extended any of her conversation invitations, neither was she humming or resting her forehead against the window.

"What has he done now? Taken to overseeing the labs with his legs bowed?" she replied, in a voice suggesting that she really did not care to know. Still, she had asked, and that was enough of an opening, particularly if I ignored the latter half of her question.

"Well," I said, perhaps too eagerly. "Remember how you commented just last week that Mrs. Chavez is really starting to show?" Mrs. Chavez, who, like Felicity, is a math teacher, announced just after the Christmas holiday that she was pregnant.

"I do."

"Well, Mr. Matthers has taken to asking her, every time he sees her in fact, whether she has ever experienced a miscarriage. On Thursday, four or five of us were in the lounge, and we all heard him. We knew about it already, of course, because Mrs. Chavez had mentioned it to several of us." This made it sound as though I was one of the people that Mrs. Chavez confided in, though that was not the case. "Then, Ms. Gutierrez scolded him right there in front of everyone. She told him that it wasn't proper to ask any woman, but especially a pregnant one, whether she'd ever had a miscarriage."

"And has he stopped?" Felicity asked, showing more interest than I expected.

"Well, I haven't heard of anything else, but I left right at the bell on Friday. I had the show, you know."

The show, because I realize that I haven't explained about the shows yet, was a cat show in Los Angeles, for which I left immediately after school on Friday, returning Sunday afternoon in time to grade a set of mediocre essays before picking Felicity up from the airport. Felicity and I are both highly skilled cat judges and, as such, find our services requested at cat shows all over the world. When we were hired at the school, the principal, who was a cat lover as well (though of the mixed-breed, pound-affiliated variety), was quite accommodating about our obligations. In turn, as a gesture of goodwill, we put forth that, except in cases of emergency, we would not accept judging duties that resulted in our being absent from work at the same time. Thus, Felicity agreed to do the Hong Kong show while I stayed behind, holding up our end of the bargain, teaching while she was off, as it turned out, having her head shaved.

By this time, we were pulling into the school parking lot, so Felicity was preoccupied, taking it all in after a week away, her head pivoting in tight, frenetic movements, like a sparrow's, which might have been the way she always moved her head, though, in the past, her hair was there to soften things. We got out of the car, walked across the parking lot and through the front doors, our paths diverging immediately—mathematics left, English right.

And so, I did not tell her about the other incident, the one that had nothing to do with Mr. Matthers at all. It happened on Friday, third period, with the tenth graders, of whom I am rather fond. I had started them on Salinger, despite the fact that another English teacher, whose name I shall not disclose, had suggested that Salinger, with all his "New Yorkiness," had little to "say" to a group of students who had grown up here in New Mexico.

"I believe that Salinger has something to *say* to all tenth graders," I had replied, perhaps overearnestly. "I myself was once a tenth grader growing up in Minnesota, and I found that he had plenty to say." I do not buy into this idea that one learns more from literature that is familiar; in fact, it seems only logical that one would learn most from subject matter that one has not already mastered through the daily grind of ones existence, which is what I shall tell her the next time she bothers me about Salinger.

I arrived in the classroom just as the bell was ringing, for I had paused briefly outside Mr. Matthers's room on my way back from the teachers' lounge, which is where I generally spend second period, my free hour. When I entered the classroom, the students were unusually still, already in their seats and seemingly engrossed in their Salingers. I felt a momentary thrill at being proven correct, but I had not turned to my right as I entered, so I did not yet know what was there, written in large letters on the blackboard.

"Good morning, class," said I, then waited while they responded in kind, for one of the things that we had been working on was the forgotten art of basic, cross-generational politeness. They always had plenty to say to one another, but on the first day of class, they had stared blankly at me when I greeted them, and so I had related the story of my sixth-grade teacher, Mrs. Kjelmer, who required us to line up at the end of each day and pass by her on our way out of the room, pausing to shake her hand and thank her for some specific contribution that she had made to our educations that day. I am fairly sure that we did not find this odd or extreme, but my students had stared at me in horror as I recounted the tale, a few of them even gasping, as though each day had ended with the beheading of a student rather than this basic gesture of appreciation.

Having acknowledged their return greeting with an inclination of my head, I turned around toward the board, and there, in an awkward teenage scrawl, was their summary of my relationship with Felicity:

MISS LUNDSTROM & MISS SHAPIRO ARE LEZZIE LOVERS!!

My immediate reaction, as you might expect, was akin to my feelings upon takeoff—that is, I felt remarkably close to crying out, "Stop the plane!" Instead, I did what a speech teacher long ago had advised, which was always to act in opposition to what one's nerves dictated. Thus, instead of mumbling and stammering my way through a demand to know whose work this was on the board, I turned back toward the class and asked, in a very precise, audible tone, whether anyone could recall my position on the ampersand.

There they sat with their mouths drifting open like a choir fading out after a sustained high note, and so I took several steps backward toward the board and pointed, with a surprisingly steady finger, at the offending ampersand. "This symbol, as you may recall, is called the ampersand. Like all symbols used to replace perfectly good words, it is, in my opinion, a symbol primarily of laziness and should be tolerated only on signs or in computer programming." With the side of my hand, I deftly swiped at the ampersand, then picked up a piece of chalk, and neatly wrote the word *and* in its place.

"Well," I said, turning again to the class. "Who would like to go next?"

They were familiar with this exercise, of course, for each time I handed back a set of essays, I selected five particularly poor sentences from among them, which I copied onto the blackboard.

Then we worked our way through them, one at a time, making corrections and revisions. Nonetheless, I was surprised when Keith, a short boy with a purple smattering of acne, raised his hand.

"Keith," I said.

"The exclamation points?" he asked.

"What about them?" I prodded.

"Do you really need two of them?" The students understood how I felt about the exclamation point, the impact of which I illustrated early on by passing around a print of Edvard Munch's *The Scream.*

"Good," I said. "Though I think that begs the question, 'Do we really need even one?'" I held the chalk out and Keith came dutifully to the front of the room, erased the exclamation marks, and inserted a simple period in their place.

"Well, I suppose that naturally brings us to the excessiveness of all-uppercase lettering, does it not?" I said, the students nodding as I rewrote the statement in lowercase, retaining the essential capital letters, of course.

We turned our attention to word choice then, with Clara S., as she always signed her name, suggesting that *lezzie* seemed "informal—or something."

"Hmm," I replied. "Yes, I suppose that a case could be made for informal. Does anyone else have any thoughts on the word *lezzie?*"

"It's spelled wrong?" suggested Beth, an exceedingly poor speller who walked with a strange, gliding motion, as though she were skiing.

"I know," cried Manuel, who was the sort to answer only those questions that the other students had already, and unsuccessfully, attempted. "It's prejudicial." He sat back with his long arms crossed triumphantly, a gesture that did nothing to endear him to the other students.

"What would you suggest?" I asked.

"Lesbian?" Manuel replied after a careful pause, having the good grace to uncross his arms as he spoke. Still, the other students became quiet, unsure perhaps where *lesbian* stood on the "prejudicial" scale, but I was saved the need to make a reassuring response by Tina, a shy girl, partial to plaid, who asked, "Isn't that redundant? I mean, you know they're lesbians because they're both women and they're lovers." Had I been in a different frame of mind, I might have turned the discussion to her seemingly unconscious reference to me and Felicity in the third person, though hadn't I been urging the students all year to please, oh please, just distance themselves a bit from the text?

"Nice work, Tina," I said, and she blushed deeply, in keeping with the type of personality that is attentive to redundancy.

The critique session took nearly half an hour, at the end of which the students slumped in their seats, looking dazed and exhausted. On the board was our final revision: *Ms. Lundstrom and Ms. Shapiro are lovers.* Of course, we had changed "Miss" to "Ms." in both cases, for, as I pointed out to them, Ms. Shapiro and I were not schoolgirls, nor was this the 1950s.

Felicity and I were introduced six years ago by a mutual friend whom I shall call Sally. Sally and I had, once upon a time, been English majors together, but she had gone on to accept a position, temporary she assured me at the time, with a company that replaced windshield glass. The company, however, was not accustomed to having employees who could put an estimate into proper letter format or utilize the semicolon, and soon she had been promoted to regional manager. There was a long period after college during which Sally and I were not in contact, but when I moved to the Twin Cities, I called her and we met for lunch. She looked nearly the same, although puffier and with a penchant for purple, and when she asked what I had been doing for the last fifteen years, I blurted out this parallel list of accomplishments: I had earned a Master's degree, done some teaching, and established that I was a lesbian.

Sally was new to the idea of knowing lesbians and admitted to being somewhat nervous, though she seemed unable to articulate the source of her nervousness. I have found that, when presented with this revelation, many people take a careful step back, keeping their mouths shut for fear of saying something wrong, but I have always found myself more charmed by those of Sally's nature, those who barrel right in, unaware that a list of right-and-wrong-things-to-say even exists. Thus, while Sally confessed to a certain nervousness, it was certainly, and refreshingly I might add, nothing that compelled her to err on the side of caution. She telephoned not long after our lunch meeting to announce that she had just met another lesbian, suggesting, with much enthusiasm, that I might wish to meet this new acquaintance, a woman named Felicity whose windshield had been shot out by a neighbor who resented people parking on the street in front of his house.

"And why might I want to meet somebody with such a ridiculous name?" I asked.

Sally paused, for I don't think that it had occurred to her that her suggestion might be met with anything but equal, possibly greater, zeal. "You're of the same ilk," she said at last.

Assuming that by "ilk" she meant a shared orientation, I replied that her "lowest common denominator" approach to matchmaking was a bit insulting.

"But you're both lesbians," she insisted indignantly.

"That," I explained, trying to be gentler, "is the 'lowest common denominator' to which I refer. It is a necessary factor, true, but it hardly qualifies as, well, ilkiness." In her defense, she did not know the special attachment I had to the word *ilk*.

Sally, however, was of a persistent nature, and so, several weeks later, when she and I again met for lunch, Felicity was there as well, though I learned afterwards that she had been no more apprised of this meeting than I. At the time, I was putting the finishing touches on my dissertation, which dealt with the practicalities of teaching grammar and writing to older-than-average students. I had discovered, for example, that in a class made up largely of women in their fifties, coordinate and subordinate clauses made sudden sense for them when likened to marriages, the former a marriage in which the two parties were equals, the latter a marriage in which one party was dependent on the other for meaning. In my dissertation, I had neglected to mention, as a corollary to this discovery, that many of the women steadfastly purged their writing of all subordinate clauses following this lesson, suddenly seeing something shameful in each *if* and *because*.

I arrived for lunch that day bearing a list of problematic sentences from my dissertation, hoping to review them with Sally in order to ensure that my meaning, as I intended it, was patently clear, even to the less engaged reader. I saw no reason to alter my plans simply because Felicity was present. In turn, she felt that it was perfectly acceptable to interrupt me and my troubling sentences almost immediately with the following observation: "You have no control over what the reader thinks; you do realize that I would hope. It doesn't matter *what* you intended."

I'd had my fill of critical theory by that time, so I certainly did not need to be eating lunch with some amateur reader-response critic, but when I suggested, coyly, that perhaps she had been reading too much Stanley Fish, she stared back at me blankly. "I don't believe that I am familiar with Mr. Fish's work," she replied, overly politely I felt. "I'm simply making a point about the way that people communicate. This conversation is a perfect example," she added, pointing her fork at me severely and, I might add, not unbecomingly. "I'm *saying* one thing, but you *think* I'm talking about something else entirely, about some Fish fellow, whom I've never even heard of."

I will admit that her use of "whom" left me undone, even with that preposition dangling unattractively at the end, but then I'm afraid that I've always been attracted to such things, the ability to differentiate between subject and object forms, a refusal to use *if* when the situation requires *whether*.

"This," she was saying, "is what makes mathematics so appealing. The number one is simply that—one. Everyone who sees it thinks the same thing." She looked smugly at me across the table.

"Yes," I replied. "But numbers are just as much symbols as words are." I had nowhere to go from there, but I insisted on babbling on. "This," I said, pounding the table, "is a table, the actual, tangible thing, not to be confused with the word. The same can be said for your number *one*, I am afraid." I sketched out the number in the air between us.

Of course I was ashamed of myself, using basic Plato to impress this woman, though, to her credit, she did not look impressed. There was a moment of stiff silence, which compelled me to continue. "To quote one of my students, 'Why is a sheep a sheep and not a rock,'" I said lamely, a bit of irrelevant nonsense to end the discussion, but to my great pleasure, she laughed. Sally, in case you were wondering, was still present, sitting there eating her Cobb salad and, I was to find out later, listening to us argue and regretting the fact that she had ever thought us *ilkstresses* (my word, of course, not the windshield-fixing Sally's).

Over the next few days, Felicity and I did not discuss her baldness or the incident with the chalkboard or even the ongoing escapades of Mr. Matthers, who had gone on to post several signs in the teachers' lounge announcing that he was interested in acquiring used Tupperware, the word *used* underlined thrice. She made a point of emphasizing her busyness and her jetlag, and before we knew it, it was Friday and I was off again, this time to a cat show in Scottsdale, and when I returned on Sunday evening, via a taxi as we had planned, Felicity was gone. I'm sure that to the average, discerning reader, this comes as no surprise, and so I am embarrassed to admit that I never saw it coming.

She left a short letter, of course, in which she explained that she had moved into a studio apartment downtown and purchased a used car, drawing entirely on her "own funds," she was careful to note. The car, she wrote, had belonged to one of the teachers at the school, but she did not refer to this teacher by name, an omission that struck me as a total denial of the degree to which our lives were intertwined. She acknowledged this interconnectedness only at the very end when she wrote that it was her desire that we not "advertise" the change in our relationship at work, that she did realize there would be speculation and gossip, particularly after she filed her new address with the school secretary, but that she hoped we could "absent ourselves from such conversations and treat one another with the politeness and friendly rivalry accorded colleagues."

I was most bothered by the reference to her "own funds," for I was not aware of any funds other than the meager sum of money that resided in our joint checking account, though the mystery of these funds resolved itself soon enough. I made a quick sweep of the house, noting that she had taken all of her books, an easily accomplished task for we had never merged our collections, but left those that we had acquired together. Appliances and kitchen items also remained, though when I counted the cutlery and dinnerware, both of which we had purchased in sets of twelve, I found that each set now consisted of eleven pieces, a consolation, for had there been two of each missing, it would have suggested a situation that I lacked the emotional wherewithal to face.

One of my suitcases was gone, but I forgave her this, for I had taken her suitcase with me to Scottsdale, the suitcase that we always fought over because it was light and maneuverable and orange—easy to spot on the luggage carousel. I fetched it from where I had parked it just inside the door and, not one to let sorrow sideline the moments practical requirements, began to unpack—placing clothes in the hamper, hanging my toothbrush in its usual slot, though both were now available, and transferring the set of essays that I had graded on the plane into my briefcase.

Inside the suitcase's small, inner compartment, which over-zealousness required that I check even though I had not used the compartment, I discovered a piece of paper folded carelessly in half. It bore a pinhole near the top, and several Chinese characters marched down one side, so I knew immediately that it had been left behind after Felicity's less-methodical style of un-packing, carried out exactly one week earlier upon her return from Hong Kong. The rest of the text, which was in English, read thusly:

NOTICE

Kindly to all hotel guests.

A Hong Kong film company has need of the following:

1. Several women (Caucasian) to serve as extras. Roles require British Victorian maidens, but as there is no speaking requirement, Americans and Australians are acceptable. Costumes provided. No stipend, but scene involves eating. Real food provided.
2. Caucasian woman, any age, for horror film. No speaking, but must be willing to shave head on camera. Upon completion of baldness, a fee of $2500 (U.S.) will be paid in cash.

Interested parties should please inquire from Mr. Simon Woo, front desk, for contact particulars. Thank you.

I read the notice twice, the English teacher in me making mental corrections, before tucking it away inside my desk, in the note-book containing this account, and though I tried to sleep then, I could not. Finally, I rose, retrieved this notebook, and proceeded to read back over my text thus far, but gone were my student days when everything seemed clearer in the middle of the night. I did realize, in looking back over what I had written, that I had said nothing of Felicity's hair, beyond noting its absence. For the record, it was blond, though not purely so, but I dislike expressions such as *dirty blond* and *dishwater blond*. Perhaps what I most admired about her hair, purely from an aesthetic point of view, were the two patches of white hair that grew in little tufts on either side of her head, directly at her temples. A beautician told her once that these white patches were caused by the use of forceps during childbirth, which I liked to think was the case, suggesting as it did that her stubbornness-bordering-on-truculence had been there all along, making its debut in her unwillingness to cooperate with her own birth, and while the beautician had seemed confident of her theory, she had also maintained with equal assurance that she herself had been born with the ability to understand both German and Chinese, so you can understand my reluctance to put full faith in her explanation.

When I parked in the school lot the next morning, I looked around at the other cars, wondering which was the used car that Felicity had purchased with her own funds, the source of which I had identified but did not wish to dwell upon. She and I did not cross paths that morning, which was not surprising, for, as I have already indicated, math and English occupied different sides of the school. I made it through my first class and chose to spend my free period in my classroom rather than in the teachers' lounge, so I was there, sitting at my desk, when my tenth graders arrived, Salingers in hand. It was impossible, of course, that they knew anything of our breakup, but I could not shake the feeling that they sensed something, for they struck me as oddly muted that morning, restrained, like caricatures of what they believed perfect students to be.

I handed back their essays, the ones that I had graded on the airplane in a state of oblivion as my bald girlfriend was transporting her few possessions, via her new used car, to her studio downtown, but when I turned toward the blackboard to copy out the five worst sentences, something struck me, perhaps the memory of the last sentence that we had revised, pushing and prodding it into some sort of straightforward, grammatically sound ideal: *Ms. Lundstrom and Ms. Shapiro are lovers*. In any case, as I stood there at the board, chalk in hand, set to record their most recent transgressions, I began to sob. I did so quietly, of course, but eventually they understood that something was amiss, and I felt them become perfectly still behind me. For several minutes, I stared at a particular spot on the blackboard, at what appeared to be the remains of a letter *b*, composing myself, and then I turned to face my tenth graders, wholly unprepared for the looks of sheer terror and helplessness that sat upon their faces. We stayed as we were, facing one another, I in front of the blackboard and they, sitting erectly in their seats, eyes focused uniformly downward, with the exception of Tina, my timid, plaid-wearing redundancy expert, who sat in the back row regarding me closely and nodding.

"Class," I said at last, "please forgive me. I am not in the habit of indulging in such outbursts." At hearing me sound reasonably like myself, they tilted their faces upward again, relief settling collectively upon them; I recalled, in that instant, the vulnerability of youth. I would like to say that this put me fully in charge of my emotions and that the remainder of the class passed without incident, but that was not the case. Rather, as the tears began to flow once more down my face, I blurted out—in an attempt to explain myself and perhaps offer reassurance—these words: "Ms. Shapiro is bald."

Dance for Me

AMINA GAUTIER

From *At-Risk* (2011)

The girls on Lexington had it the worst. Hated maroon skirts the color of dried blood. Navy blazers complete with gaudy emblem. Goldenrod blouses with Peter Pan collars. And knee socks. Actually, knee socks weren't so bad. Knee socks served their purpose in the winter, keeping sturdy calves warm.

The girls on East End wore gray or navy skirts, plain and not pleated, with a white blouse, sweater optional.

Multiple skirts were another way to go. We had our choice of navy, gray, maroon, and an unpleated light blue seersucker meant only for the spring. The choices allowed us to pretend we weren't really wearing a uniform. We hoped merely to be thought eccentric. Girls with a penchant for skirts with panels. But we fooled no one. Our uniforms, our talk, our walk, our avid interest in grooming and normal people's clothing, and our daily preoccupation with what we would wear on upcoming field trips when allowed to be out of uniform filled our time and conversations. We had a special way of standing that was part lean, part slouch, as if posture was too much of a bother to consider.

Nameless, faceless on a school trip, we stood out. Solid-colored blouses, pleated skirts, knee socks, and loafers, bluchers, or oxfords. Private school girls. Not to be confused with Catholic school girls. Or reform school girls (how many times did the kids in my neighborhood look at me in condescending pity?). Not to be confused with the girls from *The Facts of Life*. They were boarders. No matter how many times I tried to explain this, the kids in my neighborhood persisted in calling me Tootie.

We attended a second-tier all-girls school. It wasn't as illustrious as the private schools on the Upper East Side nor as seedy as the ones in Midtown. We clung to our small but unique differences. For example, having our choices of uniforms made us the envy of the other all-girls schools. Girls were sure to take it out on us during soccer games. Secondly, there was our partnership with a nearby all-boys school, our "brother" school two blocks away, which allowed us to have kissing partners whenever we put on a play.

At school, there were the WASPs and the JAPs. And me. Girls with last names for first names. Riley. Taylor. Haley. Morgan. Hayden. Girls whose names are meant for a boy or girl, depending.

I'd never told anyone this, but I always felt naked in my pleated skirt, vulnerable. There was a trick to rolling the skirt that would take several inches off, a way of folding tightly and minutely that would allow one to hide the extra material beneath a shirt if tucked then pulled out just enough to camouflage the extra bulk. Only I didn't know it. I'd seen it numerous times, jealously watching girls enter the bathroom with skirts that covered their knees and walk back out with skirts that skimmed their thighs, but I still couldn't get it. The lines of my pleat were never quite right, always drooping in the front, making me look slightly off kilter.

It was lunchtime and I was in the school's bathroom with my stomach bared to the mirror as I tried to roll my skirt when Taylor and Ashley entered and headed for the stalls, deep in conversation. Neither of them noticed me.

"Well, I wouldn't go with a guy from Buckley, that's for sure."

"I might not get to go at all. We're supposed to go to the Hamptons and my dad really has his heart set on it. How am I supposed to get out of it?"

"I don't know. I so need a new pair of jeans. Do you want to go to the Gap today after we get out of chorus?"

"Um, yeah. Hey, did you hear Heather's parents let Chase go to Cabo San Lucas with her for spring break?"

"No."

"They even paid his way."

So caught up in eavesdropping on their conversation, I didn't hear the squeal of the bathroom door the second time it opened. Heather walked in alone and went straight to the mirror. She frowned slightly when she heard herself being discussed. Then she went into a stall near theirs.

"Who said that?"

"Heather, that's who."

"I heard she broke up with him."

"For the coxswain? That's like way over."

"What happened?"

"He dumped her for a girl from Chapin."

Two toilets flushed simultaneously. By the time Taylor and Ashley emerged, I'd whipped out my Carmex and pretended to be carefully moisturizing, all thoughts of fixing my skirt gone. They washed their hands and walked out without looking at me.

Once they left, Heather came out of her stall.

Moments like these were common. They happened several times during the day—self-reflective moments where girls met in between classes, gathering in bathrooms and on stairways to consider the grave issues of the times and their place in the world. Usually the person being discussed wasn't present.

Heather was still standing there. Her eyes met mine in the mirror. "It's not true, you know."

"What?"

"I never went out with that guy. Never even kissed him. He was a total turd."

I shrugged. "Okay."

She scrutinized me. "You're in my class."

I nodded. "Yeah."

"Do you know about the party on West Ninety-first this Friday?"

"At Trinity?"

"Are you going?"

I pretended to give the question some thought. The parties were hosted by coed private day schools who issued invitations to certain schools, who then issued memberships to certain students. She knew I couldn't go. The memberships were a subtle way of excluding the undesirables. The membership lists went out in sixth grade. The scholarship girls who came in through the enrichment programs started in seventh grade. There was no way ever to be included on the lists, unless someone sponsored me, which no one ever did. I had no plans to go to the party this Friday or any other Friday and she knew it.

"I wasn't planning on it," I said.

"Oh. Do you know how to do that new dance they're doing?" she asked me. "You know the one that goes like this." Heather's gyrations resembled nothing I could identify.

"Um no, I can't say that I know that one," I said. "Sorry."

"Maybe I'm doing it wrong," she said.

"Maybe."

"It's called running something."

"The running man?"

"That's it!" She touched my arm. "Do you know it?"

"Sure."

"Can you show me?"

I looked around. "Here? In the bathroom?"

"Yeah." Heather smiled at me, warm and eager. I really didn't want to. I wasn't a very good dancer and I didn't like to perform. At home, I would sing only in the shower, and I danced at house parties only when the lights were very low. But I danced for her, awkward at first, since there was no music, but she didn't seem to notice or mind. Once I started dancing, her eyes never met mine. They were riveted instead to my legs and feet. I had a feeling she wanted to take notes.

"That looks so hard," she said.

"It's not," I huffed. I danced harder, wanting to show off. I was silently repeating the words of a popular song in my head to give myself a beat. I danced harder as I tried to incorporate moves I'd seen on *Video Music Box*, getting ahead of myself and quickly losing the beat. A video diva I had never been, watching videos only on Saturdays when my mother was out. I was losing my rhythm and running out of breath when she finally said, "Wow. You're good. Really, really good."

I stopped and took a deep breath. I smiled. "Thanks."

That evening, our phone rang, something it hardly ever did. My mother eyed the phone suspiciously, letting it ring three times before picking up. "Hello?" she answered warily, frowning at the unseen offender who'd interrupted her silence.

"Yes, hold on." She held the phone out to me. "It's for you?" I ignored the question in her voice and grabbed it.

"Hi, it's me."

"Hi. It's Heather," she said, as if I wouldn't know her voice.

"Hey."

Who is it? my mother mouthed silently.

Heather, I mouthed back. *From school.*

It had been my mother's idea to put me in the enrichment program that had given me a scholarship for the all-girl's school, a decision she'd come to regret in the face of my loneliness and unpopularity. Now, she hovered and tried to listen in, filled with hope.

Heather's excitement came through, giddy and loud. "You're coming! You are so coming," she shrieked into my ear.

"What are you talking about?"

"The party this Friday. Did you forget?"

"No, I remember."

"Well, I got you in. I sponsored you," she said. There was a pause in her voice, as if she was waiting for something.

"Thanks," I said.

"You don't sound excited."

"I am."

"You are going to go, right?"

I didn't answer. I was taking my time to think about it. Although she'd sponsored me, there was still the question of clothing. I had nothing suitable to wear. The dance would also end late and I didn't think my mother would want me riding home from Manhattan to Brooklyn that late at night by myself. "Well—"

"Nadira is going," Heather said, as if it made a difference.

Nadira was the other black girl in our class. She'd been at the school since kindergarten. There were a number of affluent black and Asian girls in my school, and we claimed no kinship with one another. If I closed my eyes and listened to them speak, I wouldn't know they weren't white. Though Nadira and I belonged to the same race, she had more in common with the white girls. She and they lived in the same neighborhoods, had the same friends, values, and ideals. They listened to z100 and sang classical in the choir. Like the white girls, she could not dance. I couldn't either, but no one knew that. They all took it for granted that I could.

"I'd like to, but I don't think my mom will let me because it ends so late."

"Tell her that's no problem. I wanted you to stay over. I'm having a little get-together at my house after the dance. You know, an after-the-party party. Just a couple of girls. A sleepover. Taylor. Maya. Ashley and maybe some others. Ask your mom if it's okay."

I held the receiver to my chest. "Mom? Heather wants to know if it's okay if I sleep over at her house this Friday." Heather lived in a penthouse on Ninety-fifth and Park. Of course it was okay.

Heather invited me to sit with her at lunch the next day. Four girls smiled at me as I sat, and then they continued on with their discussions.

"I have this body suit and I'm going to wear it with my white jeans," Maya said. The other girls nodded their approval.

"You should wear your hair half up and half down," Heather told her.

"I don't have anything to wear. I'm going to need something new," Taylor said.

"Let's go to the Gap after class today and find something," Ashley suggested.

They were all wearing fleeced pullovers in different colors from L.L. Bean or Patagonia over their collared blouses and they were wearing heather gray leggings beneath their pleated skirts. None of them had on socks. Their feet were bare in their loafers, docksiders, and bluchers.

I excused myself to go to the bathroom. There, I peeled off my socks. Ashley followed behind me. When I stood up, socks in hand, she said, "Um, do you think you could show me the dance you showed Heather?"

The next day, I was back in the bathroom, showing five new girls. For the next two days, Heather brought girls to me and we took them into the bathroom to teach them the steps. For the next two days, I danced and danced on the cold white tiles while white girls leaned against sinks and stall doors and watched. The dancing, I thought, brought me respect and admiration. Through it,

I was redeeming myself in their eyes. I was, after all these years, good for something.

The day before the dance, Heather caught me on my way out to the train station. "I've been meaning to tell you this. About the party on Friday." Hands jammed into her jacket pockets, she stood on one foot, the other snaked around her calf, rubbing the back of her leg with the toe of her shoe.

My stomach tightened. Now she'd tell me it had all been a joke. They'd been teasing me. Making me feel as though I fit in was a prank some upperclasswoman had put them up to. "What about it?"

"Well, I know I told you there were just going to be girls at the party, but I wanted to make sure you'd come. There are going to be a few guys there, too. Don't worry, they're cool. They're guys I know from St. Bernard's, Allen-Stevenson, Buckley, and Collegiate."

"But—"

"They're going to sleep in the den. We'll meet them at the party and they'll come back with us. Is that cool?"

"Yeah," I said, relieved that her groundbreaking news had nothing to do with me.

"Good. Look, the girls and I chipped in on this. We were wondering if you could score us some weed? We want to have some real fun. I hope this is enough," Heather said, pressing crinkly bills into my hand. She patted my arm and stepped off the curb to hail a cab to take her home. I clutched the money in my hand, walked down Lexington to catch the four train, and rode home.

When I got home that night, I searched in my mother's sewing basket until I found her seam ripper. I removed the deadly thing and carefully pulled off the stitches surrounding the little horse on the back pocket of my jeans.

I changed into these jeans, a trial run for the real test tomorrow. I was surprised to see myself in regular clothes. I changed shirts and threw on a light jacket. I counted out the money Heather had given me, folded it neatly, and slipped it into my pocket.

"Where are you going?" my mother asked when she saw me at the door.

"Out."

She didn't ask for any further explanation. Something had changed between us ever since the phone call. My blossoming friendships pleased her. My mother was as happy as if the invitation had been extended to her. Just yesterday, she'd put her hand on my shoulder while I was washing dishes. "I just want you to be happy," she'd said, her guilt now assuaged.

There was a store two blocks away that I knew was just a front. I'd gone in once to buy snacks and everything they sold me was expired, stale. I pushed through the door and walked in. One teenager hunched over an arcade game and two lounged against the corners of the wall. Twenty-five-cent bags of popcorn, potato chips, and cheese curls, ten-cent lollipops, and five-cent Peanut Chews and pieces of Super Bubble were behind a counter covered in Plexiglas.

I walked up to the counter.

"Can I buy some weed here?"

I could feel everyone look at me. The man behind the counter squinted. He cleared his throat. He took a long time before he spoke. "We got soda and chips. What you see, that's what we got."

"But I want to buy some weed," I said. "I have money."

"We sell candy, soda, and chips," he said. "You wanna buy some candy?"

I didn't know what else do to. I was frustrated, wanting to argue. He knew it was a weed spot; I knew it was a weed spot. Was there some magic word I needed to say, some secret code that would let him know I meant business?

I pulled my money out and held it up to the Plexiglas. "Open sesame," I said.

He shook his head. I walked out.

A minute later, I felt someone behind me. I turned. I recognized him from the store; he'd been playing Pac-Man. "What was you doing in there? You crazy or something?"

I walked faster. "Leave me alone."

"That was real stupid. What, you not from around here?"

"I live here," I told him.

He didn't believe me. "Where?"

"Miller and Pitkin."

"I live on that block and I never seen you."

"Well, I go to school," I said.

His lips curled up then. They were full, made brown from smoking. His eyes were large, round, sleepy. He was older. Beautiful. I felt my mistake. "I didn't mean it like that."

He walked by my side. "So why you wanna buy weed?"

"Just to try it," I said. "For fun."

"You ever smoke a blunt before?"

"I didn't want a blunt. I wanted a joint."

He looked at me like I was stupid. "I was going to buy it for my friends," I said. "They asked me to get it for a party."

"So, you still want it?"

"Five dollars for a nickel bag, right?"

"You been watching too much TV," he said.

He refused to give it to me out on the street.

"Let's take a walk." We walked past my block and past the intermediate school to the park.

He stopped when we got to the swings. He sat down on one and backpedaled with his feet. "Come here."

I stood between his legs; we were eye to eye.

"What's your name?" he asked.

"You don't need to know."

He nodded. "So, you like white boys."

"No," I said.

"Black guys?"

"Nope."

"Girls?" he asked, his voice filled with disbelief and excitement.

"I don't like anybody," I said.

He pulled me toward him and kissed me. The faint sweet scent of smoke clung to his chin and I knew that I would smell of him. I had a feeling as if I were waiting in the subway for my train just before it pulls in and it was rushing down the track, blowing its dirty hot wind underneath my skirt, caressing the bare skin between pleats and socks. I tried to pull away but felt his hands cupping my butt, felt him slip the bag of weed into my back pocket. He turned me away from him, adjusting me so that I sat on his front thighs. Pretending to put his arms around me, he slipped his hands into my front pockets, seeking until he found my folded cash. Slick, I thought. Smooth. To anyone passing by, we looked like two fools making out in the park.

The party, because I had longed for it, was a disappointment. The deejay could not mix one song into another. The lights never got very low. We stood in a papered gymnasium, in jeans, stretchy shirts, and too many coats of mascara. Girls from different schools divided themselves accordingly. Even without their uniforms, I could pick out the girls from Brearley, Chapin, and Spence. The boys Heather knew didn't show up until the end of the party. The only people I really knew were Heather, Taylor, Maya, and Ashley, and every time I saw them, they were all dancing, proudly showing off the moves I'd taught them. I ran into Nadira once that night when we were both getting sodas, but she didn't speak to me. I held up the wall all night. No one asked me to dance. I held my plastic cup of soda and thought of my mother at home, sleeping blissfully, happy and proud.

I had only one chance to talk to Heather at the dance. She came over to where I stood on the wall, her face flushed from dancing. "Did I do okay?" she asked me.

"You look good," I said.

"How do you like it?"

I shrugged. "It's okay."

"Aren't you dancing?"

"Nobody asked me."

"They probably don't want you to embarrass them," Heather said. I didn't bother to tell her that the dance I'd shown her was the only one I knew. "Don't worry," she said. "The real party starts when we get to my house."

At Heather's house, we had carte blanche. Her parents were asleep. Heather brought out the alcohol, I pulled out the small bag of weed, and we wasted no time getting drunk and high. A boy Heather had introduced as Gabe wanted to play a version of spin the bottle.

I was the first victim. Gabe and I looked at each other across the thin neck of the bottle, unsure.

"He's never made it with a black girl before," Taylor said.

"So?"

"Go in the closet with him," Heather suggested. "Show him how it's done." She clapped me on the arm and gave me a push. Gabe held out his hand and I got up, unsteadily, taking it. I wasn't sure that I wanted to go, but I went.

We sat in the deep closet; the hems of Heather's jackets grazed the tops of our heads. I decided I couldn't, wouldn't do it. Gabe slid a finger up my arm and I shivered, backing away. "Wow, this closet is really big, huh?"

"It's cool," he said. "We don't have to, you know, I mean unless you want . . ." He looked hopeful even in the dark.

"I can't," I said.

"Maybe if you touch it." He took my hand and rubbed it against his denim crotch, his hand over mine.

"I'm going to be sick," I said.

"Whoa, wait a minute," he said. "Okay."

"Sick sick sick," I said.

He leaned back, but in a minute he asked, "Can I touch your breasts?"

"I don't think so."

"Just once?" He reached under my shirt. My bra was lace, one of my mother's cast-offs. My underwear did not match, but I knew he would never know that.

"Hey," he said, feeling the lace cups of my bra. "Whoa. Hey."

"Whoa. Hey," I said, mocking him, feeling suddenly warm.

His hand closed over my breast and squeezed. It made me think of the old-fashioned cars in a Bugs Bunny cartoon. "Beep beep," I said, then burst out laughing.

He laughed, too, and then the two of us couldn't stop laughing. We fell against each other, laughing. Then he pulled me through the jackets and across his lap, pushing his tongue into my mouth, banging his teeth against mine, kissing me wet and sloppy. I tasted the strong flavor of weed on his tongue and thought of the boy who'd sold it to me, how beautiful he'd been, how though we lived just a few blocks apart, we were strangers. Like the boy pressing himself against me; we were from different worlds. They were both from the real world, their own distinct ones, but I was somewhere in limbo. Set apart, I didn't know how to let either of them in.

Gabe's hands were tugging my shirt down, and I knew that in a minute they'd be working the latch of my bra, but I didn't stop him. In the dark of Heather's closet, I tried to see what Gabe saw.

I pictured an image of myself that was Heather's body and face, only it was black and it was me. I saw how much of me would change; I saw the girl I would become. And I decided to go ahead and miss myself right now, knowing that the girl I would become wouldn't know how to appreciate me at all.

Thieves I've Known

TOM KEALEY

From *Thieves I've Known* (2013)

A boxer's offense is designed to create openings in the opponent's defense and to land blows to the vulnerable points of the head and body from the waist up. Power originates as she pushes off from her feet; its degree depends upon her ability to link the muscles of the legs, the back, the shoulders, and the arms into a chain of force. A boxer's attack consists of such basic blows as left jab, right cross, left hook, and uppercut.

Helen, fifteen, throws a hook from her left foot, covers her mid-section, ducks, takes a hit on her padded headgear, feints with the left again, listens to her trainer's voice, mumbled through his mouthpiece: move back and back in, keep me in the center, I'll kill you near the ropes. Move with your feet, keep your waist straight. Next time you lean back, I'll knock you down; and when she does lean back, he does knock her down, with a strong hook to her forehead and a sudden shove of hips. After the fall, she stares at the tubes of fluorescent lights above the gym, the glow of the streetlamp through the windows, the nightbugs outside. She presses her gloves against the canvas, feels the cold lick of sweat against her T-shirt.

I haven't started the count yet, he says. Not even in the corner yet. You wait till five before you get up. Think about where you are, and think about what put you there. Three, You know I'll push hard now. I'm going to see what you've got left. Five.

Helen stands, punches her gloves together, hops on her toes. He is a head taller than her, wider in the chest and waist, with longer arms and better technique. Dark hair covers his chest and shoulders. He moves in and she sidesteps, takes another jab to the head but slips in one of her own. He chooses not to cover, tries a jab and misses. She has already turned, gives him a hard shot to the ribs and then a harder one still with the other arm. Before he can wrap her up, she steps away, covers her head as she was taught, swings to the center of the ring. She hears the slap of her punches only now, seconds after they landed. Because she holds her ground, he tries a cross and it glances off the top of her skull, but he pays with two blows to his ribs, the other side this time. He steps away and circles the ring, keeps a distance from her. He notes that she has been practicing.

I'm going to knock you down now, he says, and again, he does. A flurry of hooks and crosses, most of them missing. She plants a strong jab in his gut, hears nothing, moves back, which was the mistake: he connects to the side of her head and then with the right square to the nose, her headgear saving the bone from cracking. It's only after she falls, after her feet fly from the canvas, her back slapping flat against the mat, that she hears his grunt of surprise. Not now, but from seconds before, the jab to the gut. She looks at the fluorescent lights again. She tastes the blood in her mouthpiece as he retires to the corner.

I haven't started yet, he says. The words come out without vowels. Helen shakes her head, sits up but does not rise. Two, he says. You've got me thinking now. Got me thinking this'll go an extra round. I'm not going to push it hard this time, or maybe I will. But if I'm smart I won't. Five. Stay down. I'm thinking I might not bring all I got here. So what are you going to do?

Keep you moving, she says. I'm going to move around.

Get up now, he says. And make sure you do that.

On the train, Omar, twelve, finds it hard to understand the mumbled voice of the conductor who announces the station stops. He likes to talk to his mother on the train, though she doesn't ride with him; it keeps people away. He thinks about his brother and the belt. A woman with a baby sits across from him, and a man dressed in two heavy coats. Give me your belt, his brother had said to him through the broken glass of the warehouse window. What do you want my belt for? Just give it here. So, Omar had handed it over and watched as his brother wrapped it around his arm. The boy took out a needle from his sock.

His brother often talked as he was shooting up. Mama's too fat, his brother had said. She eats too much.

When he was younger, when he'd handed the belt over, Omar hoped he'd always live with his mother, thought about no matter how old he became, the three of them would still live in the same house. I don't want no skinny-bones mama, he'd said. She isn't a girl. I don't want to sit on the lap of no skinny-bones girl.

He takes the steps from the subway station two at a time, watches his frost breath as he comes above ground. The abandoned car in the lot near the station has a cracked windshield with blood and a few strands of hair, and in a lot not unlike this one, a month before, two kids were trapped in an abandoned refrigerator, suffocated. Omar likes the tugboats in the harbor, he can see their red running lights from the top floor of his apartment building, but to get there—to the top floor—he has to pass the steps on the sixteenth, the hallway with no lightbulbs, where, often enough, he can hear a man crying. But Omar has never seen this man, thinks he might be an old man, by the sound of the voice, takes the steps one at a time when he passes.

If he sits on the rooftop—his legs hanging over the side—at sunset, Omar can see the rats emerge from the riverbank. They look like an army of insects from where he sits. They cross the lot where the car with the cracked windshield sits, they pass over the rolls of carpets, the broken chairs and the trash and the abandoned tires.

It's the last day of the month, this day, and Omar passes his own apartment building, passes the cemetery with the broken headstones—no one has been buried there for years—passes the piles of trash in the graveyard, the oil drum filled with wood and fire, passes, for all he knows, the skeleton his friend Toomey had seen, not rising from the ground, but laid in a corner, never buried, the bones as gray as the sky. Omar keeps his eyes on the tallest building on the street, where, on the fifth floor, he hopes to find his mother. A rent party.

He thinks about the baby on the train. Its eyes closed, wrapped in a green sweater, its mother's—sister's?—enfolding arms swaying with the rhythm of the railcar. More than wanting to live with his own mother, and long before even stepping on that train, before stepping on countless trains, Omar had wanted a baby boy of his own. But only you know that.

Winston, thirteen, takes the handkerchief from his pocket and wipes the spittle from his grandfather's chin. The old man turns the key in the ignition of the truck. It's older than Winston, abandoned in their backyard for almost as long as the boy can remember. The boy had shoveled leaves and twigs—a bird's nest?—from the seats before they'd entered. The windshield is cracked in the corner—no hair or blood, simply a crack, a rock left on a road years before. Unlike his grandfather, who is gaunt, mostly bones, skeletal, Winston is a big boy, bigger than most in his school. Fat. Fat fingers, fat toes. He's only eleven but thinks as he gains age he might gain the person inside himself whom he wishes to be. The old man, his name is Winston too, coughs, and Winston wipes again with the handkerchief.

The truck is not going to turn over. The engine in the truck— the starter—is not going to turn over. Winston looks out the windshield and sees, in the distance, the sunflower fields bend-

ing with the wind. To the left he sees the lights—green and red—
of the Ferris wheel of the traveling carnival. From this distance,
a long distance away, it looks slow, but when he'd sat in one of
the cars with his father, it had seemed fast, rising and falling
above the lights of the spook house and the ticket merchants—
and he hopes, if the starter turns over, that he and his grandfather might drive there. Might ride the Ferris wheel together. In
his pocket he carries all the money he has to his name (seven dollars and change). But the starter won't turn. Winston, the grandson, knows little about trucks or cars, but thinks, as his grandfather turns the key, that something is being burned out. That the
more the key turns, the more something is being lost.

He'd ridden the Ferris wheel only once. Had not budgeted—
his father's word—correctly, and had left that seven dollars and
change at home. He'd blown most of his money on the spook
house, which his father had refused to ride with him. He'd sat
alone, that first time, in the front car, had screamed when the
dragon had bent at the entrance, fire glowing in its belly, and
had assumed (Winston) that he'd be scorched before he even
got inside the house. The pirates had swiped their sabers above
his head, a witch boiled the skulls of children in her cauldron,
and the bony white hands of skeletons had barely reached him,
clicking against the top of the rail car. The giants appeared after that. I want it to be quiet in here, the man in the car behind
him had said, and it was only then that Winston could hear his
own screams, had felt for a moment outside himself, had wondered, hearing that man's voice, what his classmates might think
of him. I can't help it, he'd said, I'm scared. Had said that with
the weight of the two dollars he'd paid for the ride. Two dollars,
he felt, earned him the right to scream. More pirates had been
next, and the goblins after that. Finally, the ghosts, white sheets,
through which he could make out the people, and he did not feel
so afraid. But he continued to scream, wanting his two dollars'
worth, until the cars exited the house and he saw his father wait-

ing near the ticket booth, arms crossed, the Ferris wheel turning in the black sky behind him.

Looks like you were scared, said his father.

No, Winston had said. I loved it.

The starter turns over. Winston looks behind him, through the glass of the rear window of the truck. A thick cloud of smoke—as big as a giant's fist—blows out into the air. Beyond, Winston can see an orange glow, not the sun, which was setting in the opposite direction, but something else, something almost as big, glowing and stretching toward the sky.

His grandfather says nothing, has said nothing for almost a week. He switches the gears into Drive, and the truck sets off across the yard, spitting a trail of white smoke and mud.

A boxer's defense is designed to prevent the jabs, hooks, and crosses of her opponent from reaching the vulnerable areas. It is also intended to leave her in a position from which she might score with her own punches. A boxer avoids an opponent's blows by using correct techniques in blocking, parrying, ducking, and slipping.

Helen showers, dresses, ices down her left elbow where a bruise has already formed. She waits for her trainer at the ringside of the gym, watches two young men wrap each other up near the ropes. An older man separates them, gives them a silent count, steps away, and the shorter of the two men takes a shot to the head, swings wildly, and is hit again. Helen examines her cut lip in the reflection of the windows. She waits for her trainer for a half hour, watches the two men in the ring. When she gives up, she exits through the back door, walks through a cloud of cigarette smoke, the stares of the boxers, walks the long road home in the dark.

She unlocks the house quietly. Her mother is likely asleep. In the kitchen, Helen takes her brother, two years old, from his daybed, wakes him, wipes his nose with the sleeve of her shirt. She sets him on his feet, steadying him with her hands gripped beneath his arms.

Her father was a pilot when she was younger, had a prop plane that he flew out of Juneau, ferrying supplies to homesteaders, taking Helen with him on occasion. She'd sit at the window as he flew low over the inside waterway, watching for pods of orcas or the hump of gray whales against the white crests of the sea. On the brightest days, the green treetops stretched for as far as she could see, and her father, holding his hand up against the sun, blinded from the horizon, seemed to fly on instinct. When they reached the lighthouse on Hawkins Point, they turned landward, flying over the black rocks and the white dots of eagles' heads, sharp and clear in the branches of the tallest evergreens. Even then, Helen knew life would not last this way, sensed that she would always come down, knew that high expectations led to disappointment.

When she'd left him—been sent away—she sat on the bollard of the ferryboat, alone in the stern, her face wrapped in scarves, watching her breath disappear in the mist from the ship's wake. The ferryboat pitched and rolled with the waves. Above the stern, a line of gulls stretched and dived at fish in the water.

Her baby brother neither smiles nor frowns, looks at her with great curiosity, moans for a moment, then is silent as she removes her hands, lets him stand on his own. The expression on his face changes, the first thought of doubt. His knees give way, and she catches him, leans forward and slips her hands against his ribs. On the ferryboat, she'd sat in the cabinhouse next to an old woman, had stored the woman's duffle bag in the rack above them where the woman could not reach, had stood on the armrest to pack it in. The woman had slipped her a piece of chocolate, and though Helen would have preferred to save it for later, to savor the thought of the candy waiting in her pocket, she ate it slowly, nibbling at the edges, letting the chocolate melt on her tongue. They'd played cards, she and the old woman, every afternoon on the three-day trip—gin rummy, crazy eights, and bird's cage—had eaten their soup on the starboard benches, had looked through the woman's binoculars at a sea otter, at the weekday fishermen pulling in their crab traps. She still wrote to Mrs. Lange, once each Christmas so far, and once in the summer, received letters back. Beneath the locks of gray hair, Helen had noticed the woman's ear, the top half missing, a stub on the skull, and the woman, noticing Helen's stare, had said, A donkey bit that off. I got too close when I was a little girl. My father took that donkey out to the field and shot him after that.

Helen sets her brother straight again. Locks his knees into place. He continues to watch her, as if her hands, her arms, were connected go his own body. When she lets go, he watches the hands move away, his eyes begin to water. He takes a step toward her as she pulls away, keeps his feet. He wants those hands back. Takes another step, keeps his feet again, loses his balance, straightens himself, has a look of surprise for a moment, and in that moment loses his balance again. He falls back before she can snatch him up. He moves faster in that fall, it seems, than her trainer has ever moved, and before the child fully realizes he has fallen, she has him in her arms, pushes his head against her neck, begins a song that he recognizes. His fall is forgotten, if it ever happened at all.

What is it out there that points the right way? Omar feels this, although he doesn't think it, not exactly, as he makes his way through the snowflakes mixed with rain, his feet slipping against the sidewalk. His thoughts are on his mother. When he opens the door to the tallest apartment building, the air is only slightly warmer, and a sourly unpleasant odor drifts from the hallway. He takes the steps one at a time, knows better than to trust the railing, passes a man at the top of the stairway who mutters, Works, man, works, takes the rest of the steps, moves faster, up to the fifth floor. He passes the people, the bottles in the hallway, finds the apartment and then the bedroom.

His mother is a small circle in the center of the bed. She is alone, and for that Omar is grateful. She is no longer the fat woman that his brother had spoken of, taking the belt through the broken window. She is skin and bones. He takes a cloth from his pocket, has brought it for this very purpose, runs cold water over it in the bathroom. Returns and wipes his mother's face. Touches the sores on her lips, wipes the blood away. She stirs, opens her eyes, doses them again, A dead rat lies in the corner of the room. You're good to come get me, she says, mumbles the words to the point that he can barely make them out, but he's heard them before. Soon she'll try to convince him this is as good a place to sleep as any, will ask him to slip up next to her. Let's go Mama, he says. In the ten minutes you want to sit here, we can be home.

She squeezes his hand, tries to sit up, leans back on her elbows. They can hear people begin to dance in the next room, can feel the bass of the stereo through the floorboards. Omar wishes he'd turned on the lights. He kisses her on the forehead, is trapped by her arms, still strong, even at this time. He looks out the window at the river. His mother, he is sure, is kind to other people, treats people better than anyone he knows. He believes his mother means everything to him. We could be at the bottom of the stairs in two minutes, he says to her.

Longer than that.

A year before, he used to look out on that river. He thought there might be another boy, a lot like him, on the other side, but now be doesn't think so. His mother rises, sits up, rubs his shoulders with her hand. Kisses him where he kissed her. She stands up from the bed and stumbles to the bathroom, and in seven minutes, they'll reach the bottom of the stairs.

That boy on the other side of the river, way on the other side, miles and states away, watches his father from the cab of the truck as his grandfather drives through the ruts and ridges of the back lawn. His father stands with arms limp at his sides, as surprised as the boy at the movement of the truck. The man disappears around the corner of the house—the two Winstons disappear around the corner of the house—and the truck creaks and bounces onto the state highway. Above them, the stars are clear. They drive on, slow; cars pass them on the left side as the older Winston shifts to higher, then lower gears. It seems to the younger Winston that his grandfather cannot decide on something. They drive in the direction of the carnival, Winston can see the Ferris wheel turn, remembers his father sitting next to him on the ride—the only ride the man took that day—and knows that the carnival is not his grandfather's destination.

Maybe the creek, he thinks, but not likely. If a raindrop fell in that creek it might travel south to a larger stream, and a river after that, might find its way to where three rivers meet, might choose the smallest of the three and turn eastward, rolling over rocks, fish, hollow reeds and old tires, rats. Might be observed from a rooftop by a boy near Winston's age. But Winston doesn't think of this. He thinks of the snake his grandfather had caught at the creek, had pinched it near the back of the head, lifted it from the mud, showed Winston how to hold it, watched as it crawled up the arm of his grandson, had seen the fear and the delight in the boy's face.

But they pass the turnoff for the creek, and soon after, they pass the carnival. Winston's eyes follow the Ferris wheel as it rises above them, a hundred yards from the shoulder of the road. The older Winston follows his grandson's gaze, watches the lights of the Ferris wheel in the rearview mirror. He has a clarity of thought for a change: that would've been a good place to stop. He has no idea where he is going, recognizes this fact, and in recognizing it, knows that he has come through the fog of his own thoughts which, God knows, he's been trying to come through for the past week.

But even as he keeps his eyes on the road, edges the steering wheel to the right, he keeps the picture of his grandson in his mind. The boy's father had considered him a halfwit. The word had bothered the older Winston. He'd seen it hang in the air like a weight, had thought he might keep it from settling around the boy's neck. On the days when the father worked, the old man had taught the boy how to drive the tractor in the fields of his neighbor's yard. The boy was tall for his age. His feet could touch the pedals if he sat forward. The old man thought he might teach the boy a trade. Farming took not great thoughts, but a focus that he was certain the boy had. He'd taught him how to bale hay and how to lead the cows in to milk, how to hook up the machines. He'd taught him how to catch a snake—that was for fun—and earlier still, years before, how to tie his shoes and how to read. He thought he might be teaching him something here, in the truck, had started the old clunker with that in mind, in his fogged mind, but what that was he was not now sure.

On the windshield the reflection of the carnival lights dim, and another set of lights shines brighter. Blue lights. The old man checks his mirror and sees the sheriff's cruiser closing the distance on the highway.

God dammit, he says.

Hey, says the younger Winston. That's your mouth.

The old mail neither stops nor speeds up. The cruiser rides close to his bumper, and the lights glow strong against the windshield. The deputy switches on his siren, follows close, and when, after a minute—two minutes—have passed, calls in to the switchboard for backup. On a straightaway, he moves the cruiser to the left lane, comes even with the truck. Beyond them, down the highway, Winston can see the same glow he'd seen from the farmhouse. Not the carnival, and not even now the lights of the sheriff's cruiser, but a glow greater than any of those things, as bright as the moon, even at this distance. It burns orange against the skyline.

The deputy, now ten minutes past his shift, had taken the call because it was an easy one: an old man and a boy in a truck, to be pulled over and returned to a farmhouse five miles back. The deputy has a boy of his own, is a first-time father, had seen his boy walk two days before, had caught him as he fell, had been thinking about that as he called in for backup. He pulls level with the truck, in the opposite lane. They're not moving very fast. He smiles at the old man. Doesn't see any reason to be rude, had not been raised that way. He points to the side of the road.

The old man looks at this deputy. The man looks like a boy himself. The older Winston takes in the smile. Takes it for a cockiness that the deputy had not intended. The old man raises his right hand and extends his middle finger. Next to him, his grandson—a bit of a prude when it comes to language—likes that. The old man can hear the boy's laugh.

You do it, he says.

No way, says Winston.

The deputy loses the smile and sets his foot against the brake. Ahead, he can see a long line of cars, blocking the road in both directions, stretching toward an orange glow in the distance, bright as the moon. He seems to register this—the deputy does—thinks he might see the source of the glow and hopes he will not. Thinks of his son again, and then of the boy in the truck. He presses down on his brake and gives the old man some room.

Slipping is avoiding a blow by moving to the side, a counterpunch follows to the right if she moves to the right. A left from the left. A duck is a bend to escape an opponent's blow. The hands are held in punching position so she might retaliate as soon as the opponent's arm passes over her head.

Helen tapes her hands, makes fists as she sits on the sink in the kitchen, watches the shadow of her hands against the floor.

Outside, she ties the punching bag to the largest low branch of the spruce pine, fifty yards from her house. She warms up, counts to four hundred on the bag, her fists working from memory. She watches her white breath in the air. She hits the bag like it was made of glass, hits it solid and light, hits it on the backswing so as not to break it. Years from now, will she stand on a corner at two in the morning, waiting for someone who never shows up? She thinks this at around three hundred. Wonders who that person might be. She sees the portholes and hatches of the ferryboat, feels the warmth of the bourbon slide down her throat, just a nip—Mrs. Lange's word—try it if you like it. She hadn't liked it at the time, but likes it now, doesn't taste the bitterness or the sting while punching at the bag. It warms her: the memory, the taste, and the movement around the tree.

Helen reaches four hundred, stops and moves to the other side of the bag, moves beyond glass, thinks of the bag as rubber, bouncing back, bouncing faster the harder she hits it, if she keeps the right rhythm. She thinks of her trainer. Then, tries to think of the ferryboat instead of him. He's twice and a half her age. He's ugly. She'd like to break his nose. Thinks that she might slip in one day, with practice, with repetition, with guile and deceit, and smack him a good one. She smacks the bag a good one and loses the rhythm, tries to get it back, fails. She stops the bag and starts again. The uppercut is a blow delivered with either hand and in close quarters. The boxer finds this blow most effective against an opponent boxing in a crouching position.

Omar crouches like a boxer, as if he's waiting for the blow to come, waiting for his chance to cross or jab, but he crouches for neither of those reasons. He holds the weight of his mother, half her weight. Even with her skin and bones, she is still heavier than him. He's a small boy. A squeak next to Winston, if they'd ever stand together, he's not as solid or defined as Helen. He holds his mother's weight up in the rain and sleet with his legs pressed with each step against the sidewalk. He accounts for a slip with each step, although he never falters, not any time between the apartment buildings, eight blocks. He keeps her talking, keeps her awake, lets her take her weight back, takes it on again.

I rode that bike down that hill, you remember, she says.

Omar doesn't know what she's talking about.

My mother said we'd go biking, and I used to fly. There was a group of boys, and when they saw me come by, one of them said, "That girl is too fast, we're going to have to cut her down." And I was like, that's right, cause I'm like a fast speed.

Okay, says Omar, I hear you. He wipes the rain from his eyes. They didn't catch you, did they?

Oh, they caught me.

C'mon Mama.

All right, she says. They're still chasing me. We better hurry up.

Omar looks ahead in the sleet and rain. They've got a long way to go yet. He takes on the weight. I won't let them get you tonight, he says.

They're off the road—Winston and his grandfather—they broke a fence and carved up a farmer's barren cornfield with the bald tires of the truck. If it had been before harvest, the older Winston would have stopped the truck. He's thinking smart now, wants to keep in motion. The sheriff's cruiser follows behind them, through the field; a scarecrow is run down, falls in the glow of the blue lights. The deputy switches on his wipers to get the straw off his windshield. Winston—the older one—sees the scarecrow fall in his rearview mirror, thinks about how someone had stuffed the old shirt and pants, painted the face, maybe a mother and her kids, He doesn't think much of the deputy for knocking it over. He—Winston—is senile and dying, and even he'd thought to turn the wheel.

The younger Winston thinks this is great fun. Better than the spook ride and the Ferris wheel put together and then some. Yet he knows, can feel in his bones, that they'd paid no admission price, that they'll pay a price at the end of this ride instead. He wants this ride to go on and on, so that they won't have to pay. He feels that his grandfather will pay a large price, and yet he senses that he—the younger Winston—himself will pay longer. Will not lose his seven and a half dollars, but will lose something else when the ride ends. It's like driving the tractor—don't tell your father, the old man had said—and he feels this same dread, this same delight, as they come clear of the fields. Winston looks back now through the window at the blue lights of the sheriff's cruiser, and farther still, the orange glow a mile down the road.

And then they're in the sunflower field. The old man chooses not to avoid it, can't see a way around it. Tall stalks fall in the lights of the truck, the blue lights of the sheriff's cruiser flashing against the windshield, the yellow heads of flowers snapping and falling against the hood of the truck, flying through the side windows. The younger Winston collects the heads of the yellow flowers in his lap, listens to the pops and snaps of the stalks against the fenders, the tires. The flowers reach in the window like arms, like the hands of skeletons. When they come clear of the field, the silence seems to swallow him.

Ahead, right in front of them, he sees the ditch; they both do, but too late. Their brake lights warn the deputy, who slows in time to avoid it, but the front end of the truck, its wheels spinning in air, smashes into the opposite bank. Winston feels himself falling, feels the thick fingers of his grandfather's hand against his chest, but it was the seatbelt that saved him, saved his grandfather too. He hears now, seconds later when it seems quiet, after the deputy has switched off his siren, the shatter of the windshield. He sees the broken blue shards on his lap, on his shoes near the floorboard. The yellow heads of sunflowers lie on the floor. The boy believes he's bleeding to death. He studies his arms, his ankles.

You cut? says his grandfather.

I don't think so.

His grandfather has a gash on his hand, a small one. There's a little blood there.

You ready to run? says his grandfather.

Winston is still looking for a death wound. Let's stay here, he says.

The old man looks through the back window. I got to keep moving, he says. Already, they can see the white beam of the deputy's flashlight through the back window.

Come or go, says the old man. He opens his door and kicks off the glass. He moves faster than Winston has ever seen him move.

Let's stay here, says Winston, He doesn't want to touch the glass in his lap.

I'll see you again, says the old man. And he's off, out of the truck—Winston can hear him splash in the creek. The boy thinks of snakes. He watches as the old man's white head disappears from the flashing blue light. It enters the darkness beyond Winston's sight.

The deputy watches the old man go. He calls out for him to stop. He thinks about his training, moves beyond it for a moment. He could plug the old man in the leg: he's a good shot. It's not much of a distance. But, he doesn't even unlatch his holster. He climbs down into the creek, feels the water soak his boots and socks, slips a little in the mud.

You all right? he says to the boy. He shines the flashlight in the boy's face, checks for firearms, a knife to the heart. The boy is terrified.

That your grandfather?

The boy nods.

He got a gun on him? Any weapons?

The boy shakes his head. He won't hurt nobody.

He almost killed you, says the deputy.

Winston doesn't like the man's tone. It reminds him of his

teachers at school, the way they mix concern with a shake of their heads, the downward turn of their lips. You can do better. This is all right, good even, but you need to concentrate, focus, you know what I mean?

I don't, says Winston.

You don't what? says the deputy.

I don't know.

All right, says the man. He unclips the latch on his holster. You stay here. I'll be back in a few minutes.

Winston watches the man's head—black hair—disappear out of the blue lights. The boy picks off the glass with his fingertips, drops the shards on the floorboard. Nicks his finger with the last one, puts the finger in his mouth, tastes the blood. He is sure he has betrayed his grandfather. Doesn't exactly know how, but is sure. He picks the yellow flowers off after that. When he climbs out of the cab, splashes into the water, crawls up the bank of the ditch on hands and knees, muddying both, he is convinced that the accident, the ride even, is his fault. He watches the blue lights hover across and around the ditch, and he watches for the white and black heads in the creek. Can see neither. A woman in the farmhouse has come out onto the porch. She stands at the railing, arms crossed, looking at her sunflower field, looks at where Winston is looking.

He sucks at his finger, tastes no blood, wishes he had left with his grandfather. He feels completely alone at the edge of the ditch. Abandoned maybe. Feels like no one—not his grandfather, not the deputy, not his father, not the woman on the porch—will ever return to him. Behind him, he hears the hum of the engine, not from the truck, but from the deputy's cruiser. When he turns, he sees, in the flash of the blue lights, the keys hanging in the ignition switch.

The left hook is a short, bent-arm blow, thrown off the left foot, as the boxer turns her body to the right behind the punch. The right cross, a short or long blow, is thrown off the trailing right foot and crosses the opponent's right arm. The body is turned to the left, with the left arm and hand in the guard position.

Helen opens the window on the second floor, pops out the screen. She takes her baby brother out onto the rooftop. She likes it up here, believes her brother does too. She looks down at him. He's wrapped in a sweater and blanket. She rocks him against her shoulder.

She remembers the coastline from the ferryboat. The waves of the sea breaking against the black rocks, seeming to continue toward the mountains. The mountains seemed as waves themselves, the landscape of the sea the same as land. She'd thought this, had said it to Mrs. Lange, and Mrs. Lange, holding her cards to the tip of her chin, had stared out at the sea, at the Inside Passage. In that moment, a man with a cast on his arm had crossed the deck. It does look like that, the old woman had said. They seem to go on and on.

Helen remembers this. She hums a tune to her brother, rocks him in rhythm with her thoughts. Sleeping beside Mrs. Lange that night, she'd heard the woman mumble in her sleep. She was sure she'd not misheard. You're not going to let another man hit you like that. They were alone, no man around. Helen had sipped at the flask of bourbon, her second taste, still bitter and harsh in her throat. She looked down at her cards. Solitaire. Felt the dip and roll of the ship for the first time that day. Heard someone latch a porthole closed. She'd played a card.

Now, she feels the warmth of the child against her shoulder, feels herself slip on the roof. She presses her feet against the shingles, holds her brother tight against her shoulder. Tomorrow, the trainer: she's going to break his nose.

Winston finds it—the sheriff's cruiser—a lot easier to drive than the tractor. His feet meet the pedals easily. He turns off the radio, grips his hands on the wheel, keeps the tires away from the edge of the ditch. He's moving fester than the tractor, than on any ride at the carnival. After only a minute—two—he can see the nods and dips of the two heads in the stream, the one behind closing the distance.

Behind him, the older Winston can hear the footfalls, the splashes of the deputy. In his youth, he'd have left the man far behind. Twenty years ago he would have left him behind, had always been a good runner. The ditch reminds him of France, near the Moselle River, of a ditch he'd run through in the war. Artillery in the distance, and German voices behind him. He kept low and kept the pace. He outran them. And later he was shot in the back by another American, a boy—he'd always assumed—who shot at everything. He lay that night in a foxhole. His wound was packed but not sewn. The pain was distant, a dull morphine pleasure. The foxhole was deep and he'd stayed quiet. He was nineteen and watched the snow and the tracers falling from the sky.

Blue lights above him now in the ditch. He glances behind him. The deputy is closing the distance. The old man hears his grandson's voice, and up the ditch he goes. He is not without skills, even with his mind failing. He gets into the cruiser. Shuts the door. He puts his seat belt on. He wants to be a good example for the boy.

The younger Winston takes out the handkerchief; there's spittle hanging off the old man's chin and he wipes it away. Carefully. He wants to apologize, for not following, but he can't quite make the words. It's a ride, he thinks. This whole thing. He wants it to go on and on. Through the windshield he can see the orange glow in the distance. It's just over the next hill. They can make the road easy from here. The boy can feel—even as he presses on the pedal, even as the cruiser moves forward, even as he tries to say what he has to say again—the hand of the deputy on his arm, through the window, a vice, like one of his teacher's at school. The boy presses hard on the pedal, lets go the handkerchief.

The deputy, his other hand on the rooftop, hesitates, feels the slap of mud against his legs, feels the motion of the cruiser, feels his boots dragged across rocks. He can imagine his head run over in blue lights. He thinks about his baby son, decides, lets go of the boy's arm. As he slides to the ground, the back tire rolls over the man's boot, breaking five bones and fracturing two more.

When they reach the apartment, Omar sets his mother against the wall, closes the door behind them, pulls her up before she can sit down, presses his hands against her ribs. He looks up the stairway. Two minutes you think? he says.

Three.

Three then. He wipes the snow and rain from her hair, off the crown of her nose and cheeks. He wraps her arm around his shoulder and takes the stairs, letting her lead, pushes at the small of her back.

Why you pushing? she says.

I'm trying to help.

You're being rude.

I'm not meaning.

Meaning and doing are two different things. Your brother never pushed his mother like you do.

Omar says nothing.

If your brother was here, I'd already be up these stairs.

He takes his hand from her back.

Don't make that face, she says.

I'm not.

I'm looking at your face and you're making it right now.

He hides that face, looks down at the stairway, sees the cracks in the wood, a dark stain on the floorboards. He waits, listens to the silence between them. In that silence, she takes his hand, squeezes it, leads him up the stairs. As he follows her, he feels as if he's learning a trick. He's adding to his bag of tricks: keep her talking, wipe her face with cold water, give her a goal—five minutes, three, ten. Turn on the lights. Pout a little. He's going to get this right.

She stops on the staircase with a flight and a half to go. Give me a push, she says. These old bones aren't going to make it.

It's a wood yard, says the younger Winston. They sit at a road-block, the blue lights still flashing above them. Another deputy walks down the line of cars ahead of them. He's checking licenses, looking in backseats. Behind him, dark smoke pushes across the road. The fire in the wood yard is a deep orange, tinges of blue and white in the center. It's a huge fire—even many miles back, a deputy with a broken foot can see it. But it puts the younger Winston in mind of the carnival. He remembers the spook house and the fire in the dragon's belly. He'd screamed, though he doesn't scream now. He's tempted though. He watches the fire-men spraying white mists of water over the blaze. They'll not put it out for a long while. By the time the road is open again: an-other boy, miles and states away from here, will have unlaced his mother's shoes, tipped a mug of water to her lips, pulled the cur-tains closed from the glow of the moonlight. He'll take a blanket from his own bed, Omar, cover his mother. He'll slip in next to her and sleep. But Winston doesn't think of this. He can't see any of these things. He sees the fire only. Even at this distance, he can feel the heat of the blaze.

The older Winston has a fog in his mind. He's confused, but at least he knows it. But he doesn't know if the fog is coming in or going out. He sees, ahead of them, another deputy. The one checking the licenses. Three cars ahead. The man wears a cow-boy hat. Silhouetted against the fire the deputy looks like a ban-dit, or the Lone Ranger. The deputy gives the license back, sees the blue lights. He looks. He knows this cruiser, but he doesn't know the two people in it. He passes the next car. Keeps his eyes on the two Winstons. But he doesn't know their names. He holds his hand up to shield against the lights. He tries to see into the cruiser, he's level with the car ahead. He studies these two people in the cruiser. The older Winston feels the fog slipping in.

The younger Winston, he's been waiting. He has his hand on the seat between them. What do you want to do? he says. He's said it three times now. There's no answer. He grips the edge of the seat hard. Looks at the deputy.

He wants then to reach into his pocket. Take out his wallet. Pay the deputy. But the man doesn't approach the car. Winston wants to pay the price for this ride now, before the price is named. He thinks the ride might could go on. Thinks maybe if he moves fast enough, he might get a bargain. He believes the price to be paid will not be found in his pocket. He reaches there anyway. The deputy, watching the boy, doesn't see a boy. It's a big boy. It's an adult. The boy's hand reaches for something, and the deputy unclips his holster.

The older Winston reaches forward. He's not sure if he's got this right, but he reaches out of sight of the deputy. The younger Winston watches the hand go. He wants that hand to go on and on, knows that the ride is still on, as long as that hand moves, as long as the deputy's hand moves, the ride will not end. The old man flips his wrist and the engine dies. His hands are still moving. He takes up his grandson's hands, slowly. He's gentle, this man, with this boy. Always. He puts their hands on the steering wheel.

The uppercut is a blow delivered—well—up, with either hand and in close quarters. The boxer finds this blow most effective against an opponent boxing in a crouched position and moving in.

It's the morning. Helen walks the three miles to the gym in a white fog that hovers over the gravel and the farmland in wisps and strings, in fingers. She smells smoke and watches the first orange rays sift through the white fog.

She's been told where the key is. She undresses near the ring, hears the door open across the way. Slips into her shorts and T-shirt. She tapes her hands, and watches her trainer undress, tape his hands. She skips rope. Three hundred.

In the ring they say nothing. She ties his left glove. They crouch in the center of the ring. He ties her left, then her right, shows her again how to tie with a glove on. How to make do. They take a minute in their corners. Here, they are their own trainers. When she talks to herself, she sees his face. She listens to his instructions.

In his corner, he sees a girl. Not this girl—the one behind him—but another girl. He sees his mother as a child. He's seen her in black-and-white photographs, and he remembers a story now. His mother is nine years old and reaches for a piece of fruit in a street cart. He can't remember the fruit now. Let's call it an orange. His mother is looking like a buyer, but she means to steal that orange. Her brother lies in a bed, asleep. When the boy—the boxer's uncle—wakes, someone will wipe his chin, will help him walk, might offer a piece of fruit. The boy will not live out the year. But his sister reaches for an orange in a cart on the street with a picture of her brother in her mind. She has black curls and tiny hands. She watches the merchant, pretends to be a buyer. She squeezes the orange while her brother, blocks and blocks away, sleeps, while the merchant turns, while, years and decades later, Helen says, Ready?

The trainer turns and looks at this other girl.

Do you know what I'm going to do? he says.

No.

This merchant. Decades before. Let's give him a moustache. He sees the girl. The merchant is quick and tall, and two steps away. He's got long arms and angry hands, and he's caught his share of thieves in his day. This little girl looks at him. She's nine years old, but will one day be someone's mother. She puts the orange into her pocket. Brazen. Her eyes ask him a question: are you as fast as I am? He doesn't have to answer the question. He believes he's plenty fast. He moves, sudden, and grabs her. He's going to show her now. He's going to show what he does to thieves.

But he is completely mistaken. He looks at his hands. He holds nothing. And now he has one less orange. He grabbed air. He looks around for the girl, for the boxer's mother. But she's long gone. She's slipped away. Because that is what a fast speed does.

The trainer moves away from his corner.

Do you know what you're going to do? he says.

Yes, says Helen.

What's that?

Keep moving, she thinks, but she says nothing. She lets go of the ropes, fits her mouthpiece to her teeth, walks to the center of the ring, meets him, and moves in.

A Difficult Age

HUGH SHEEHY

From *The Invisibles* (2012)

The man is the corrupt dream of the child,
and since there is only decay, and no time, what we call days
and evenings are the false angels of our existence.

—EDWARD DAHLBERG, *Because I Was Flesh*

Look at it this way. Fourteen years old and I stand six feet two inches high, a lummox with charm like the muttering lord of the dead. Last summer most of my mom's breasts were removed, which is no excuse, though it is a reason I began to hate everyone. She shed her hair; I grew mine to my shoulders and dyed it black. Once partners in sarcasm, observers of amphibians in our Black Swamp surroundings, the parent-child duo that chatted past the zero hour, we have become strangers, willing to hurt with words. To ease life I roam the downstairs, now that she's as bald as Lionel, the boy on our front porch, listening after the doorbell's echo, his pipe-thin arms short and flared.

Lionel's baldness is self-imposed, and to ensure that no one mistakes this, he wears a heavy chain-link necklace and a black Megadeth T-shirt that portrays an emaciated man sweating bullets out of his forehead and chest onto a wooden table. Lionel is my age, has hounded blue eyes and crooked teeth, and lives in a slab house on the south side of this large park of Black Swamp forest, in a neighborhood of slab houses, a neighborhood with snarling dogs and no government, alongside the railroad tracks. He is my best friend, and for a long time was my only friend, until Brooke became pregnant, around the time the surgeons cut the tumors out of my mom. Until Brooke began driving him over in her old blue Stingray, the rumbling and rusted wonder of our minds, Lionel was forced to ride the dirt trails on his secondhand mountain bike to reach my house through the riparian forest.

I open the door. He waits, immune to the October cold, on the flagstones. Up high the clouds lie back over the stick trees. Brooke waits in the running car, her little eyes crinkled as she smokes a Kool.

"Don't ask," says Lionel. "Don't even bring it up. She got really really pissed off about five minutes ago, and before she got pissed off she was already crazy. All right there, big guy?" He claps my shoulder, laughs nervously. Being so much smaller, he enjoys the idea of pushing me around. I hardly notice this. He slips past me and opens the front door. "Hi, Mrs. Wheeler, bye, Mrs. Wheeler!"

My mom's up in her room, watching the TV shows we once watched, in the days she had breasts and long messy hair and did more than eat frozen dinners in bed. Skeletal, loose-skinned, and bald like an old man, she sits under blankets and pink wool cap next to the much-hated wig of bouncy brown-blonde hair on the nightstand, the lesser world of *Cheers* going on inside the television, her gun in a drawer and her ranger's uniform hanging in the closet, the park service radio burbling on the dresser. At the sound of Lionel's shout she savors a blend of fondness and anger. She won't call back, though she smirks, and not because teasing Sam has once again irked Diane into a sexy shouting match. She is getting slowly better, putting all of her power pills into a pile. Her strength is returning, having once left her stoned and waxy in a hospital bed—that night I sat in the waiting area I half-expected to see her ghost wander past the nurse's station, as if in search of a restroom. Instead we came back here, where she glides through the kitchen in a pink gown. She sniffs the rot in the room and tells me to sweep the sparrows out of the fireplace, to repair the screen at the top of the chimney. She watches, silent, vigilant only until the job is finished, then departs without a word. The commercial break echoes from her bedroom, and the quiet fills with her steady breathing until her door shuts.

When I think of her coming out of there, I shiver a little.

In the sound of ticking clock-and-quiet house and disconnected surf of radio static, I ask Lionel if he was able to get the item that he promised to bring today.

"Patience is divine, Wheeler," he tells me, tilting his knobby head. His maverick wink says yes, he has brought the highly experimental drug that he promised he would bring, but that he is also going to proudly be a pain in the neck about it. I follow him to the car and sit in the backseat, among crumpled fast food sacks, and give the brooding, unspeaking Brooke directions on the mazey park roads to the pond where the rangers never stop. In the front seat Lionel fast-forwards through the new Fishbone cassette, looking for a part of a song that he feels is currently the best expression of young black anger.

We are only young and angry, I point out. Not black.

"Two out of three ain't bad," Lionel mocks, in a dull voice. He knows his theories precisely, like inventions left lying around his personal laboratory. "That kind of thinking isn't going to bring people together, Wheeler."

Though everything's changed since Brooke drove him to my house two months ago, I've come to feel that it always goes this way, me in the backseat staring out the window, while Brooke drives and Lionel sits shotgun, pontificating in his small cutting voice. It's hard to keep in mind all that's changed, except that two months ago I wouldn't have considered smoking crystal-form cocaine. The word "crack" belonged to undead grown-ups that herded in unnamed ghettoes and to the straight-up cops who hunted them.

Lionel sometimes remarks, *How quickly and cruelly the outer world relates to you.* At times I have replied, *How quickly, Lionel? How cruelly?* and at others, *Lionel, could you relate that to Shut the fuck up.* More and more lately, I've been saying, *Yes, yes, how quickly indeed.* When we left my dad behind and came to the park, my mom tried to convince me of our safety here. "Things are going to get a lot easier," she used to say. "You're not going to believe it." She was looking out into the woods, reading about the school system. All along the cancer was inside her.

It's not saying I'm bitter, like kids they make TV movies about, just that I'm feeling open to a new way of living, a new way of thinking, once Brooke parks the Stingray on the broken-up blacktop beside a long-unrented cottage of decaying logs, once we are climbing from two open doors into the sweet pungent autumn with instantly cold throats. Beyond our clouds of breath, a single fisherman sits in a lawn chair down on the dock with his line out in the dark pond, a bobber among the reflections and moss and leaves. It's Fritz, the harmless, muttering old German who catches and releases the sunfish and bluegill that otherwise have the run of this body of water. He wears a thermal flannel shirt and a hunter's cap and smokes a corncob pipe.

Brooke fears rangers, jails, courtrooms, and parents. Before the pregnancy she dated the quarterback of the football team. She sold brownies at the bake sale and wore glitter lipstick. She shivers and hugs herself in her thin suede jacket, and I stand beside her to murmur that all will be fine. This forest is my area of expertise. Lionel strides on ahead of us, stubby arms swinging, no jacket for him, into the opening in the trees that we have gone into many times before to drink Old Milwaukee and smoke the occasional joint. This is a special occasion, however—momentous is the word, really—and my fear is gone now that I know for sure that Brooke, being with child, will say no to smoking crystal-form cocaine. If my mom had smoked crystal-form cocaine while she carried me, I don't know what I'd tell people.

We linger, she short and delicate in a way that makes me hide my hands in the kangaroo pouch of my hooded sweatshirt.

"What if he sees us?" she hisses.

"Don't worry. He's just this old guy." My whisper does not convince her, and she only follows so as not to be left alone with the half-blind old man sitting with his back to her, once I've almost disappeared from her sight down the trail into the leafless dog-woods—she catches up at a stumbling, paranoid jog. It's embarrassing to see an older girl unnerved, so I don't mention to her that when I look back Fritz has turned in his chair to watch her through his thick bifocal glasses, chewing the pipe with his old teeth. I look a second longer to make sure he doesn't feel ignored by me, until he jerks a nod. Maybe a long time ago in the Black Forest or wherever, kids would meet in the woods to get it on. I go after Brooke, a step behind her, into the den of leafless branches, with my head down.

Our spot is a flat dry bank between an isolated chunk of granite and a bald cypress. Lionel crouches on the boulder. He hops down as we squeeze through the branches of young basswoods. He pulls a small pipe from one pocket, from the other a small bag of dope and a little smoked glass vial that I recognize as having contained pure caffeine at one time in a cabinet in our General Science classroom. The day Mr. Clayborn got that stuff out so we could estimate its melting point, boys from our class stole them to flash such vials in the corridor and joke that they contained what Lionel's actually does. Explaining that he's already broken up the crystal, he twists off the lid and shakes frosty nuggets onto the swirl of twiggy pot in his bowl. Observing ritual, he balances the pipe on the toe of an Airwalk and searches out his cigarettes in the vast pockets of his jeans. "Wheeler?" He offers one, totally solemn, and I take it, light it, and pull out the bottle of apple-flavored wine I have stolen, smuggled, and hidden in my shirt as a surprise for my friends on this occasion.

"Thank God," says Brooke. She uncaps the bottle and drinks from it, watching Lionel and me smoke our Camels. "You guys are fucking crazy," she tells us between slugs, eyeing the pipe balanced like a hacky sack on Lionel's shoe. "That stuff can make your heart explode. What if you get addicted?"

"Then we get addicted." Lionel glares at her like she's his little sister, whom he had no choice but to bring along this one time. I happen to know that he loves her and wants to adopt the baby when she has it. He tells me all his secrets and thoughts. He imagines putting the baby into a car seat once he's got his license. He says he sees them moving into a slab house in his neighborhood together. He'll be a construction worker, come home to her in the evenings. Then I'll stop by, and we'll drink beer in the living room. Lionel believes his love is all the more legit because Brooke annoys him—this time because he has conducted actual research on this particular chemical under the reading lamps at the downtown library, and he is confident that the first-timer-hooked story is falderal meant to deter us from passing into an alternate world that could lead to a higher reality. This higher reality stuff isn't very clear to me.

"That's the problem," he says. "The way the system is set up. So you won't see that every second is another chance to shoot into another dimension."

Lionel winks at Brooke, then takes the first hit, mouth puckered hard around the piece, holds it and blushes, and quilts my face with pot smoke. With a hurry-up motion he hands me the pipe, and then, with an audible heartbeat and damp armpits, I'm doing it myself, staring directly into the disapproval of too-thin, pretty if slightly buck-toothed Brooke.

A ball of tension in my chest releases into a greater tightness that makes me understand for the first time that my mind is a part of my physical body. There I am, standing on taut legs, laughing with Lionel, as Brooke freaks out and drinks green wine from the bottle, the three of us on the mud bank of a still pond under a spry autumn cloud.

This is all that happens.

As far as I know.

That makes me laugh like I've never laughed before, so hard I think I'll break my chest, and Lionel walks up with a cackle in his throat and punches me in the cheek. I bop him in the middle of his bald head and he goes down, laughing, on the hard bank. We sit together, painless, sharing a pipe, and drum our legs on the bank. Brooke calls us idiots, but more importantly, the autumn is its naked self, bold and inelegant, and hard like a new tooth driven through a baby's gums. We laugh hard and cry and get scared and laugh hard, and Brooke stares at the pond and shakes her head, drinking wine and being pregnant.

On our last night together my dad stands in the red bathroom with my mom's hair in his fist. He uses his knuckles to point her eyes directly into the toilet. He shouts in a voice torn down to a squeak, that she has to take the fucking cabbage out of the fucking toilet. This during the period we believe that alcohol does this to him. The toilet is empty. Nonetheless my mom, wide-eyed in pain and by now done talking to him, lowers both hands in, hoping, I guess, to catch my dad's hallucination in both her palms as she lifts them out. She tries not to get the floor too wet.

After he passes out I climb out from under their bed, from under his flung out arms and the broad shining slope of his belly. My mom has been preparing for this, and the duffel bags are out of the closet. She composes her clothes and hair enough to go outside, composes her head enough to drive the car. She kneels beside me, and we look at the snoring, slobbering disaster that is my dad. She breathes hard and I breathe hard and we both smell like the kind of tears that don't mean anything, the useless tears that continue to fall after the reasons for the pain are isolated and as uninteresting as childhood toys.

We drive to the house of a friendly ranger my mom knows. We stay in his stone cottage less than two miles away, but I don't see my dad again until we go to the courthouse. He wears a suit, his face sickly white-and-yellow, his guido hair combed back. Except for the tattoo of a five-pointed star on his right ear, he does not resemble the oaf who raged in our house throwing unbreakable plastic dinnerware and glassless photographs and tackling heavy wooden chairs, searching for nonexistent friends and sometimes naked when he'd fabricated a coyly hiding lover. In the court he is frightened and sick, as the clerk reads from my mother's testimony about some things he's done, which I remember well, which he says he does not remember. He scares me most like this, braced in agony, without his usual, unkind happiness.

A psychiatrist questions him for a week and takes pictures of his brain that are blown up and colored for the benefit of the judge and lawyers. He is diagnosed as schizophrenic, and when they tell him this in the courtroom he weeps. He has not had alcohol to drink for almost a month by now. Lighter and sweaty and shivering, he stutters when he tries to talk after the judge asks if he has anything to say.

He looks at us at our little table, me in my suit and tie, and says, "I-I-'m s-s-s-sorr-ry," as if he has eaten a speech therapy student, who is speaking from inside his stomach.

My mom maintains an upright posture in her gray suit, her face smart and ready. She is nearly free, and looking past the present, she hardly knows he is there.

They move my dad into an institution in the farmlands north of Lima, Ohio, but he doesn't know where it is. He doesn't know that we move east along the lake, not because he's vindictive and murderous but because he takes Thorazine. He can't keep drool in his mouth.

I don't miss him. In six years I'll take an unannounced trip to

Lima over Christmas break, in an '89 Accord, and be informed by a doctor there of my dad's release after three years due to cuts in hospital funding. My mom will apologize for not telling me. She will be forty-one and still bald, and it will be easy to forgive her. When I drop out of college that spring I'll drive to Panama City, where he's thought to have gone in search of a climate conducive to heavy drinking and homeless living. After a week of talking to volunteers in missions around the city, I'll be directed to a block near Buccaneer stadium, and he'll be the old man in mesh shorts sitting in the shade of a viaduct. The star on his grimy ear will look like a tattoo of used chewing gum. I won't know if he knows me, but like I think we're bros, I'll buy two forties and sit with him. After saying a few planned things, I give him my goddamn beer and leave him there.

This is what happens in Mr. Clayborn's General Science for Freshmen, a boring required course in which I fail to foresee an oncoming disaster. In this class students sit in pairs at green Formica lab tables, and since Lionel and I are lab partners and contemptuous of our childish peers, we sit together and sneer at our surroundings. Our table is in the back corner beside a cabinet in which a pig fetus, a pine rattlesnake, a mudpuppy, and a cow's heart float in jars of formaldehyde. In the larger cabinet behind us are stored seriously unstable compounds and elements, all of them in smoked glass jars. Several times per class period, Lionel and I wish they would explode. Lionel is one of three Advanced Chemistry students in the freshmen class, and as far as we know he is the only one who's noticed this powder keg in the classroom. Today we feel especially superior, fourteen-year-olds who have smoked crystal-form cocaine and survived without becoming addicted to it. Every few minutes I write into Lionel's notebook: *You a fiend yet?*

"No," he whispers.

How about now? I write.

"Not yet."

Today Mr. Clayborn lugs in a large cardboard box containing his taxidermic collection of roadkill. Mr. Clayborn, PETA member, boombox-toting founder of Right Now!, faculty advisor to the freshman class president, master of the a.m. glad-handed greeting, how we scorn you. You and your box of preserved armadillo, jackrabbit, chipmunks, guinea fowl, raccoon, and squirrels. Lionel and I are cool as gargoyles as our classmates express chirpy excitement about today's plan to pass around animal corpses.

Mr. Clayborn's nose wrinkles as he breathes through his mouth, out of breath and flushed from the exertion of carrying these dead animals up two flights of stairs, a light fog in his glasses. "I thought you guys might want to get a good look at an armadillo's feet."

Lionel opens a turquoise folder and mutters into it, "I thought you might want to get a good look at my balls."

Mr. Clayborn holds up the small, armored, pig-faced animal so that we can see its wicked-looking black claws. "This guy is my favorite. It's truly a wonder that such a timid beast is endowed with such dangerous natural tools." It is this verbal excess that pushes Lionel into the airless realm of disbelief. On the desk he tilts our worksheet that features diagrams of the animals in Clayborn's box. He scribbles neat, elaborate notes in the margins with a number 2 pencil. By the time the armadillo reaches our table we have thoroughly studied, written about, and added genitals to diagrams of the jackrabbit, the squirrels, and the raccoon. All of the lab groups are working at what Mr. Clayborn deems a medium noise level. I am well-informed of what Lionel expects of me, and I wait until a girl in the front asks a complicated question and Clayborn is preoccupied.

I'm nervous, and Lionel is right there beside me, urging through thin, excited lips, "Do it, Wheeler, do it, get us in trouble. You think you know how much but you never will if you don't do it." With a newly sharpened pencil he traces a five-pointed star in the middle of our worksheet until the paper tears. "Come on, come on."

As Mr. Clayborn explains a squirrel's digestive system to a pair of girls up front, I take the shiny armadillo in both hands. It's light and hollow and football-sized. I pretend to weigh my options, letting Lionel's words tickle until I can no longer control myself. I twist off its claws quickly and, snickering, hand it to Lionel, who breaks into hard laughter at Mr. Clayborn's alarmed shout. As the teacher rushes to us, slamming hips against tables, Lionel drives his pencil up into the armadillo as far as it will go. He holds it up by the eraser, offering it like a Popsicle, and Mr. Clayborn swats it out of his hand so that it hits the floor and cracks.

"Oh my God," Brooke says as we wait in the long line of cars leaving the parking lot. She quickly smokes, trying to ignore the faces of her old schoolmates as they walk past us to their parked cars. She tells us, "You guys are assholes, in addition to being idiots."

Behind the rebukes she is amused, holding back a smile, and I think that perhaps she is baiting Lionel, to get him to joke with her. She's not used to him being such a grouch. It almost makes me talkative, but I don't want to get involved in their relationship. Except for the grunt with which he confirmed my story, he has made no sound since getting into the smoke-smelling car. He ignores her and holds his eyes on the blasted sky, and Brooke gives up on him for the moment.

We wait in full sight of her old friends and the quarterback ex-boyfriend she blames for her predicament. They stand in a stylish group beside the tennis courts, staring as we roll past, and the quarterback ex-boyfriend will not take his eyes off of Brooke holding the steering wheel and staring ahead. He's hoping she will let him look into her eyes, and then talk to her for just a minute, put his hand near hers, and so on. Brooke is strong under this pressure. She finds me in the rearview and asks about the headlines of the school paper, whether the editors are holding up without her.

The quarterback ex-boyfriend stops trying to get her attention and fumes at Lionel. Either Lionel doesn't notice, or he doesn't care. I worry about all this. This quarterback ex-boyfriend will stare all the way across the cafeteria at the empty table that Lionel and I share at lunch. I am bigger than he is, yet the flawless muscular black boys from the football team follow him like a bodyguard, and like the other white kids in this school I fear these stronger, handsomer black boys. But the quarterback ex-boyfriend's anger with Lionel is undercut by his ex-boyfriend sadness. I've been by his locker, and there are pictures of him with Brooke taped all over the door. At the moment I passed, two of Brooke's old friends were comforting him as he moped. Lionel says he is a pussy. It is not Brooke's quarterback ex-boyfriend that has made Lionel sit like a stony god of hatred in the front seat.

"Lionel, what's up with you today?" Brooke is cautious with him, asking gently, then respecting his silence as we escape the school grounds and cross the road where the subdivisions end and the farmlands begin on the way to the lakeshore.

Lionel will not admit that Clayborn caught him tongue-tied in the principal's office. It's too embarrassing for him. I don't like to think about it, but the truth is that Mr. Clayborn turned out to be tougher than we'd expected. He knows what Lionel and I are about, the ideas we have, even the way we view the teachers. Neither of us was prepared for this revelation. We could only dodge his eyes and listen. He sat on the edge of the principal's desk, as the principal supported him by repeatedly looking at us and then at his wristwatch. He pointed a thick Clayborn finger at each of us, one at a time. "This alternative education you're investing yourselves in isn't going to pay off, unless you guys are trying to find out what the floor smells like in Stryker, because that's where this kind of behavior is going to take you." He said this to both of us but the conversation was between him and Lionel. And when Lionel opened his mouth, Mr. Clayborn cut him off. "What do you think, that nobody's done any of this stuff before? You think you're Butch Cassidy and the Sundance Kid."

"He doesn't even know what he's saying," Lionel tells Brooke and me, as he and I prepare to smoke more crystal-form cocaine and disappoint Brooke, in our spot. "He couldn't possibly understand the subtlety of our project." He does not attempt to explain this subtlety. It seems best not to ask him to. We all three sit against the granite hunk because Fritz the German lunatic has moved from his usual place on the dock and relocated directly across the murky water from us, shrunk by a hundred yards' distance, and though I don't think he can see that far I'm not very comfortable with the possibility. Even if we did not drink wine and beer and smoke cigarettes and crystal-form cocaine, I don't believe I would want anyone to see the three of us out here. My friends don't embarrass me, but I'm not sure we'll always be friends.

Lionel produces a spike of fire with his butane lighter and sparks a bowl. He exhales and gives me the pipe, then lays back against the boulder with his arms relaxed at his sides. Like a toy bald person. His chest rises and falls faster, and he grins his cottonmouth grin and tells us, "Yes. Fuck Clayborn. I'll kick his ass with thoughts."

I'm slow to smoke and I hold the pipe to my lips awhile. Brooke has developed a small double chin, which Lionel and I agree is very cute. She hides her pregnant belly under sweatshirts and coats, though Lionel has touched her bare skin and felt the baby kick. He tells me she would let me do this as well, that it's not a couples thing, but I said no thanks. I'm not interested in touching her, or in babies. She smokes and blows rings, pensive and sad and resigned to look over at us for a reason to smile, and she sees me holding the pipe like I am. She rolls her eyes.

"You two," she says, and looks away. It is as if we have once again caused her to catch us wearing her bras on our heads, and it is no longer funny. In a way we have come to enjoy this general feeling. I light up and enjoy what's left of the day in this season of diminishing afternoons. It's cold with a gonna-storm dampness, and we are all three in jackets beside the pond full of sunken leaves.

Lionel believes that Brooke is tougher than either of us. He tells me this as we smoke cigarettes under the clean autumn night sky. He is thinking about their future together, which is what he thinks about when Brooke is gone and he is tired of thinking about getting even with Mr. Clayborn.

Today Brooke went to a sonogram reading with her quarterback ex-boyfriend and all their parents. Strictly political. She disobeys her parents most of the time and does what she wants to but says they deserve to have a daughter once in a while. "So much wiser than us," says Lionel, a little high from this afternoon. "She's *tough*."

I'm inclined to agree with him.

When the school nurse interpreted the blue plus sign on the home test for her, Brooke knew she was as good as expelled. She pulled off her senior class ring and squeezed it in her fist until she felt sweat or blood. That summer she could get an equivalent degree and depart from her academic days in virtual obscurity, without throwing a mortarboard or a party in her parents' backyard. She wanted none of it, nor did she want the words being said by the young nurse sitting beside her on the tightly made white cot.

The nurse, a graduate of a women's college who trusted her youthful sensibilities to overlap with ours, was saying a lot of words, and one especially. Options.

Brooke pushed the hand from her elbow and walked out of the office. She took the dizzy road to her boyfriend's chemistry class where, between teacher and chalk equations and twenty-two concentrating adolescents, everyone knew something had gone wrong. A few kids later bragged that they had guessed she was knocked up, but no one claimed to have the intuition to predict her next move. No one would have believed that story, because we all knew that people would meet up years later and still express excitement and surprise over the new confidence that she displayed as she lifted her quarterback boyfriend's pen hand by the wrist and confiscated his highlighter and then planted her sweaty ring in the center of his palm.

It was the twin of his, and he had paid for both. To wear them had been his idea, like they were teenagers and tacky and also engaged, and Brooke wanted no more reminders.

With the ring in his hand her quarterback boyfriend became her ex. People said he was totally still and that he didn't lift his head until she'd turned away. Now that she'd done what she came to do, Brooke's strength began to leave her, her shoulders fell, and she rushed toward the classroom door, almost tripped, then disappeared clattering into the hall. The class sat stunned through the long, shrill bell.

I wonder what she does all day while we sit at school. When I ask Lionel, he tells me, "Stuff that pregnant dropouts do." It troubles him, too, the mystery of her. Moonlight falls blue on his head as he smokes and thinks of her, off with the strangers she knows.

I imagine her routine involving a quart of mint chocolate chip ice cream, a television, and all the sadness that a person by herself can work up. Maybe Brooke and my mom watch the same programs while I'm at school all day. Maybe they could get together, get their schedules lined up.

My mom is called to the school the day that Lionel sets off the explosions in the senior bathroom. This is after the paramedics rush six football players out of the school on gurneys, Brooke's quarterback ex-boyfriend among them, sitting up in goony anguish over the terrible bleeding burn on his throwing hand.

I walk into the principal's office, escorted by two city cops who are good at scowling. There's my mom, sitting across the desk from the principal and Mr. Clayborn. She has put on jeans and pulled a pink T-shirt over a thermal undershirt, beneath which she wears a bra that reproduces the bulge of breasts. She is wearing the wig of bouncy blonde-brown hair that she hates like a curse put on her alone. By the light glaze on her blue eyes I see that she had not planned to leave the house today. She has a hard time keeping her head still and probably wants to take a nap. When the principal voices concern that she might pass out, she holds up a bony hand and says, "Huh-uh." She reaches out her shaking hand for me, and I sit facing her so that she can try to pulverize my shoulder with her weak grip.

"You," she says, almost as tall as me but oh so brittle. "Did you do this?"

"No." I didn't. It was the first of our experiments for which I was demoted to observer status. Lionel didn't trust me to handle the potassium hydroxide. He thought I'd bring it into contact with a microscopic piece of water, and so he dried the sinks in the bathroom himself, stuffed the drains with paper towels, and then sprinkled into each a few white crystalline flakes. The potassium hydroxide flakes resembled the crystal-form cocaine that we have smoked in our spot near my house. Lionel dismissed my analogy with a callous bah-and-wave. He peeled off latex gloves and said, "If you want to smoke it, I suggest you wear a gas mask."

I had only meant that there was perhaps a noticeable cycle in our experiments. My point was lost, in the gloom of the bathroom, on his single celebration bounce. He led me out into the hall, where we hung out next to a window with the view of the lot of gleaming student cars and waited for lunch to end and the football team to trash the senior bathroom, according to routine. As they roared past us into the brick-walled lavatory, none of them noticed us, except for the quarterback ex-boyfriend, that melancholy ad model whose diminishing power was to make you feel sorry for him. He moped at us, and we stared at him, invincible nobodies. As the daily riot started inside, Lionel and I headed for the doors to the gym hallway, for we were scheduled to be physically educated.

The first bang sounded just as we reached the end of the lockers. It was as if a big, steel pocket of air had burst, followed by shouts in the bathroom, the sounds of boys directing one another in matters of first aid. We stopped. Someone shouted some nonsense about a gun, and girls began to scream from the bathroom down to our end of the corridor. The second explosion sent us all running out of the school, Lionel and me at the front of a teeming mob of panicked teenagers. He was trying very hard to laugh at what he had done, but like me he grew quiet once we stood behind the fearful, gossiping, overreacting crowd in the parking lot.

For some time he looked down at his Airwalks, and then, as if something had occurred to him, his face hardened like that of a guy going out to the firing squad. He took his cigarettes from his pocket and lit one. There was nothing he could do, now that he had done what he had done. Suspicions about his involvement were only as natural to the principal and Mr. Clayborn, the keeper of volatile chemicals, as was their dislike of a kid who shaved his head and wore pictures of zombies on his shirts and who sneered at them with all the calculated ferocity of a fourteen-year-old. Lionel was who he was, and I admired him for it. He sighed and wearily smiled and looked over the crowd and the school like he owned both. He smoked an illicit cigarette on school grounds, knowing he would be lucky to finish it before they marched out to seize him. I looked across the heads of the crowd to the shining school doors, where there appeared, no mistake, Mr. Clayborn, who immediately saw me, the marker of Lionel's location.

Clayborn was not graceful in his apprehension of my friend. The cigarette fell to the blacktop and continued to burn, as its owner was dragged off by a nearly violent science teacher into the crowd of impressed students. I was surprised to be left standing alone, but the students were watching Lionel. It was as if I, the biggest freshman in the school, had somehow been overlooked. I went in with the crowd when the fire trucks left and attended what was left of gym class. No one bothered to change for the few minutes left, and we were shooting around in our school clothes when the cops came into the gymnasium and asked Ms. Nagle which kid was me.

Expecting to be handcuffed for the first time in my life, I tell Mr. Clayborn and the principal that I am not responsible for the chemical mines. They confer, and Mr. Clayborn suggests that I wouldn't have known about these compounds. "He's not in the advanced class with Lionel. And I just don't think Francis would do something like this."

To my disbelief and great guilt they believe me. My mom is willing to let them believe what they want to. She has her own plans for me. The principal sends the policemen away. I am told that as we speak Lionel is waiting to be taken to jail. The principal and Mr. Clayborn are oddly compassionate as they tell me this. They treat me like an old friend, and I squirm in my chair. From these men I expected nothing less than persecution and torture. For some reason they now view me with eager curiosity in their middle-aged faces.

From his perch on the desk, Mr. Clayborn says, "I know that you went along with him because you didn't want him to feel alone. I understand. He's a bright kid, and it must have hurt him to be wrong about a lot of things. Why was he so unhappy? Was it his family?"

Who can say? A fourteen-year-old boy, no matter how tall and physically mature, cannot. My mom is one person in the room who is aware of this.

"I'm going to take him home now," she says. She's exhausted, and these men are crazy to her. At the door she tells them, "Lionel was his best friend."

She's driven the cruiser and I sit shotgun, trying to see into the backseats of the police cars parked along the curb ahead of us for Lionel's bald head.

"They already took him away," my mom says, as she starts the engine and puts the car into motion. The school is five stories, orange brick, looking down on a broad lawn with four black walnut trees and, across the highway, fallow soybean fields. Once, the sheer size of the building in the middle of this nothingness shocked me, as it does again now. I want to never go back. I want to run away or kill myself. I want an unimaginable fate to lie in store for me at home. As we get farther away from the school, driving in silence, these things become less and less likely.

When we've gone a mile or so she switches on the radio and sings along with some band of whiners from the sixties. Her voice is soft and harsh, but she can bellow when she feels like it. Great, I think, sing me to death. I have a sour mouth. I realize that I know this song. I've sung it before, with my mom, on the road. She turns to me, slowly saying the words as though to remind me of what they are, though she knows that I do. It's not okay to laugh, even though she's teasing me. What am I going to do? Pout? I give it up, lie back in my seat, and sing along.

That afternoon I don't know what to do with myself, and I sit on my front porch smoking cigarettes and checking to make sure my mom isn't moving around downstairs. I'm not in trouble, just brought home early, cautioned. I'm sitting on the flagstone front porch, paranoid, Camel to my lips, when Brooke pulls into the driveway.

She is glassy-eyed and grimacing, more unhappy than I've seen her. I worry she's abandoned Lionel and gone back to her quarterback ex-boyfriend. She mentions none of this, just says that she wants me to come with her out to our spot. On the way she bitches about how stupid it was of Lionel to try to kill her quarterback ex-boyfriend (for this is how she interprets his act) and then to get caught doing it.

"What's he trying to do?" she asks. "Punish me by taking all the men out of my life?" She is through with men, she says; she will become a born-again virgin and live in France as a nun.

We weave fast through the stripped trees, and I look out for rangers and hope against a second encounter with the authorities in a single day. Not soon enough we are parked, and she is slamming out of the car, cussing out the gray disturbance in the sky, telling Fritz the crazy and now startled fisherman that he can go fuck himself too, and then running down the leaf-covered trail to the boulder, with me jogging in pursuit.

She stands at the edge of the pond and utters a valedictory to love and life as she knows it, and reaches into her purse and brings out Lionel's pipe, wrapped in tissue. She has it ready to smoke, and preserved this way, packaged, rubber-banded tight. "I've decided to kill the baby," she tells me, theatrical and self-pitying.

Of course, she's been trying to kill the baby since I met her.

"Oh for the love of Pete, don't stand there!" she shouts at me in disbelief. "Come take this thing away from me."

I do this, look at the packed bowl, a real winner, and put it in my pocket. Later I'll trash it. Crystal-form cocaine is not something I want to be smoking by myself.

Brooke sniffs and dangles a crushed pack of cigarettes. "These, too."

I store these with the drugs.

"Anything else you'd like to give me?" I ask.

Brooke surrenders a miniature bottle of Jack Daniels. She sighs and cocks her head at me, dainty but for her protuberant belly under her gray peacoat. She's out of tears and anger, and I can see that she's done what she's come here to do. I guess she's making a lot of quick adjustments now that Lionel's in trouble. In irony I offer her my arm. She takes it, and we walk this way to the clearing, to her car.

Fritz is standing at the end of the dock, his pole beside his mucky galoshes. He's got this big painter turtle in his hands.

Brooke stops. "What is it?" she asks.

"Ach," says Fritz, holding his rod to the dock with a galosh. He's biting down on his fishing line, keeping it taut so the turtle's head stays out of its shell. Its neck fully extended, the turtle frantically paws the air.

The line falls out of his teeth, and Fritz roars at the turtle, "What are you doing awake?" The turtle's head goes into its shell, and Fritz's throat catches like he's going to get upset.

I go over and take the line, and standing over the old man's uneasy breathing, I sort of pull the turtle's head out of its shell with the line. The poor animal's wrinkly neck is taut and it hisses at me, but Fritz says not to worry, I won't break it.

"I'm going to go, Wheeler. I'm going to leave you here." Brooke pouts on her way to the driver's side. I wave okay and stand closer to Fritz to help him get the hook out of the poor turtle's beak. It upsets Brooke that I do not chase her, and she sits a moment in her car, watching us, furious and prettier that way, in black eyeliner.

"My friend is in love with that girl," I tell Fritz.

Fritz says, "That girl is a bitch. Eiskalt. Your friend is a scheisse."

I don't argue with people who are insane or old. It turns out I can hold the turtle's mouth open with a key as the old fisherman pulls the hook from the upper part of its beak, chipping it, but getting it out of there. The car starts and kicks up gravel. Fritz and I look over, and Brooke is staring straight at me, a second before she drives out of my childhood. There's an understanding of this between the three of us, before it slips out to a place beyond words, and she squeals her tires.

"There we are," says Fritz, "good as new. Almost."

I step away, and he releases the turtle into the cold autumn water.

From that moment I know Brooke won't come to my house again by herself. As it will turn out, she will never return to the house where I stay the next four years with my mother. Lionel will be released from the Child Study Institute when he is eighteen, and we will not resume our friendship. By then Brooke will have a daughter and be married to her disfigured quarterback ex-boyfriend. Lionel will swear off terrorism and go live in some mountains somewhere to write poems for kids. Sad local Christians will put him in their newspaper, and I'll read the article about his struggles and poverty and his vision of peace-loving kids. An hour later I won't be able to recall any of it verbatim.

I will hear of Brooke's divorce in another city, and after I have forgotten about it, I will come into the watery state of the present moment, being twenty-three years old, a door-to-door book salesman passing through Missouri. I am the weirdo on the doorstep, the ogre in the trenchcoat, leather attaché in hand, preposterous, quoting Faust to housewives.

"A man is being made," I tell them, accept their rejections, and traipse away across their dry autumn yards.

At a house in the suburbs, Brooke answers the door, older, sturdier. An attractive woman with a serious life, or at least she dresses this way. We share surprise, silence, and nervous laughter. We find we are happy to see one another. Each of us is happy to see how well the other has survived. There is an offer of coffee in the wood-paneled dining room. An introduction to the little girl spying on us from the kitchen doorway. Auburn pigtails a mess, the emcee of the great room. Through the passageway I see there are toys scattered across the white carpet—the plastic castle and the pretend-beach of naked, sunbathing dolls, beside the many pages of blue construction paper that Brooke explains make up the broad and deep Pacific Ocean.

I think it for an instant only, but Brooke perceives my flinch. Our chatter fails as the daughter she once forsook for two months comes into the room, sensing something wrong, and wants to sit on her mother's lap. She is too big for this and sits there blocking Brooke's mouth, furious at my intrusion, shoulders hunched up beneath her tiny ears.

I want to tell Brooke what Lionel once advised me, that when you remember something you're not proud of, it's best to think of the outcome as inevitable. It helps to pass the memory, he said. Instead I finish my coffee. Brooke sees me to the front door without the pretense of a smile, and we resume being the people we tell ourselves we are.

The Hired Man

GREG DOWNS

From *Spit Baths* (2006)

George Washington was dead. Not exactly front page news. But the way George Washington died, that was what disturbed Tom Floyd. April 1778, Valley Forge, sailing on the Schuylkill with Hamilton and Laurens and von Steuben, George Washington stood at the bow, his surveyor's hand shading his eyes. When the hull struck a rock, George Washington fell forward, his arms waving like wings. Then he was gone, the water smoothing away the memory of his fall. Hamilton and Laurens and von Steuben shucked their shirts, dove into the river, but they could not find him. Upstream at Valley Forge, the soldiers hauled the shad nets in by hand, Greene and Ludwig tallied the loaves for the spring-time feast, the fiddlers celebrated a winter's passing. And Washington tumbled southward, through Philadelphia, the Delaware Bay, the Atlantic Ocean. The currents lifted his shoes, his fabled gold watch chain, his ivory teeth. His bare feet cartwheeled above his unwigged head; his body danced over the sharks.

Five months and twenty-three days before he discovered the truth about George Washington, Tom Floyd finally accepted retirement. His wife, Stephanie, took hers a year earlier, but then she liked being home. Bad students couldn't drive him out, not their unexcused absences, in-class chatter, chalked-up erasers, ill-intentioned caricatures, not even the bag of dog shit some dumb ass left on his desk three years ago. No, it took an expert, an administrator, to wear down Tom Floyd. Eleven guest speakers assigned by the district in one goddamn week, AIDS, drugs, gangs, guns, the procession of fear. After number nine, Tom Floyd signed the form he'd been keeping in his desk drawer. In the three minutes before number ten arrived, he carried the form to the office and gave it to the bookkeeper.

If Tom Floyd thought teaching was boring, he should have considered retirement. Even took up smoking again, until Stephanie made him quit. He wrote family histories and carried them out to the glider, where Stephanie read biographies in the afternoons. "This ain't another letter to the newspaper, is it?" she'd ask, teasing him. What she cared about was inside their fence line. Not strangers, not politics. After folding back the corner to mark her page, Stephanie would go to work on his history, scoring his loose sentences, his sloppy grammar. She asked questions. "Your great-aunt Jean really took a steamship through the Panama Canal? Grandpa Louis played exhibition basketball against the House of David All-Stars? Your people did some crazy shit."

"And I married you," he said.

"Take a rest before you make your corrections." Stephanie lifted her legs, opening a spot for him to sit. Stephanie laid her feet in his lap, and he felt himself getting big. "Good grief," she said. "Leave it to a white man to get excited over a comma splice." She laughed. "Just wait till I finish this chapter, and I'll take you upstairs. Paul Robeson's father is fixing to die."

"If Mr. Robeson's death doesn't put you in the mood, nothing will," he said. But she liked order. Finish what's in the left hand, then worry about what's in the right.

For Christmas, Tom Floyd started Stephanie's family histories. No small present, finding information about dead black people. It required driving trips down past D.C. to Virginia, where her family had been kept before emancipation. He flipped through old plantation books until his eyes hummed. When he returned, Stephanie was reading by the sunroom window, waiting for him. A plate of cookies on the sill, covered by a white dish towel. He'd been smelling those cookies since Baltimore.

This trip, his third, Tom Floyd found the George Washington story in an 1827 plantation journal, between two long entries about the New Orleans cotton market. The woman who kept the journal owned Stephanie's great-great-grandfather, Immanuel Carter. Immanuel warned his mistress about the rumors, to keep his family out of any trouble that might be coming. The slaves up at Mount Vernon, Bushrod Washington's people, were telling the whole neighborhood about the two George Washingtons, hoping to shame old Bushrod into freeing them before he died. Loud talking could lead to trouble. But that was the only passage in the journal that mentioned the rumors, or Immanuel Carter.

Hamilton and Laurens and von Steuben tied off on the east bank of the Schuylkill. They kindled a fire to dry their trousers, covered their groins with their shirts, slept on the grass. Their dreams horrified them; they saw their bodies hanging from trees, their limbs fed to hogs by the Hessians the British hired. Each man woke with thoughts of running to Philadelphia, of surrender, but no one would say it aloud. Hamilton lifted the trousers from the tree, still wet. The men put them on anyway. As they bucketed water onto the fire, a hired man walked from the woods into the rock-strewn field and began to break the ground with a hoe. He was tall, lacking teeth, and he hoed with silent fury. No farmers' curses, no hired man's laxity. It was the silence that inspired Hamilton's idea, and von Steuben's concurrence. Laurens needed convincing, but what were their options? Surrendering? Serving under that fool Gates? The hired man—they never asked his name—listened quietly. The colonists could not survive without a leader. If he would only say yes, he could give up the hiring-out life, own entire plantations in Virginia and hundreds of niggers to work them. Would he try it? The hired man, the new

George, scratched his face. "I'll want teeth," he said. They did not ask if he left behind a family, a past, a life. The wind had died, and they began to row upstream. Laurens and Hamilton, being younger, took the first turn. When they were tired out, von Steuben took one oar. The new George picked up the other, then, remembering himself, gave it back to Hamilton.

Every October, Tom Floyd had presided over a weeklong mock trial of George Washington. Traitor/hero, racist/emancipator, aristocrat/democrat. Even the dumb students loved trials; they learned their legal phrases, with their cynicism, from the television. After the prosecutors pronounced George's guilt, the defense his innocence, Tom Floyd gave the verdict. "You're both right," he said. "He's guilty and innocent. Just like the country. It's not a single thing, good or bad. It's big enough to be worth arguing about, to be worth keeping together." But if Washington was small, a fake, a hired man, what did that say about the country he founded? For the first time, Tom Floyd was glad he had retired. For all his limitations, he never once knowingly lied to them.

All the "Washington" signs on the Richmond–D.C. connector sickened Tom Floyd. False advertisements. Every April, he chaperoned a daylong trip to the capital; the students loved to watch the clouds scoot across the reflecting pool by the Washington Monument. Every year, it softened him, seeing these Philly kids toe up to the water's edge alongside the other history tourists, school groups from improbable places like West Des Moines, Muscle Shoals, East Lansing. Unlike by color, by accent, by pride, but here they were. Americans. Tom Floyd came late to patriotism; he'd entered teaching to avoid Vietnam. Over the years his students got darker, more skeptical, and he needed to remind them, and himself, that they were all in the same boat, that they weren't just floating free. Stephanie believed in a lonely world, and that drove her into herself, her biographies, her backyard, her clannish friends. But Tom Floyd still had his hope.

At the harbor tunnel, he passed his five to the toll taker, got three ones in return. The JFK tollbooths took a fresh five. So it wasn't until the Delaware Turnpike plaza that he looked at the dollar bills he'd received as change and saw the hired man grimacing at him. Fraud. He passed two fake Georges to the toll taker, and the gate lifted; the guilt bled from the Schuylkill to the Delaware to the Potomac to his fingertips. The third bill he dropped onto the passenger seat, on top of the journal pages the library staff copied for him. He had circled the name Immanuel with a black pen, so Stephanie could find it.

Near the Philly airport, he cut along Island Avenue, through the full and forgotten streets of Eastwick. Half the businesses in the city advertised history: the line of women at the window of Liberty Steaks, the pigtailed girl dragging her father toward the Independence Water Ice stand, the delivery truck for George Washington Pretzels idling in front of Franklin Market. Tom Floyd wanted to tear the picture of George Washington off the truck. He wanted to attack the country, so that he could be roused to defend it. When the light changed, the car behind him honked, and he drove through. He'd save his words for Stephanie, who would argue back, who was tough enough to tire him out.

At home, Stephanie was knitting in the sunroom. As she finished each row, she looked out to the street. When she saw Tom Floyd, she raised her hand to wave. Then she put down the half-finished scarf, a blue one meant for him. Tom Floyd grabbed the papers and the dollar bill from the passenger seat.

"What's in your hand? You find something for me?" Stephanie stepped out onto the front step, holding a plate of cookies in her hands.

At the base of the steps was a latticed bin that covered their garbage cans. Tom Floyd stopped there, looked up at the sky. The streetlamps ruined most of it, but he could see a few stars, small hammer points. Some of the stars, he knew, had been dead a long time, thousands of years, and yet, from the Earth, they still spar-

kled. When the new George arrived at Mount Vernon, at the end
of the war, his people lined the driveway. As he stepped down
from the carriage, Martha waited for him. He gave her his arm,
led her inside. If she noticed the new man beside her, she never
said so.

"You coming up? Or I got to come get you?" Above him, Stephanie shook her bangs from her eyes. It felt good to be missed.

But her mood wouldn't last. Stephanie didn't care about
George Washington. He would argue, throwing off his burden,
and she would seal her cookies in Tupperware, let her bangs
shield her eyes, retreat behind her books. The cookies smelled
the way her wool scarves felt on his skin. If the stars could burn
falsely, why couldn't he?

"I didn't find nothing, baby," Tom Floyd said. "Just some trash."
He crumpled the diary pages into his fist, tossed them into the
garbage can. Then, just this once, just for his own soul, he threw
the dollar bill in, too. As Tom Floyd walked up the steps to his
wife, Stephanie set the plate on the windowsill, so that he could
come close to her, so that she could kiss him.

Side by Side

CATHERINE BRADY

From *Curled in the Bed of Love* (2003)

Wonder is not what Bill should feel after a truck smashes into his car at forty miles an hour, but he does. He is amazed that he could step unscathed from his crumpled Toyota, amazed by the way his body absorbed the impact. The stack of bones in his spine jumped, scattered, and then resettled, as if his bones had been momentarily freed from their tethers of muscle and tendon and ligament.

Everyone, even the paramedics who came to the scene of the accident and assured Bill he would be in pain tomorrow, seemed as amazed as Bill. You escaped with your life, said the cop who made the report, both of the paramedics, the shaken driver of the truck.

Even Bill's wife, Pam, says so when he comes home to tell her what happened. He finds her in the backyard, barbecuing even though the fog is rolling in, visible as exhaled breath in the cold air. Their old house didn't have a yard, only a rectangle of concrete patio, but here they have a lawn, flagstones, a flower bed. The grass is already jeweled with beads of condensed water. Bill has an impulse he's never had before. He takes off his shoes and socks to cross the lawn to Pam. His feet sink in the damp grass, so cold. With his two hands he mimes for Pam the collapse of his car and watches her face shift, like another kind of mime, from nonchalance to concern to fear. She puts both her hands on his cheeks. They've come through a bad patch recently, and it's good to see that inside his wife, this is what was waiting for him.

She wants him to go to the emergency room right away, and when he refuses, she wants him to lie down. But he feels good. Woozy and only slightly achy in his joints and completely let off the hook, the way he feels when he is coming down with the flu. Bill walks away from Pam and drifts across the wet grass. He imagines his feet leaving a slick snail's trail on the wet lawn. Delicious cold pricks at his toes. He watches the pine tree at the back of the yard shiver a little in the wind and he waits. He has a beatific moment coming to him.

The closest he ever comes to that clarity is when he takes the Vicodin his doctor prescribed for back pain. Throw in the daily dose of muscle relaxants, and Bill can feel mighty fine indeed. Maybe the recognition of having been spared comes grain by grain, like some sort of time-release medication. Maybe he is just distracted by all the trivial ways in which, it turns out, he hasn't been spared. The morning after the accident, Bill decided to call the doctor and discovered he couldn't lift the phone book. His doctor said he had whiplash and he could only expect his pain to grow worse. When Bill called the truck driver's insurance company to file a medical claim, an agent informed him that the truck driver—that man who'd had tears in his eyes when he saw Bill climb out of his car—was claiming the accident had been Bill's fault. Every day, Bill, lying on the sofa with ice packs strapped to his lower back and neck, has to field calls from the bullying substitute who has been taking his high school English classes until he gets back on his feet.

How thin relief seems compared to the leaden compactness of pain. It doesn't keep Bill from being bored with watching TV all week. Sick of Oprah, he wonders how he might find a witness to vindicate him. There must be plenty of them, maybe even someone he knows—the accident happened at rush hour just a few blocks from home. He takes a poster board his son used for a science project and writes a plea for help in large block letters on the back, and at 4:45 he walks to the intersection. He wears the poster like a sandwich board, held in place by twine looped around his neck. Even fortified with Vicodin, he can't stand the strain of holding up the sign with his hands.

Standing on the corner, inhaling the sweet fumes of car exhaust, Bill is encouraged by the fact that so many cars go by. Hundreds every minute. Someone in one of these cars will know what happened to him.

When a van pulls up next to the curb and honks, he is disappointed to discover that the driver is his wife. Pam leans over to unlatch the passenger door for him. "Get in," she says. "Hurry up. Before one of the neighbors sees you."

Bill climbs into the car—slowly, fine-tuned to the compromised functioning of his body. From the back seat, his kids stare. Pam has to pick them up from the after-school program now that Bill can't bring them home with him after school. This has been rotten for her. Ordinarily Bill fetches the kids and does the little daily errands, the late-night run to the grocery when they're out of milk, the kids' dentist appointments, the dry cleaning.

Bill rolls up the poster board and holds it between his knees. "I thought it was worth a shot," he says. "Too many good drugs, I guess."

He's sure Pam will tell him he's crazy, right in front of the kids.

"Let the insurance company handle it," she says.

When they pull into the garage, Pam jumps out of the car to unload groceries from the back, where the bags have been shoved in among the accessories she carts around for the houses she stages. With the bare minimum, Pam can furnish an empty house from her inventory or repair the bad taste of sellers who don't know how to arrange their possessions in a cunning way.

People don't just sell a house in San Francisco anymore, not in a market pitched to frenzied desire. Spending a few thousand dollars on Pam's fee and a coat of paint and artful flower arrangements translates into tens of thousands in the actual offer, more like a miracle than an investment.

Pam issues instructions while the kids are still slamming the car doors shut. Arianne is to go and empty the hamper into the laundry basket so Pam can get a wash in, Liam has to set the table, and Bill needs to help them start their homework. Juggling two grocery bags and her purse, Pam frees a hand to grab the mail and uses her elbow to switch on the light on the stairs.

Bill lies down on the sofa to ice his back and tells the kids they have to bring their homework to him. Arianne wants to know why he can't come to her room to help her with long division. She stabs her sheet of notebook paper with her pencil. "See? I can't do it in my lap. It won't work." She begins to weep. "And I can't find my right pencil."

She insists on using only a pastel mechanical pencil for homework. She clips her hair into a ponytail with an elastic hair band that must be new every day, cried this morning because Pam hadn't done a wash, and the shirt she always wore with her corduroy pants was still in the hamper. She can't bear to lose things and accuses her little brother of stealing them when they go missing. Her sneakers must be wiped clean every night or she won't wear them in the morning. She's ten. How can she have so many requirements?

Bill promises to buy more mechanical pencils tomorrow.

"No you won't," Arianne says. "You won't even drive."

These tiny probes of hers uncover such large flaws. "I can't," Bill says. "Not with my back."

"You don't look like it hurts," Liam says.

Through the soft haze of the drugs, Bill reaches for Arianne. His hand cups her skull, bumpy, somehow stubborn beneath his fingers. She nudges his hand away with the pencil. Liam asks Bill what he should do for his book report. How blank and erasable their faces are, how much like any other kid's face, lips and nose still smudgeable and cheeks smooth and eyes another kind of indefinite. Not written on yet. How large would Bill have had to make the letters on his sign so that they could be read by people in moving cars?

Bill is tired from doing nothing all day. He keeps his eyes half closed even when Liam punches his arm. His children swim like tadpoles in his dimmed and narrowed field of vision. They bicker with one another, a persistent butting of dissatisfaction. Tadpoles. Balls of blind guts with a tail for motility. Pam hollers from the kitchen that Bill could at least keep the kids out of each other's hair. Sounds are as buffered as the pain signals arriving like huffing, smoking locomotives in Bill's brain.

Bill flips through a magazine while Pam conducts business on the cell phone, rearranging the appointments she had to cancel so she could bring Bill here to the back clinic. He can't drive yet. He made a stab at going back to work; he spent one day in his classroom, talking to his students about *Huck Finn*, and whether he stood or sat, any single position made his back hurt. He was up and down and up and down until the accumulated pain at day's end made him wish he could hang himself from a hook.

They didn't expect this would take all morning. The specialist examined Bill in less than fifteen minutes, but the X ray he sent Bill for required an hour's wait, and now they are waiting again for the specialist to interpret the results. When Bill stood in the dark X-ray room, holding his breath while the technician took the picture, he had a moment when he thought he might faint. He felt queasy, as if the injury had been inflicted fresh, first by the doctor's hands during the exam—mere touch inflaming every nerve in his back—and then by the technician's hands as he positioned Bill before the plate that held the film.

Bill watches Pam punch out numbers on the phone, demolishing her list of calls, brisk and chatty. She smiles as if the person on the other end of the line can see her, keeps trying to tuck a loose strand of blond hair back into her ponytail, smoothing her hair in place, this quiet gesture betraying her anxiety only to him, like a private gift of love. His wife. His sweetie.

What was that bad patch about anyway? Irrelevant stuff. Bickering over Bill failing to put up the screens on the windows or not talking to Pam the right way about things. So what? What did they even have to discuss? Whether Liam needed to be tested for learning disabilities because he didn't like to read, Arianne should be coaxed to make more friends, or Bill should think about moving into administration. Whether Bill complained that Pam had missed the school play and most of Liam's soccer games because he resented her for being the big breadwinner.

Is that all it was about? The housing market in San Francisco has cooled a bit, but when it was peaking, Pam worked like crazy; everyone in real estate was scrambling to make a buck before the bubble burst. The houses Pam staged sold for 8 percent more than comparable ones. She kept her cell phone on the table when they had dinner; in real estate you worked the hours when clients were at leisure to tour houses. She adopted the habits of the realtors who supplied her with clients; she wore a lot of perfume, bought handbags that matched her shoes, indulged in a lavish gift exchange with the realtors. They sent Pam wine-and-fruit baskets when a sale closed, and she boxed for them leather desk sets and raku bowls. In the worst of the frenzy, Bill, not Pam, woke up sweating in the middle of the night, began talking in his sleep. Loud enough that Pam would have to elbow him to shut him up.

Bill stands up to relieve his back. Pam looks at him. "Does it hurt?"

He has to take a breath before he answers. "I just got this weird stabbing pain. Usually it's a dull ache, this dense sensation."

Pam laughs. "Dense sensation? This isn't English class. You don't have to interpret it."

Bill laughs with her. "I'm beginning to understand how hypochondriacs get the way they are."

"The back X ray will turn out to be a waste of time," Pam says. "You should push this doctor for an MRI."

Another insult to his precious pain. Bill's doctor was reluctant to refer him to this specialist and noncommittal about whether seeing a chiropractor would help. Walk, the doctor said. Walk for forty minutes a day. Now the specialist seems convinced Bill's pain stems from nothing but tendon and muscle damage. He authorized the X ray only because Bill asked for it.

"What if I insist on an MRI for nothing?" Bill says. "This is my manhood at stake here, honey."

Bill can't tell if the walking is doing him much good. He goes out in the neighborhood at dusk and walks streets he has only ever driven through. Their new neighborhood has stucco houses with tiled roofs and soothing green lawns, a far cry from their old neighborhood of ticky-tacky boxes built in the sixties. Bill savors the flower beds, the trees, the flagstone paths, and wrought iron fences of this neighborhood, all the ornamentation that evinces a careful husbandry. He feels sorry that he teased Pam when month after month last spring they spent their Sundays hunting for just the right house. On his walks he has scouted a couple of houses for her, come home to announce For Sale signs on lawns, and she's about to sign a contract for one of them, a house left empty by its former tenants. Now he takes a proprietary interest in that house, in all the houses whose gardens and window treatments he has memorized in his slow pacing. The lit windows, tantalizing behind drawn curtains, beckon him, and on those rare occasions when he passes an uncurtained window, he slows to seize this glimpse through a peephole into another world.

A nurse opens the door to the inner office and calls Bill's name. The back specialist doesn't smile when Bill enters his office, and Bill immediately begins to sweat. He knows too many people who've had back surgery and were the worse for it. Or who went from specialist to specialist until finally and too late someone discovered the damage.

The back specialist clips Bill's X ray to a light board. Bill can read nothing in the swirly grays that make his solid skeleton look as if it were made of smoke.

"There's mild joint damage," the doctor says, tapping the X ray. "But that could be arthritis. A simple fact of your age. It proves nothing."

What can Bill say? *I demand an MRI for my dense sensation!*

When Bill comes out to the waiting room after just a few minutes, Pam looks up expectantly. He's ashamed he has so little to report to her.

Bill shrugs. "Whiplash doesn't show up on an X ray."

She smiles. "But that's good news."

"How can it hurt like this, and nothing shows up?"

"Get that MRI," Pam says. "So you can put this behind you."

When she stages houses, Pam does simple things like remove ruffled valances from curtain rods, set out a wine rack on a kitchen counter, move sofas and chairs in from the walls, set out towels of a certain delicious color in the bathroom, replace a spider fern with a blooming phalaenopsis. Pam can predict what triggers wanting, and it's so simple, nothing complicated about it, nothing hidden from sight.

Bill nags the kids to make lunch for school the next day. He has to stand over them every night to make them do it because they can't manage it in the morning. Five nights a week, nine months of the year, minus four weeks vacation—that's one hundred and sixty times annually. When he made dinner earlier—forcing himself, because it hurt and Pam couldn't be expected to carry him forever—he wondered how many times a day he checked his pocket for keys, calculated how many leaves of lettuce he washed every night, how many dinners—assuming they had dinner out an average of once a week—he would have to make in this decade and the next and the next. Maybe when Bill's bones jumped and scattered and snapped back into place, they landed wrong. Maybe a disk presses on some secret nerve or occludes the flow of blood to his brain.

While Pam finishes the day's calls, Bill stands over Liam and Arianne to make sure they brush their teeth, which they should do for a full 2 minutes, or 728 minutes a year, and as he kisses them good night and tucks them in, he totals the number of bedtime kisses he has given them so far in their lives. Thousands.

Pam comes into the living room after she delivers her kisses to the kids. She twirls. "Free at last," she says, which she says nearly every night after they get the kids into bed. She sits on Bill's lap, facing him, straddling his legs.

He's a little surprised. He thought she might be mad at him. He has refused to get an MRI, couldn't come up with a better reason than embarrassment. Pam will shrug off clients who insist on leaving their bowling trophies on the mantel, and she has apparently cut her losses with him too.

Pam unbuttons his shirt. "Now let's have sex."

There's something about her bluntness. It's good for him.

Pam kisses him and slips her hands under his shirt. Then she gets up and leaves him. She has gone to brush her teeth and get ready for bed. Like a commercial break. They'll meet in the bedroom and take up again as if there were no interruption.

While she's in the bathroom, Bill strips off his clothes and gets under the covers, shy. This is the first time.

Pam talks to him while she undresses. She hangs up each garment as she removes it, snapping out wrinkles. In bra and underpants she removes her jewelry and her watch. The chunky metal links of her watch make Bill think of her heavy key ring, the one she drops in the bowl by the front door when she comes home, carefully tagged keys to all the houses to which she has access. Keys. Checking for his keys in his pockets, two dozen times a day. Fingering the key he lifted from Pam's key chain yesterday, stroking it in his pocket while he took his daily stroll.

She crawls into bed with him. "I did three houses today, way too many. It's so hard to turn down work right now. Everybody's holding their breath, waiting for the market to slack off. Be glad you don't have the stress I do at work."

No. Now that he's back at school, the only pressure he gets is from students who want to know when he'll hand back the last papers they turned in. Sixteen hundred pages per class per semester. Yesterday, for maybe the thirtieth time in his life, Bill talked to his students about the river and the shore in *Huck Finn*. He was saying something about the river, the fluid freedom of natural man, the search for meaning, when he felt a sharp pain in his back, pain like a directional arrow instead of the usual seeping ache. It made him think that there was something he could do—something he had to do—to relieve it. Like hunger, it condensed his attention to meeting a single demand. He was in the middle of a sentence. Something about Huck's journey to find meaning. "Find meaning," he said. But he was listening to that other demand. "Find meaning . . . in the meaningful." And all the rest of the day, he felt a craving he could compare only to hunger. A craving he could plan for without being sure that this was what he was doing. When he slipped the key into his pocket, he didn't know that he would use it; he didn't know if it was of any use in staving off this sensation.

Pam kneads Bill's trapezius muscles. "I've been wondering if I should try something else," Bill says.

"What do you mean? Go into administration?"

Pam's touch confuses him. Too light. He's gotten used to the chiropractor, who seems bent on remolding his flesh with her hands. She was interested in the types of his pain. She had him fill in a diagram of his torso, locating every emanating source of hurt in red ink. Then she sank her fingers right into the core of every glowing ember, an artist.

Bill traces figure eights on Pam's arm until she shivers. He says, "Really something else. Something entirely different."

Pam kisses him, tugs his chest hair in smooth circling motions. They're married people all right. They don't bother to demarcate sex from the chitchat that ends their day. She says, "A year ago I'd have told you, get a real estate license. We'll go into business together and make a killing."

"I wouldn't like all those forms you have to deal with when you sell a house," Bill says. "But I don't know what I could try. You're good at figuring out what people want. What do you think I should do?"

Pam moves her hand down to his belly. "I never know too specifically. That's the whole point. If people are still living in the house, we make them take down the family pictures, anything that makes the house seem as if it belongs to someone else. The trick is to give the buyers room to imagine themselves in the house. You set out place mats and pretty dishes and wine glasses and the buyer is like, yeah, if I lived here, I'd have wine with lunch every day. They can see *their* life, only nicer."

It doesn't make any sense to Bill that he wanted to go inside that empty house, that he wants to again. Really he wants to go into all the other houses he walks past. In neighborhoods like theirs, people always draw the curtains so you can't look in, as if to shield the inner sanctum of all that visible cherishing and flaunting. He had to get in somewhere.

It was just an empty house. Pam had not yet transformed it with her props. Sometimes she borrows things from their own house, filches a Moroccan pitcher or a framed watercolor that proves essential to achieving the desired effect.

Pam fishes in Bill's crotch. "Do you enjoy your work?" he says.

Pam giggles. "Which work? What I'm doing now?" Her efforts

are producing instant results. "Yeah, I enjoy my work. I'm good at it. That's always gratifying."

Bill's hands scout the solid surface of her. "Is this gratifying?"

He smells her perfume. He wonders how many dabs are in a bottle, how many days of smelling like jasmine. Sometimes when he wakes at night he feels as if the air in the room has thickened with this scent while they sleep. An odor so strong it drowns the smells of the body.

When he enters her, he feels pain spread like warmth across his lower back, like a large hand pressing on his hips from behind. That pain plants itself behind every thrust of his body, and Pam braces him with her hips from beneath. Slap, slap, slap, his hips against hers. A metronome beats out the time, the steady pace of his strokes. Every human on earth must do this to the same rhythm.

"Pammy?" he calls.

Slap, slap, slap, steady and unending as the sound of the ocean.

Bill retrieves his kids from school in a rental car. The kids climb in, banging backpacks and slapping their rumps on the seat and slamming their elbows in that way that kids need to smack you with their physical existence.

"How come you're driving?" Liam says.

Bill shrugs. "I usually do," he says.

It's time. Pam is right about this. If he can do nothing more about his back, he just has to pick up where he left off. It takes only forty minutes, total, to make the circuit from his school to the kids' and then home.

Arianne fidgets, her legs making slick sounds on the vinyl of the car seat. "You forgot to sign my permission slip," she says.

"What permission slip?"

"I gave it to you yesterday," Arianne says. "You lost it."

Even when he can't remember how he must have sinned against his daughter, she always makes him feel he deserves to be accused. "If you gave it to me," he says, "then its somewhere in the house."

"I was supposed to turn it in today," Arianne says.

Bill is distracted by a light change. He has time to brake for the yellow light, but only if the driver behind him doesn't expect him to squeak through on the yellow. Reacting to a light change is no longer reflex but a futile attempt to read someone else's mind. He brakes, and the car rocks, and he can't help looking in the rearview mirror.

"Whoa, Dad!" Liam says. "You're scary."

Arianne's rump swooshes across the seat; her elbows go smackety-smack on vinyl. "My teacher says if I don't bring it in tomorrow, I can't go on the field trip."

"We'll find it," Bill says, trying to sound soothing. He has students like Arianne, kids who always rush into class late or are dismayed to discover that a paper is due or redden with humiliation when Bill gently corrects something they've said in class. These kids remind him of cartoon characters; every emotion registers on their faces as an abrupt infusion of shock, shame, or despair, and no mishap ever registers as less than catastrophe. It helps to divert them to task—have them scrawl the due date on a binder or open their books to the third chapter or answer the next question he's posed for discussion.

"We'll look for it as soon as we get home, and we'll put it in your backpack," Bill says.

"You don't remember what you did with it," Arianne says.

Bill's hands on the steering wheel seem to bear the weight of the wheel and the column that holds it in place. "Sure I do," Bill says.

Arianne kicks the back of the seat. The impact shudders up his spine.

As they approach the next intersection, the light turns yellow. The Jeep behind him is awfully close. But Bill brakes for the yellow light. In the rearview mirror he sees the Jeep grow rapidly larger till it blots out its own reflection. As the truck did when it hit him. Anticipation keens in Bill like hunger. The Jeep's tires squeal on the asphalt, and then the driver gives Bill the finger. When the light turns green, the driver of the Jeep leans on the horn.

Be reasonable, Bill tells himself.

Arianne wails. "You don't care about me! You don't care about anything! And now I won't get to go!"

Bill accelerates jerkily and careens into the left lane to get away from the Jeep, but the Jeep swerves with him. Bill slams the brake, though the light at the next intersection is still green. The Jeep's tires make a whining sound as it skids. Arianne emits a tiny squeak.

Bill doesn't mind that it hurts to twist around in his seat to look at Arianne. It should hurt. "Not another sound out of you," he says, "or you walk home."

She stares back at him in silence. But her body seems to vibrate and shimmer, to be blurred by the incessant needs that swarm about her. Bill has to remind himself, this is my daughter. My little girl.

He drives on, gripping the steering wheel, hunching over it in a way that he knows is not good for his back. When the Jeep swerves around him, he slows to let it pass. Be reasonable, be reasonable, he tells himself, until they arrive home. Pam pulls into the driveway right behind them, home early. She gets out of the car to wait for them, strands of fine hair drifting free of her ponytail, just like usual, her body quietly countering her strictness with it. Liam jumps from the car—the bang of the door, the slam of his backpack against it, so much announcement—to run to his mother. "Dad's a lousy driver," he hollers. Pam laughs and lifts him off his feet, and then she snags Arianne. She leans close so Arianne can snuggle against her and murmur and sniffle against her chest, and then she booms her answer, as loud as Liam's judgment of Bill's driving.

"No!" Pam says to Arianne. "She didn't say that, did she? That teacher is really an idiot! I'm going to have a talk with her."

Pam sends Arianne into the house to take her pick of the Godiva chocolates some realtor sent today (diverted to task, Bill thinks approvingly). How firmly in place Pam is, how simply her feelings are translated into deeds.

When Bill approaches her, Pam gives him a peck on the cheek.

"She whined the whole way home," Bill says. "She worries me." What he means is, she bothers me.

"You have to learn to ignore her. She's a twitchy kid, just like my brother was. She'll outgrow it someday." Pam laughs. "And she left her math book at school. She said you rushed her. I told her you'd go back for it."

Forty minutes, round-trip. Bill doesn't think he can do it. Anything could happen on the road at rush hour. He feels the way he felt behind the wheel of the car, as if things in his field of vision are arbitrarily swelling, bursting the constraints of perspective, and then shrinking back into place.

"With my back like this," he begins.

"I've got about eighty calls to make before I'm through for the day." Pam swats him lightly. "Just take a Vicodin when you get home."

Bill wakes in the night, his heart thudding. Why? He managed to retrieve the math book, Pam finished her calls in time to join them for dinner, and they watched TV afterward, relaxed. He lies still, soaking up the pain he feels whenever he wakes, the pain that seems to locate for him the parts of himself. He listens for some noise in the house, some clue to what woke him.

He decides to get up and check on things. He pulls on sweatpants and a T-shirt and moves quietly through the house. He listens at the door of each kid's room. He looks in on Liam, curled in a ball at the foot of his bed, but when he tries Arianne's door, it opens only a few inches before he meets resistance. She has rigged up some kind of spiderweb of twine between the door and the doorjamb, with tape clumped here and there. He reaches in and feels for the doorknob, clotted with tape and twine. Don't ask, he tells himself. You don't want to know.

He goes to the front of the house and looks out the window at a silent street. He thinks about waking Pam. *Just take a Vicodin.* His back hurts enough that he'd have trouble going back to sleep anyway. Walking relieves his back pain. He could take a walk. He grabs Pam's clump of keys from the bowl by the door, and again something not exactly like intention directs him down the hill toward the empty house with these keys in his hand.

It's peaceful to be alone on the street with all these darkened houses around him. He could walk right up to anyone's windows and peer in. When he gets to the empty house, he has trouble locating the correct key on the key ring in the dark, and then he has a hard time fitting it into the lock.

He steps into the house and calls "hello?" into the echoing emptiness. And then he booms into the empty space, "Hello!" He flicks on the light switch in the living room. It's as naked as it was the first time he came. Pam hasn't gotten to work with her usual efficiency. His nostrils itch. Something about a house that's not lived in makes dust collect everywhere, silt the air. He has the urge to turn on every light as he moves through the house, to enter every room so that he can silt the air with himself. He flips one switch after another as he goes, on and off, opens closets and yanks on pull chains to light the naked bulbs inside, looks in the empty medicine cabinet in the bathroom, slides on the slick wooden floor of the hall as he heads toward the bedrooms. He finds a receipt wedged beneath a baseboard. He remembers packing up their old house. You always leave something behind, cannot completely erase the traces of your life within four walls.

He ends up in the kitchen, where all the cupboards are disappointingly empty. He turns on the tap and water pulses noisily from the faucet, forcing before it an explosive rush of air. When the water flows in a steady stream, he cups his hands to drink it. He lies down on the linoleum floor. The cold hard surface eases the ache in his back. He watches a branch scratch against the window above the sink. There's something drowsy-making about the fluid motion of the branch.

He wakes for the second time that night with a thudding heart. Only now he is blinded by light. That light seems so omnipotent and obliterating that the terse voice he hears seems to emanate from it, and he can't identify what is being said any more than he can identify any human source for it. A rough hand grips his shoulder and forces him over onto his stomach, yanking his hands behind his back.

The light no longer shines in his eyes. He can see the figure of a man—someone other than the man who has a knee on his back—in the kitchen doorway, the dark clothing, the peaked cap, the bulky outline of the belt that must hold a gun, another long-handled flashlight. He shouldn't have left lights on all over the house. He should say something to these men. Appease them.

He hears the clink of handcuffs being locked over his wrists. The sound of Pam's heavy watch ringing on her dresser, the sound of her clump of keys pinging when she drops them in the bowl. He wonders where he left the keys. He wonders what she'll do when his call wakes her. He blinks when the flashlight beam sweeps over him again, spiderwebbing his vision.

Why didn't he hear them trying the door, issuing an order into the silent house? And what intruder was his daughter expecting, preparing for, with the twine and tape Pam kept for packaging her gifts to the realtors?

The cop above him says something and tugs on Bill's shoulder. To comply, to get up from the floor, Bill has to fold his body to leverage his weight onto his knees. Pain balls up in Bill's lower back, a fist ready to strike, a separate existence within his existence.

Bill has that dizzy sensation he had when his back was x-rayed, a fearful and thrilling anticipation. He twists to get to his feet, deliberate now, anxious to force the torque in his spine, to flush from cover what's inside him.

Marguerite Howe

PHILIP F. DEAVER

From *Silent Retreats* (1998)

I think back on all the waitresses I've watched—roadhouses, coffee shops, airport restaurants. I watch them because it occupies
me while eating lunch, and admittedly maybe because I'm lonely
in a way women never understand, and probably because I'm
tired of watching soap operas in these canned-decor motel rooms
with their high traffic bedspreads, tired of stripping down and
taking futile, half-sleep, beer-induced naps, lulled by the sound
of cars out on the highway where I should be.

And I watch because waitresses are fascinating, the way they
cope with routine, their eyes down, their thank-you's flat and
self-protective. Sometimes I might say something to them or
write a note to them on a napkin as I leave, or I might leave saying nothing but taking a little of them with me in what I've seen
and wondered. Sometimes coming out of the restaurant is disorienting, like coming out of a movie. I scan the terrain for clues as
to where I am, what year it is. Waitresses deal with you as a customer, and in that way are a lot like the rest of the world. But by
observing and wondering, I do at least manage to keep myself
from thinking about all the other things I think about when I'm
on the road.

Like all the times I bashed my head. Like the dizzy hour in the washroom back at South Ward, sixth grade, sitting on an old porcelain sink, staring down at the gray, matrix-marble floor, smelling the powdered soap and wadded paper towels, the whole room gray from the gray of frosted-glass windows serving as shelter from a gray day. Then a cloud like a gray whale, in from the corner of vision, and slam. When I wake up there's blood, a wide lake on the marble floor. I think to myself that there's been a disaster, and in a way there has, one of those little private ones that come back much later on. The teacher who found me shrieked and woke me up—she thought I'd killed myself. Mild kidney infection, the doctor says. That's what makes you blind. You broke your nose.

Then another time, the great family car wreck. Passing a truck on an old two-lane, we fly off the road going sixty, hit a culvert. Here's a 1958 Oldsmobile doing cartwheels down a fencerow, barbed wire, wooded underbrush, knee-high corn, flying suitcases and disintegrating windows. It lands upside down. Again I wake up bleeding. Elsewhere, someone squealing like pigs. Concussion, the nurse says—you'll be okay. Still have dreams about that one. Miss my brother Ben.

I do know about getting the old head bashed. In college I had a fight with a guy from town. The Fonz I call him in my memory. I'd gone out with his girl once. A long time after that I was going for a Coke at the bowling alley, and as I was crossing the parking lot he tore out from behind the building in an old Ford and tried to run me down. I shot him the bird; then I saw the brake lights and heard the wheels lock. He backed up. I bent down to look across the front seat at him, just as he was climbing out on the other side.

As he came around the rear of his car, I noticed that the Fonz was a little guy and I recall thinking I would win. Next thing I knew I had a bicycle chain around my head. I recall trying to go with it instead of pulling my face off, and somewhere in there my head hit the curb and the car and Lord knows what else. I finally got a hold of the little shit and decided to kill him, but some bowler pulled me off. Nasty, the doctor says—between the two of you I'll be here all night.

Anyway. The weightroom at the old memorial gym, University of Virginia, was a white cell, shaped like a perfect cube, with ancient brick walls and tall windows like the interior of an old church. This weightroom, it was not the weightroom of the athletes. It was for ordinary students. We had the pre-Nautilus machines, universals with fraying cables, free weights with old bars that were rusty and sweat-pitted. The weightlifters here were not lifting in order to make the team. At the end of it, there was not a standing ovation from the crowd and a kiss from the cheerleaders. There weren't mirrors, there weren't radios like in the beach-blanket weightrooms of the stars. There were no immediate gratifications whatever. Except for this certain girl who would pass the door of the weightroom on the way to the pool and, in passing, glance in. Half an hour later she'd pass again returning to her locker.

It was a visual thing. She had dark oval eyes, olive-colored skin, straight silky black hair. I never knew her name—in my mind, I called her simply Ann. Day after day she passed the weightroom, always that moment of looking our way. I know we all watched for her, all of us who lifted at that particular time of the afternoon, although nothing was said. I'd see her other places, on Emmett Street at the crossover for instance, or in the periodical section at the library, or drinking beer at Poe's with her sorority sisters laughing around her. Once we bumped back to back coming through the turnstiles at the bookstore. She never particularly saw me, or at least there was never a moment of recognition or acknowledgment. I was not the recurring theme for Ann that she was for me.

Anyway, I met her years later, or so I thought. And this is when I got smacked in the head in New Haven. I imagined that I recognized her at a party. In fact, this person I thought was her was the hostess of the party. It was a reception at her house in connection with a symposium we and several other Texas oil companies were attending at Yale. She was living with the artist Jerome Slater, had lived with him for a while when he was at Oxford and all during the first African tour, and his friends were at this party too, half of them gay, I surmised, and the other half, I swear to Christ, speaking French. And then there were menopausal matrons and all the usual execs and functionaries, full of mutual and fleeting admiration for one another, oil and art, art and oil, money and money, it was a great party. I was with Sarah Beecher, from our Chicago office. But don't tell my wife.

Sometimes I think back on the people who are dead. Brother Ben, seven, upside down in a cornfield. My friend Carl T. Palmer, who died in the crash of a 727 on its approach to Dulles International. I wonder what Carl thought when he heard the pine trees tickling the belly of the plane. They found his ring finger, with ring. But if there is one death among the people who are dead that makes me know I can die, I can really, really die, it is the death of Sarah Beecher in deep, cold water, Lake Michigan. I'm told Sarah was swept off the deck of a prominent industrialist's sailboat while trying, during a squall, to explain what we meant in the sixties when we said something was irrelevant. I guess that's how it happens.

But anyway, she was alive and well in New Haven the night I thought I had finally found that long-lost UVA girl, lo after fifteen years of watching for her to step out of the crowd and be like she was back in the days at memorial gym, the image of perfection, the sweet inspiration, distant and silent and coy.

Imagine my surprise when Sarah and I arrived at this quaint little Trumbull Street apartment building, climbed the narrow stairs to the right flat, and tapped on the door—and there she was, taking me away in the breeze of her dress and perfume with the startling olive skin, the oval eyes lined with dark lashes, the piercing greenish brown eyes smiling at us both. At Sarah the way beautiful women look at one another in the company of men, at me without an ounce of recognition.

"Good evening," she said. "Come in—they're just getting started in the living room. I'm Marguerite Howe." Long arms, the lovely carriage of a swimmer even then.

I watched and waited. I was going to have to ask and make an idiot of myself. I was patient, watching close, trying to make sure. From certain angles, yes. From others—maybe. A guy (Foster Petty, I called him in my mind) struck up a conversation with us that was mostly for Sarah, and I disengaged, found the perimeter of the room and took to looking at the paintings on the wall, mostly Slater's.

They were evidently from his "bridge period," bridges and bridges only, those of the old stone and old steel, and he seemed most taken by the arching formation just over the river, and by the equal but opposite reflection of the arching formation in the surface of the water passing below, which would also give you ripples of sky and river-bank trees. He would depict the birch and the sycamore, and there would be stones flat and water-swept right at the water's surface, right at the water's edge. There was one picture of a bridge over an ice-packed river, and one of a bridge vaulting a dry riverbed. But for the most part, Marguerite's boyfriend had water in his rivers, flowing steady, one must suppose, all the way down to the sea.

Presently, I went straight to Marguerite, who was standing ornamentally next to the tall, thin artist. "I hate to say this, but haven't we . . . I mean, at some time in the past, a long time ago, I think, haven't we . . ."

"Met before?" Marguerite said.

"I was wondering the same thing, exactly," I said.

"I don't believe so." She looked away. Marguerite and Jerome were so urbane and worldly that they almost collapsed from boredom. Slater came from a world where this kind of approach is not used even for the sake of humor, and he wheeled abruptly and disappeared into the kitchen.

"No, I think we have. Really."

"I've never been to Texas."

I looked down at my own name tag, *Bob Price, Market Dev., Dallas.* "Oh, that! I'm not from Texas. I'm from Illinois."

"I love Chicago. Don't I, Jerome?" Then she noticed he was gone. "I was there in 1974. I was there with Jerome in 1979—Jerome is who just left." She grinned. "He tried acting, at the Goodman. Do you know the Goodman? That was fun. I love Chicago."

"Chicago isn't it, my dear, if you'd shut up a minute."

She laughed abruptly, stonily. "Oh, this is real cute—where's Jerome." She looked back toward the kitchen.

"I'm serious," I said. "We accidentally bumped asses once in the college bookstore, University of Virginia." Her jaw may have dropped as I said this. I was losing her fast now.

"Think now. Charlottesville, '68. Jeffersonian democracy? The blessing of the hounds, the old engineering building, Mincer's, the pool at Mem Gym." I waited for her to soften. Nothing. "I can't be wrong. I'm never wrong about a face. I spotted my first-grade teacher on the ferry from Patras to Brindizi."

"I've never been from Patras to Brindizi, and I've never been to Charlotte. Don't you think I remember what school I went to? I do the Northeast mostly."

"Charlottes-ville. You *what* the Northeast?"

"Never been there. Never have."

"How can you say this to me?"

"Please," she said. "It's a mistake."

"Oh, bull."

She looked straight at me. I had decided on an impolite course of action, hoping maybe a fight would break out and I could skulk away unnoticed.

"Really," I said straight into her face. "Be serious. You used to like to swim, maybe still do. You wore your hair long. Striped swimsuit." If this was the right girl, she was going to be amazed by my attention to detail.

I looked across the room and saw that Sarah was totally absorbed in conversation. Foster was very smooth, his hair razor-cut, his tie carefully loosened, his eyebrows combed. I checked several times and Sarah never looked up.

I was beginning, it is true, to allow that this woman was not my UVA fantasy girl, only a reasonable facsimile. She was sipping an old-fashioned. We were all sipping old-fashioneds by then. Her mouth was harder than the mouth of the girl I remembered, or maybe it was her mood, or maybe the rigors of passing time. Maybe we were all harder and softer than we used to be.

"Look," I said, and I took her arm, walked along beside her. "Try to see it my way. I never make this kind of total error about a face. I have to go with my instincts."

"Would you not," she said laughing. She looked at me and I let go of her arm. Luckily she didn't dart away.

At this time, I noticed a quick, attentive glimpse from Sarah, just in the act of turning as Marguerite whispered to me, "The coffee's in the kitchen."

How do you know in the afternoon when you are drinking too much beer that you are going to need all your faculties in order to be articulate that evening? I was in a bind, being in a strange town, in the company of Sarah Beecher who, at that time, had progressed beyond relevance to feminism and didn't take shit from anybody.

Marguerite must have had a lot of parties. She knew to roll up the rug and let us spill and wet on the heavily waxed hardwood if it came to that. She was using these very hefty glasses, with a thick glass base and her initials, MMH, etched on the side.

"I can't help but notice that your name begins with MMH, and I think I even might exactly recall that the girl I'm thinking of, back in Virginia, pretty pretty girl—this whole thing is quite complimentary if you think of it—I'm sure her name was MMH, something like that almost exactly." I was laughing sheepishly. "At worst, we have a *major* coincidence on our hands."

"Look, Bob, go talk to your companion. She's lonesome for you."

"She would appreciate that—I'm serious." I turned the both of us so that my lips could not be read from across the room. "But it's you I want."

Here I achieved Marguerite's full attention. I set my sights on living through the next three minutes. The chances were fair provided she didn't shout for Jerome. The stage was set for a soap opera. Sarah's glass was already in the air, ice sailing away from it in slow motion, the drink splashing on people and causing them to contort their faces and fall away in stop-action, hurky-jerky style like when the film comes off the sprocket.

Bob, Maggie, Sarah—you think about all the soap-opera triangles you've seen. Maggie doesn't agree it's a triangle, says it's a square. Sarah's a nurse at the hospital, has many emergencies. Bob is a doctor, lawyer, and successful architect, runs a women's magazine on the side. The two women are wonderful, but different; Bob is different, but wonderful. Everyone is attracted to everyone. Suddenly Sarah inexplicably murders Sylvia, Bob's second wife's first husband's fiancée; Sylvia comes back in dreams, gives Sarah a case of the nerves. Sarah confesses, goes to jail, is found insane in a court of soap-opera law. She studies anthropology while in jail, and Maggie assists Bob at the magazine, starts her own talk show for women.

When Sarah gets out of jail, she and Maggie often meet for

*coffee, discuss Bob. Oblivious to this, Bob goes on business trips
where he has many adventures and close calls with girls on the
demographic bubble who look alike and want to be stars in the
soap operas. Finally, Bob learns that he's adopted, which makes
him sad. Sarah reveals she once knew someone who was adopted.
Maggie has a baby, puts it up for adoption. Sarah gets a job at
the courthouse.*

*Amazingly, one day the adopted child comes back and wants
to talk to Maggie. The child is now seventeen although everyone
else on the soap opera has only aged two weeks. Naturally, Bob,
Sarah, and Maggie are astonished. They meet for coffee. Someone
steps up and asks Bob to sing, so he does, to the astonishment of
the regulars in the nightclub, bar, and/or lunch counter. It turns
out Bob is not really Bob—he is David. The bad news is he isn't really a doctor; the good news is he isn't really adopted. David goes
to jail for not being Bob. Sarah asks, "But where is Bob?"*

"He's getting carried away," Maggie Howe says. The ambulance was very well lighted, large gray whales swimming. I have
no clear recollection of the following week.

Later Marguerite tried to cheer me up by telling me how this
event had really been the turning point of the whole evening. The
group loved it evidently, having a body among them. Late arriv-
als, she said, assumed it was a gangland hit which missed and
some poor bastard from Texas got nailed by accident. She did sat-
ires on the artists—the artists wanted to believe, man, that there
had been an affair, man, and this babe had kept a secret from
this dude too long, man, you know, and he had doggedly sought
to learn the truth. She had resisted, and he took her arm, man,
sex you know, and he started using this big-guy weight on her,
man, and she says enough of this shit and she pulls this little silver piece out of her purse and pop, Jack, she blows him away.
Went down like a goddamned tree. Dumb oil company guy anyway. Forget it.

According to Marguerite, it took forty minutes for the ambulance to arrive. On Tuesday, when I woke up, the doctors were on the golf course and a nurse—Bunny, I called her—with a small but crucial chip out of her nose and pointy glasses bent over me and said, "Well hello." Through her white dress I could read the designer's name on the elastic band of her bikini panties.

"What happened to me?" I asked her. No answer.

"Sarah's gone back to Chicago," Marguerite told me when she came to visit.

"What happened?" I asked her.

"Sarah said she was real sorry," Marguerite told me. "She said she didn't know why she did it. She said when she threw it she never thought she'd actually hit you. She said she saw red when she realized you were doing your thing again. She said you really bled and you never seemed like the kind of person to bleed."

I sat up, realizing I was in a hospital. My bed was surrounded by airy yellow curtains. "What happened to me?" I asked her again.

"We covered for you at home—bad fall at a party, nothing serious, you were lucky, home by Friday. Your wife bought it, we think."

"Am I okay?" I asked her. I couldn't see straight. I wasn't sure I could move my toes. She started to talk past my question again, I took hold of her arm, "I need to know what happened to me."

Pretty eyes, she looked down at me. "You got your head bashed, Bob."

You think about women. You know women aren't everything, but once in a while you think they might be. The Sarahs and the Maggie Howes, their pretty smiles and their knitted brows of concern, their hair flying in your eyes. Most of the action is mental, make no mistake. While you may bump into them at the bookstore, they may never know you exist and that you love them. Perhaps no one knows how happy it makes you just to see them walk by. You stare at waitresses. You crane your neck in heavy traffic. You become what they call a womanizer.

While I was in the hospital, Marguerite and I had several nice chats, and later she helped me get my things at the hotel and took me to the plane in her little green Rabbit. By that time I knew the whole thing had been a drunken mistake and that she wasn't my UVA fantasy girl, but she was nice, no doubt about it. She lectured me about my chauvinism.

"What's a woman to you?" she asked. She smiled at me, mercifully. "For you a woman is someone to make you feel like a boy. It isn't good for you, Bob, all these lies and deceptions. Think how it makes the women feel, your wife and everybody. Settle down. Get some character."

This is how intimate we got. Marguerite Howe has my blood in the cracks of her hardwood floor. And she told me to get some character.

I went home and cultivated a lull in my life. I imagined my brain was healing. I operated at a basic level. I decided to stop loathing my job and wanting to rush through the office vomiting into the typewriters. I tried to be faithful and truthful. My wife and I went out to eat a lot. I made it a point to eat basic foods, drink to a basic excess, stay away from the girls at the office and on the road, stop watching the waitresses, concentrate on business, and, also, I took up running. I was a little depressed, and I think now that running was a last-ditch attempt to die a heroic and dynamic premature death rather than the shameful, guilty, regressive, gluttonous, wearisome, promiscuous, and despicable premature death I was headed for. I was feeling guilty about my life, and I was thinking a lot about dying.

A shrink once told me at a party that I should give up drinking and align myself with the stars. I guess that's how those guys work. They say something like that to you and it stays in your head because they're a shrink, and later it occurs to you that you might know what they mean. I decided the reasons I was fading so fast were work, drinking, lying, late nights and pretty girls on the road, and, finally, bad organization.

I decided to address head-on, with a high heart and an eye to the future, the problem of bad organization.

I sorted everything. It was a long-range project. Sorting and labeling. I didn't just label things; I labeled the shelves I put them on. I bought staplers and note cards and a couple of two-drawer filing cabinets for the home. I had a different stack of note cards for each category of my life. Every paper clip had its place. This went on for several months. There was no doubt about it. It was a large glass, and Sarah had hit me right on the button.

In the meantime, back at work, I was doing even more driving than I used to. After Carl Palmer died on the Blue Ridge in that 727, I wasn't interested in airliners. I leased a Buick and spent my thirty-second year on "cruise."

One day in the spring of the year following the Marguerite Howe disaster, somewhere between Junction City, Kansas, and Denver, I looked into the rearview mirror and there, driving a dark blue BMW, was a beautiful woman, her hair flying in the wind, chic sunglasses, peering coyly around me. When she passed, I watched for her to look my way and I think she might have, just for a second.

I tried to imagine what she must be like, and where she must be going. I tried to imagine the silk threads in her voice, the warm breath. We were on a big four-lane, and I commenced to play a game. For no reason I would signal to change lanes, and move over into the left lane. I was about a quarter of a mile behind her. When we would come to a little rise in the road, in which for only a moment we would be obscured from one another, I'd take that moment and switch real quick into the other lane again. For half an hour I did this, supposing that she was watching my every move in her mirror.

Finally, as I was cruising along in the right-hand lane, I repeated the process again, signaling so she could see, shifting lanes, then waiting for the rise. When it came, I shifted real quick into the right lane again. When I topped the rise so I could see her, I saw to my absolute glee that she had switched to the left lane. And all the way to Denver we were never in the same lane again. I would switch, she would switch to the other. It was a coded conversation of some kind, a dance. Sometimes I would pass her and speed up ahead, and at the first rise I'd switch lanes. In the flat again I'd look back and see that she had switched, too.

Once, and this was the real surprise, I had to get off the four-lane to get gas. I knew the game was over, but I had no more gas. When I came down the entrance ramp back onto the highway—I couldn't believe my eyes—she was parked on the shoulder waiting and rushed off again ahead of me to play some more.

On the outskirts of Denver we came to a moment that, I guess, had been inevitable all along. The moment designed to resist loss. We were on a city street by this time, and finally she signaled to pull into a big, empty parking lot. Which she did. After seven hours of this strange game, there was the desire to meet, to say hello. As I went by, I saw her watching me in the mirror. I saw the realization hit her that I was not turning in, that we wouldn't meet. She looked down. I drove on, washed away in traffic. Five minutes later I changed my mind and went back, but she was gone, of course.

Anyway, I'm in a restaurant alone, on the road. I'm watching waitresses. When I leave they are completely behind me, like Sarah, like Maggie Howe. Several of them are clustered in a back booth (all the booths are vinyl, cracked at the wear points). And here comes another one, evidently off-duty. Mary Proletary, I call her in my mind. Bless her—see how she scans the place when she comes through the door. Either she knows herself in some solid, truckstop way, or she doesn't but doesn't know she doesn't.

Anyway, you can tell she pulls no punches. Her cheeks are rosy; she's still young. She isn't a quasi-professional like me, carrying flip charts and slide-tape programs around in her trunk—a labor guy, trying to live the executive illusion. Mary doesn't have to consult, tell people what they already know so they'll pay her. She never has to use the term "application-oriented" in anything she does. She never says "bottom line."

She comes into the place in her off-hours—I wonder why. I watch her. She's showing the other waitresses pictures of her baby. They peer down through cigarette smoke and black eyeliner. They smile and laugh together, rubbing shoulders as they huddle over the picture. It's interesting to watch them look at her. I'll bet they wonder about Mary, and Mary's boyfriend, whom I estimate to be a trucker from Memphis.

Mary is wearing a sundress, and I can see the straps from her bathing suit Xeroxed into her skin. Her hair is frizzed and peroxide reddish blond. Her walk is steady and solid, straight ahead. Her lower legs are full of the genes of work, her back narrow so the bones show. She's been granted seven years to flower and bear young before she plunges into the dim middle world I'm peering at her from, anonymous, scarred, guilty—futile life, totally unrelated to anything a person ever dreamed of or wanted. Lonely, burning, storms. I dread returning to the car and the four-lane highway, using the credit card to call the office and tell them the Dallas estimates drawn from Boston data.

I watch those waitresses. They wonder about old Mary, and Mary's boyfriend whom they've never seen except in the shadow of a baby's snapshot. They wonder, watching her, about how happy she seems, and how she manages to hang on the way the customer in this place tips.

The Woman with the Red Scarf

KIRSTEN SUNDBERG LUNSTRUM

From What We Do with the Wreckage (2018)

It was announced at the weekly community meeting that a new person would be joining the house: a woman, arriving from California that afternoon. They would all need to welcome her but not forget to give her room to get familiar. Anders, who had by then been at the Unity Center for nearly two months and had just concluded a silent retreat, was selected to greet the newcomer, and so after Common Lunch he went out to the porch to wait for her. Lying on the hammock, he had a view of the road, and he saw her car—or rather the dust cloud that rose with the car's motion—from a long way off. He smiled to himself as he watched it approaching—a white Fiat, ridiculous in this landscape. A car like that was as suited to the desert as a groomed lapdog.

The Center got this sort sometimes—people expecting a spa vacation and not a spiritual stripping down. They never lasted even a full week. This woman should have stopped in Phoenix, Anders thought, got herself a nice hotel room with white sheets and cable. She should have stopped in San Diego for a week at the sea. He rolled out of the hammock's hug, shaking his head, and walked around the house to the parking lot just as the woman opened her car door.

As it was, she turned out to be exactly what he was expecting: two or so years younger than he was—not quite thirty, he guessed—with artificially fair hair and a figure slim to the point of angularity. She wore an expensive-looking sheer blouse, the blush of a red tank top visible beneath it. From the trunk, she pulled a leather purse, which she slipped over her shoulder, and a hard-shelled rolling duffel. The car let out a shrill beep as it autolocked when she turned away.

Her eyes took him in with an open up-and-down sour appraisal. Anders had stopped shaving when he arrived here. He had cut off the legs of his jeans in acquiescence to the heat and had taken to wearing shoes only on long walks. No one at the center bathed more than once a week—a frugality of communal living—and most of them lost weight. After his recent week of silent retreat and fasting, Anders had lost enough that he could now feel the stays of his ribs beneath his shirt. He was a warning, a human caution sign. *When I got here, I was one of your sort,* he wanted to say. *And now look at me: a commune cliché, a dirty hippie. John the Baptist come from the wilderness, stinking of piss and honey and his own delusions. This place will wreck you.* But only people who were already wrecked came seeking here anyway.

"*Bienvenida,*" he said, raising his hand in a wave.

The woman frowned. "*Qué todo el mundo habla Español aquí?*" Perfect college Spanish.

"No, no. I just meant hello," Anders said. "Sorry. I was being casual. That's all." He looked over his shoulder. "The border's about fifty miles from here."

She squinted at him. It was bright out—the usual midafternoon desert glare blanching everything. "Casual?"

"Don't worry about it."

"But I don't follow."

"It doesn't matter," he said. She was as uptight as she looked.

He took her bag and led her up the porch steps, held the metal screen door for her, and let it slam shut at his back when he stepped inside. The temperature was noticeably cooler indoors. The house the Center occupied was old—a midcentury two-story built by some survivalist lunatic, then left to dilapidate when he died. It had been refurbished to meet code now, though only to just meet code. Still, the end-times foresight of its original owner had some use; it had been built to withstand the wild fluctuations of desert climate: thick adobe walls and tile roof, heavy wood shutters on the windows to keep out the afternoon sun, a bomb shelter below used to store canned foods. For cold nights there was a wide-mouthed fireplace at the center of the house, and the outbuilding that had once been an armory was a sturdy arts studio.

"You'll get a full tour later," Anders said. "Someone will find you before dinner. If you're hungry now, any food on the kitchen counter is up for grabs between meals."

"I'm not hungry."

He led her through the shadowed kitchen anyhow. A pile of loose vegetables from the back garden sat heaped in a wooden bowl near the sink—a bunch of arthritic-looking carrots, a jicima bulb, three fat yellow peppers—and beside them, a glass dish of red grapes and a pitcher of water. "We eat together three times a day. Dinner is at dusk."

"That late?"

"Time unwinds differently here than anywhere else I've ever been. The day won't seem as long as you'd think."

"You talk like a native. How long have you been here?"

"A while," Anders said.

The woman nodded. A sheen of sweat had broken out on her forehead and her blouse had wilted around her small frame, a damp onion skin.

He left her at the door to her room—a narrow dormitory, the

same as everyone else's, furnished with a cot, a bedside table, a single lamp.

"Is that it?" she asked, as she dropped her purse to the floor, a look of blanched worry on her face. "Will someone else be coming up to show me around?"

"Later," Anders said. "Or, if not, just come to the kitchen at dinner time."

"But that's hours from now."

"Yes," he said and smiled. "Settle in." He could have stayed to reassure her, but he turned and took the stairway up to his own room.

Later, he saw her through the open bedroom window, a wide-brimmed straw hat on her head and a white sundress swimming at her ankles as she walked. He watched her open the garden gate. Watched her choose the exposed path of the wash rather than cutting through the shade beneath the stand of pines rimming the yard. The sun hit her square and she kept going, straight out across the desert, looking wholly out of place.

How he had ended up at a spiritual retreat center in Arizona was a story Anders didn't tell everyone. It was usual to be asked—a part of regular dinner conversation at the Center, where people took an almost lustful interest in others' tales of self-destruction and grief and failure. A truly good turning-point story bought its teller credibility here, the way an evangelical's fiery testimonial could grant him proof of God's favor, or an addict's most heinous confessions could earn him the respect of a room of NA members. Anders couldn't stomach it—the self-conscious construction of a history, the vanity. Wasn't the point of coming out here to escape all that? The stories struck him as a kind of pornography, and he'd learned to give just enough to satisfy without having to strip himself truly bare. "I lost my way," he'd say, his tone somber. "I could only hear the noise, you know?" The omissions created his own brand of bullshit, of course, but he didn't figure he owed anyone anything more.

Despite this, people read his silence as pain. They assumed drugs, death, mental illness. They assumed he was running from real demons and not just ordinary life. What he was leaving out was just that, though—the banality. His reasons for leaving home were the stuff of sitcoms, not salvations: a muddled love affair, a tedious job, the messy leftovers of an only typically dysfunctional childhood. That was the whole of it. Nothing truly traumatic. At least nothing that appeared traumatic from the outside.

He had a certain guilt about it all, and in low moments resolved to grow up. Get his shit together. Stop acting the part of the wounded kid and just get back to his adulthood. He'd taken unpaid leave from his tech job in Seattle. What expenses he still had he was paying with his savings, which would eventually run out. He was burning through it all—the money and the leave and everyone's patience with him—but still he had no answers. Most of the time he wasn't even sure he had the right questions yet.

And while he was looking, Jane had kept sending him letters. They were bundled and held by the Sierra Vista post office until whoever had kitchen duties could get into town to pick up the center's groceries and everybody's mail. It was worse to read them this way—a fistful all at once—a torrent of whatever emotion Jane was feeling that week, and then several days of nothing. Jane wrote them by hand in beautiful, lush cursive, which Anders knew was her way of proving she'd won the ridiculous argument they'd had for years about technology's degradation of human relationship. She was studying to be a historic preservationist and tended to extend her affection for crumbling Roman architecture to everything old and dying and irrelevant to real life. Still, even in her antiquated penmanship, the first letters were all fresh rage, her tone hard, and her accusations on the page more difficult to ignore than they had ever been in person. He was a child. A coward. Unfaithful and condescending. A man just like his father before him.

Lately, though, almost inexplicably, she'd softened. She'd begun asking how long he'd be gone. When was he coming home? She wrote about spring in Seattle. The crocuses were up. The cherry trees bordering the university's quad were thick in pink petals. He loved that—didn't he? And he was missing it. He was missing everything. Was he missing her? She was missing him.

He read the letters and folded them and tucked them into the suitcase he'd brought, beneath the clothes he'd been wearing the day he arrived at the Center—clothes that didn't fit anymore, not physically or otherwise.

The truth was that he did miss her, sometimes badly. Most nights he lay on his cot and could not stop himself from conjuring her face above him, the weight of her body on his. Here, the slope of her waist beneath his hand. Here, the hang of her full breasts with their pale pink areolae. Her shoulders with their freckles just a shade darker than her skin, like spots of rain on a page of ivory paper. He could not stop himself.

When he could think freely again, he reminded himself that this was not about her; this was about isolation. Loneliness was inevitable and not a reason for real guilt. Certainly not a reason to return home yet.

One afternoon, not long after coming to the Center, he had called his father and told him everything. He didn't think he could marry Jane. He didn't think he could go on as he had been—bored, unhappy. It was such a predictable crisis. It made him nauseous to hear himself talk.

His father listened, and when Anders finished, he said they'd been worried. Jane had told the family he was in rehab.

"Not rehab," Anders said, though he wasn't surprised by Jane's misinterpretation of the place. "A communal retreat center. And, yes, I know how that sounds."

"No, it's a relief. I'm jealous, actually. Maybe I should come down there after all, but not to bring you home, which is what Jane suggested."

"I'm honestly not sure what I'm doing here, though."

"Yes you are," his father said. His voice was steady, sure. "You're taking the time you need. Don't second-guess that."

"I'm trying to do the right thing."

"You are. You are doing the right thing. Jane is angry now. She won't always be. And you need to know what you want, so take the time. Loneliness is nothing compared to regret. Believe me."

For an instant, the familiar tension stretched tight between them again. Anders put his head against the wall where the phone was mounted. "You regret marrying Mom?" he asked. He heard his father's breath.

"I'm not saying that."

"Leaving her—us, then? You regret that?" Anders had wanted to ask it for more than a decade—ever since his parents had split up when he was a teenager—and here it was, a prickling in his throat, a thistle, a scab picked.

His father sighed again. "I think the body gets used to certain certainties. It's bound to crave company. You're bound to want what you know. That's what I think. Sometimes I still miss how it used to be."

"God, Dad."

"I'm just being frank with you. Desire doesn't disappear just because it's irrelevant."

They said goodbye. His father promised to let the family know Anders was fine, and Anders promised not to let Jane push him.

In the next bunch of mail, then, there were more letters from Jane, these heavy with blame, but also one from his father. "You'll come through this," his father wrote. "You will."

Anders had resolved to stay another week, and that had turned into two, and two more. Jane's letters had eased up. It had become a little easier for Anders to stay away without guilt, though more difficult to find a reason to return at all to his life at home—or to any life other than this one of stillness, isolation. He'd begun to think of the desert as an island floating free from the rest of the world, disconnected, and leaving it—crossing back over to the mainland of regular life—would require a kind of drowning.

This was when the woman arrived—in his eighth week, into the midst of his confusion.

Several days later, when Anders was out walking, he saw her again. It was midmorning, bright already. She had a blanket spread beneath a willow tree, a book in her hand. She looked up when he stopped, and he asked if she'd settled in well. She said she had. She offered him the edge of the blanket, and he sat, folding his legs under him, aware of the dirty undersides of his feet. She still looked like the outside world—her hair pulled back in a braid, her skin not yet as browned as his had become. She was wearing again the white dress, the hat. She had a canvas bag, and she pulled from it a tin of shortbread cookies.

"My contraband," she said.

"Nothing's really illegal here. You know that, right? No one cares what you do, so long as it doesn't disrupt the community." He said this as he took one of the cookies. It was buttery, sweet. He hadn't eaten anything packaged since arriving at the Center, and his tongue had forgotten sugar. His mouth watered as he chewed.

"Still," she said. "It would be frowned on, wouldn't it? Cookies? I'd be judged."

"How long will you stay?" he asked.

She smiled. "I'm supposed to say something like 'as long as feels right,' but the truth is that I have a month off work. I don't plan to quit my job."

She tucked the cookies away in the bag again, closed her book—a paperback copy of a novel, the title printed in the disorienting backward and upside down letters of the Russian alphabet. When she caught him looking at it, she slid the book into the bag, too. "My grandparents were from Saint Petersburg. This seemed like a good time to brush up on the language. I've forgotten more than I'd like."

Anders thought again about her little white car, his first impression of her as someone who had hoped for a weekend at the spa and had only mistakenly ended up here. "So coming to the Center, this is a study break?" he asked. "A time-out from real life."

Her expression hardened. "Everything about me seems to offend you."

"Not offense, just curiosity."

She looked away from him, shook her head. "This place is supposed to be open, but so far I've found it exactly as narrow as everywhere else in the world."

"I think you've misjudged me."

"It doesn't matter." She got to her knees and motioned for him to stand, then began gathering the blanket. Anders stood back while she shook it, a glitter of dust rising and sparkling against the bands of sunlight coming through the willow branches. He watched her fold the blanket into a perfect square and tuck it under her arm, slide the straps of her bag over her shoulder. She looked at him. "I'm going back. If you want to walk with me, you can, but I don't need a lecture."

He nodded. "I'll be polite," he said.

They walked the rut of the wash. Under the cottonwoods, like guard dogs, squat, blue-green agave plants grew in the shade, their spikes rigid and toothed.

"They look unforgiving," she said. "That's what I keep thinking about everything here. That word—*unforgiving*." She pointed across the stretch of dry grass to the distance, where a crowd of cholla cacti stood, all arms raised and bristled. "Like that," she said. "It makes me think of a book I read as a little girl about the settlers coming to the West. At one point in the book, they see a tribal gathering. The dancing and the songs sound threatening to them. Harsh." She turned her face to him, lifted a hand to her forehead to shade her eyes. "I don't mean that the native people of the West were harsh but that the settlers perceived them that way. You see what I mean? To me, this place looks unforgiving."

"Weren't you just reading about Russia though?" Anders smiled. "All snow and ice. That's an unforgiving landscape."

She shrugged. "It's not though. Not at all. But I learned Russia first through someone else's memories, so it's a fairy tale to me." Her voice had rounded, the edges of the earlier irritation gone. She walked close enough at his side that now and then her elbow brushed his.

"Those cacti," Anders pointed toward the cluster of cholla, "they have these beautiful skeletons. You'll find them sometimes if you keep walking here. The wood left when the spines and flesh rot away looks like lace. Full of tiny holes. It's intricate, but not actually fragile."

"I'm trying to see that, but I can't picture it."

They stopped at the garden gate, and Anders opened it, let her step ahead of him into the yard. "I didn't mean to be judgmental," he said. "I've been here too long. I'm losing my manners."

She paused and frowned. "That's not a good apology," she said. "That just means you'd be a better liar if you met me in the real world." She went ahead of him across the yard and into the house, and he watched her go without another word.

The next day, though, he met her again, this time reading on the porch. Again she put her book away when she saw him, invited him to sit and talk. Her name was Anna—Annie. She'd come to the Center from San Francisco. She didn't say why. When the lunch bell sounded, they arranged to meet the following morning to walk. Anders would show her a cave he had found in a rock formation not too far away.

This was how it began, their unlikely alliance. That's how Anders came to think of it—she was a companion here where so much of the day was spent in actual isolation or in silent side-by-side work. Of course he knew some of the other residents—the woman from Texas who had just sent her youngest child to college and was searching for something of her own now; the retired Episcopalian priest; the ex-junkie whose parents had detoxed him when he flunked out of UCLA and then sent him out here; Mick, the guy who ran the place. Anders had met these people, but he didn't know them. Annie was something else.

One afternoon he took her farther out than they had walked before. A stand of willows fenced the length of a narrow creek bed. The creek was nothing but a dry gulch now; only in the summer, when the monsoons came, would it fill. Overhead, however, the willows were full and trembling with a movement like wind, though the air was still.

"What is it?" Annie asked.

"Hummingbirds," Anders said. "They're called Anna's hummingbirds. Watch, and you'll see their pink throats."

They stood still. He found himself holding his breath. Above them, flashes of green movement dipped between the trees. The birds nested here, he told her. He'd stumbled on the little grove one day not long after he'd come to the Center. Sometimes there were hundreds of hummingbirds in the trees, whole branches alive with the motion of their bodies. Before coming here, he had never seen a hummingbird in rest. It was startling.

"Why Anna's?" she asked.

"I don't know. I thought you'd appreciate it, though."

"I do. Thank you." She took his hand and held it.

"We're violating the rules, you know, touching."

"I thought you said there were no rules here."

"There is that one. Romantic entanglements cloud things. We're all here to get clearer."

"You want me to let go?" She tipped her head up to watch the movement in the branches, and he took her in. Something had shifted in her. She looked relaxed, comfortable. Flecks of light filtered through the willow branches and freckled her face and shoulders.

They walked back without speaking, hands still clasped until they neared the yard. At the gate, she dropped his hand and turned to him. "I want to ask you to come to my room." Her face had drained of its little color with the question.

This startled him. "We'd both have to leave if someone discovered us."

She looked away. "You don't want me."

"I do. I do want you," he said. There was an unexpected charge in saying the words aloud, and he stepped ahead of her through the garden and led her into the house.

In the kitchen they stopped for food, found two plates and a bowl of grapes, a quarter section of a watermelon that they carried down the hallway to her room. The space was small and close once Annie shut the door, and the air inside smelled floral and feminine. On the bedside table there were several bottles of lotions and sunscreens, and he imagined these as the source of the smell, but once they were both undressed, he understood that it was also on her skin and the sheets, the taste of her on his tongue bitter with perfume. Wearing fragrance here was a vanity, or maybe a luxury, and he wondered again at who she was and why she'd left her life for this place.

As he touched her, he thought of how cloying and artificially intense Jane could be—how different this was. Jane had not been wrong when she'd called him unfaithful. Many times he had come close to going home with women he knew from work; and once, not long before coming to the Center, he had gone home with a woman he'd met at a bar. She'd worn a green negligee, slick as a snake's skin, beneath her dress, but she'd been a cheerful and good-natured lover, easy to leave when it was over. He thought later that he ought to have been guilty. He ought to have been ashamed. It was surely a defect in him, an inherited flaw, that then—just as now—he felt only relief.

What Annie felt was unreadable to him, her face guarded. She did not speak at all while they made love, but gripped him. He came away from her hold with the red marks of her fingers on his arms, his chest—the heat of her breath humid in his ear.

Afterward, she got up and pulled on a thin robe, and they sat on the floor, their legs out in front of them and their backs against the frame of the cot. It was late afternoon. The light coming through her small window was already heavy with evening.

She settled the two plates they'd brought from the kitchen in front of them, dished from the bowl of fruit. As she did, he leaned forward to kiss her again, and she pulled away. When he touched his fingertips to the flat of her chest, she closed the collar of her robe.

"What is it?" he asked.

She sat up. She looked suddenly anguished, frill of remorse. "I should have given you the truth: I'm married. My husband is in San Francisco, working, living in our apartment."

"Why didn't you tell me?"

"Would it have changed your mind, knowing this?" Again her direct stare, her way of cutting quickly to the heart of things.

Anders stood and began to pull on his pants. "I'll leave," he said.

"Please don't leave."

"What do you want, then? Why tell me at all?"

She sighed, touched the spot on the floor at her side, and he sat again. "I don't know what I'm doing. You must think I'm terrible." Her face had gone sallow, her expression stiff. The robe had fallen open to the tie at her waist once more, and there was an intimacy that hadn't been there before in seeing her naked chest.

He shook his head. "You should have told me when we met."

She looked away. "You're disappointed."

"I'm the last person you want to be your conscience." He bit into the watermelon, wiped the juice away from his mouth with the back of his hand.

"We're having problems," she said. "My husband and I, we're struggling. It's part of why I'm here. I needed to get away. To figure it out."

Anders dropped the rind onto the plate. "I don't need to know. I told you—I shouldn't be anybody's confessor."

"You think I'm confessing?" She looked at him.

"It's useless, that's what I'm saying. Remorse, regret—whatever it is you're trying to get off your chest. It doesn't matter. It doesn't change anything now, does it?" He was disgusted suddenly—with himself and with her. He wanted to tell her to close her robe.

"You're angry. I knew you would be."

"Not angry. Just honest. You said you didn't like a liar."

"You should go."

"Yes," he said.

Outside her door, he moved along the hallway in a hurry, took the stairs to his room two at a time, anxious now to get away from the narrow room and from her—anxious to be alone again.

Several days passed. At night, unable to sleep, he took out Jane's letters and reread them. What was his obligation to her? Was he less guilty than Annie because he wasn't married? That's what he'd always told himself—they were not married, and so he was not betraying her. This was an easy lie, though, and he needed to be honest now. He needed to commit himself to honesty, at least, if he could commit to nothing else.

He began writing a handful of apologies, each one wrong, the same excuses reclothed in different words. He threw them all out. Finally, a week after his afternoon with Annie, it came to him clearly: He did not love Jane. He wrote to her with harsh focus: He was not going to come home. He could not be what she needed. He had realized at the Center that there were certain traits he could not change in himself, certain lives he could not live without hurting others. Perhaps this was a weakness in him, a pattern he could not unlearn. Maybe it was beyond that—an in-born inability. It didn't matter, really. The point was that it would be better for them both if he did not come home.

He sealed the letter and left the house. Outside, the air was cool. It was not quite dawn, and the sky was still dark blue, starred, far away, the mountains furred in purple shadow. The desert was nearly silent. It was just under ten miles to town, and he figured he could be there in a couple of hours if he ran, if he didn't stop. He'd get breakfast—a real breakfast—at the diner, and then find the post office, mail his letter before starting back. After that, he wasn't sure.

All the way there, he tried to empty his mind as he had been encouraged to do since coming to the Center. It was another of his deficiencies that he was unable to do this. His head buzzed more loudly when he tried to quiet it, his attention to every detail only sharpened when he tried to see nothing.

As a kid, he'd seen a school counselor for a few months during his third-grade year, and she, too, had tried to coach him through meditation. "Close your eyes," she'd hush. "Count your breaths. Let every thought that comes into your mind just float away." But he heard the heater in the wall click on and whir, the even thunking of the copy machine in the office next door, spitting out copies. He thought: *I am warm in my clothes. I have spit in my mouth. I have heavy feet.* In his mind, he saw his friends back in the classroom, working at their math problems while the teacher slid a new transparent film sheet onto the overhead projector. It was a racket, all this. He could not slow his thoughts—could not sit still—which was why he had been assigned meetings with the counselor in the first place. He was a failed case from the start, and eventually even the counselor recognized this, and Anders was permitted to stop seeing her.

Maybe, he thought as he walked now, some people are just restless. Maybe some people are truly unable to sit still—no matter what form that stillness takes.

He recalled the last meal he'd eaten with his parents before their divorce. It was June. A late supper. His mother had fixed salmon and had pulled and cleaned green beans from their own garden for a salad. The thick-gold light of such summer evenings was pouring into the house through the wide front windows, and when Anders sat down at the table between his parents, he'd felt an overwhelming spill of comfort, contentment. Only looking back now did he recognize his father's restlessness during that meal. The way he'd fidgeted with his napkin while the rest of them talked. The way he'd risen for more of the beans, a new fork, a second glass of wine. His mind was elsewhere already, though he would not actually leave the house for another month.

Anders wondered now how much of his father's life with their family had been a sacrifice of the self, a loss. And could Anders be angry with his father for leaving the family when he so closely understood that leaving was a method of survival? Could he hold it against Annie if she now wanted a respite from her own unhappy marriage?

It was not yet nine when he arrived in town. He found the diner, sat by the window, and watched the first of the morning's traffic passing in the yellow street while he ate his platter of peppered eggs and sausages and fried corn cakes shining with grease. He took out the letter and looked at it while he drank his coffee, then put it back when he got up to pay the check.

All the way through town, he kept his hand on the envelope in his pocket. It gathered weight while he walked, and when he finally dropped it into the mailbox at the post office, it felt like he was dropping an enormous load—a rock he'd been carrying too long, a planet on his back. As soon as he reached the Center again he went to Annie's door.

They spent the rest of her time at the Center together, meeting quietly, always in secret. His need to be near her surprised him. When she went out on errands alone, as she now and then did, her little white car pulling away from the Center's parking lot with a ruff of desert dust, he missed her. When after sex she became pensive and lay on the cot with the sheet pulled to her shoulders and her back turned to him, he grew anxious, his heart racing with the thought that she was considering breaking things off, choosing her husband. He didn't even know this man—Dmitri—but he hated him, and hated himself for the hating. Annie had told him that she'd married too young, but that she'd known her husband since childhood. Their families were close, both active in the same Russian Orthodox church; and Dmitri's father had long been like a brother to her own. She had loved Dmitri genuinely at one point—and she loved him now, in some sense, though she was no longer sure they should have married. That's all she would say. She wouldn't speak badly of Dmitri, and she never shared anything from his letters to her, though Anders saw that she was reading them. They arrived every few days in rubber-banded bundles, bricks of paper that she held against her chest as she carried them from the mail bin up to her room. Anders wondered what they contained—what professions of love or longing or obligation. He wondered how Annie felt when she read them. Guilty, maybe. Trapped. Or, worse: beloved and needed.

As Anders saw it, though, neither Dmitri nor Jane had any idea about the people they'd rooted themselves to, and there was something unforgiveable in that innocence, wasn't there? There was something blameworthy in being so blind.

"Leave him," Anders said one night. He would quit his job and move to California to be nearer to her. He could go back to school maybe, or just do something to pay the rent on a cheap apartment—clerk at a grocery store or drive a cab. "Or don't leave him, but don't stop seeing me." She could get away on weekends, he proposed. She could make up excuses about where she was going.

Annie touched his cheek. "I do have a friend with a vacation cottage in Santa Cruz. She's always looking for a tenant." It was an abstract statement, the house appearing briefly before them both, a bit of ephemera. Nothing would come of it, Anders understood.

Then, at the start of her last week, a call came for her: Dmitri was in the hospital. He'd had a migraine, which had happened before, but this time his vision had gone black and hadn't returned when the headache waned. They were running tests. It could be nothing—temporary; or it could be something serious. He was asking for her.

She explained this while she packed her bag. Anders sat on the cot and watched her clear the room of her things. The jars of lotions, the books, the white dress—she swept them all into her bag with a reckless indifference. Her face was tight again, as it had been when she'd first arrived at the Center, her expression piqued. But why? He wasn't sure. Anger at Dmitri for forcing her home early, or at herself for making it so difficult to leave? When she finished, he followed her out to her car, stood with his hands in his pockets while she loaded everything.

"I don't have your address," he said.

"I think that's best." She turned to him and frowned against the sunlight. "I feel like we did this to him. I did this to him. It's my punishment."

"You don't believe that really, do you? Life doesn't work that way." He bent forward to kiss her, not caring now if anyone inside the house saw them, but she turned her face from him.

"I don't know what I believe," she said.

He didn't wait to see her pull away but went inside, climbed the stairs to his room, and shut the door.

That evening he began packing his own things to leave.

It occurred to Anders only once he was on the road that the home he'd left was no longer his—he'd cut his ties there. He'd sent the letter to Jane.

He drove north with the aimlessness of a traveler, not a resident, unsure where or when to stop. He didn't want to return to the job he hated, but without it, he had nothing. He didn't want to beg forgiveness from Jane, but where else would he live?

Anders thought of his father and the little island house he lived in alone, and for the first time he considered retreating there. His father would take him in. There'd be long days on the beach, nights up late poking the campfire in the yard and looking for stars between the deep banks of blue cloud that always rolled in from the Pacific after sunset. It would be the safety for him now that it had been for his father just after the divorce.

But no—he couldn't go there. The house had become a symbol of his family's unraveling, and going there would be an admission of empathy for his father. He'd made a fragile peace with the past, but he was not ready to just accept the symmetry between himself and his father, or to forgive it in himself.

In the end, he drove to the house he'd shared with Jane and knocked on the door. As he expected, she took him in without any resistance. He'd just been lost, she told him. She would help him find his way again, and everything would be fine.

He fell back into the old routine: work, short evenings of numbing distractions, sleep, work again. Summer came and went, and then fall, and soon Seattle was steely with winter, the sky as thick as the gray, gray Sound, the city draped behind layers of gauzy fog that drifted inland smelling of fish and cold water. Anders didn't mind winter, actually. It was sleepy and permitted isolation without questioning. You could walk from office door to bus stop briskly, hands sunk into your pockets, eyes down, and everyone would presume you were avoiding the drizzle, not company. You could decline invitations to go out by claiming a head cold, or by simply saying, "the rain." You could convince yourself to a certain degree that your own malaise was due only to the season, the lack of sunshine—that it was the psychic equivalent of the constant damp drip of the sky and muddy choke of the landscape.

All this time, Anders couldn't stop thinking of Annie. He wanted to forget her, to put her out of his head, but she was always with him, just there behind his thoughts, the ghost of every moment. Out with friends for drinks one night, he started to mention her: "There was this woman I met when I was in Arizona—"

His friend clapped him on the back and laughed. "There's always a woman, isn't there?" he said, and Anders felt himself retreat, the impulse toward honesty slithering inward again like a snake back into its hole.

At night, after Jane had gone to bed, he often looked Annie up online, searching for evidence of what exactly, he didn't quite know.

He didn't want to wish another man dead, but what if it had turned out that Dmitri was seriously ill? Or what if Annie's unhappiness had got the best of her and she'd left him? What if she was alone now, one way or the other? What would Anders do then?

He found proof of nothing, though, just old images of her, and not even her own—photographs culled from someone's Twitter account and another person's Facebook page: Annie as a younger woman, sitting on a dorm room bed beside two other grinning coeds; a teenage Annie standing before Saint Petersburg's Winter Palace at night, her bright red scarf flying loose in a breeze, and the whole, massive palace lit a swollen gold at her back against the darkness. Anders saved this last one to a file on his computer, hid the file on his hard drive.

Each time he spoke to his father, he nearly confessed everything, but what good could come of that? What advice could his father offer that he could take? *Stay*—but his father had not stayed; he had chosen his own happiness over everyone else's.

Leave—but Anders knew what loneliness leaving brought. As it was, he decided his father would be of no help, and so he said nothing.

Only Jane was suspicious. Once he caught her scrolling through his phone messages. Another time he was certain she'd gone through the drawers of his dresser while he was at work, the clothes inside disordered somehow, though he couldn't be sure. Many times, in the dark of their bedroom when they could not see each other's faces, she asked him what had happened during those weeks he was gone. Why had he sent the letter? What had brought him back to her?

"Nothing," he said. "I don't know."

"If there was someone else, you should tell me," she said. "You have to tell me." Always the same plea, and always he responded with silence, rolling toward her, laying his palm on her back, physical reassurance taking the place of the answers he could not give.

Still, despite Jane's anxiety and against his own better judgment, he went on looking for Annie. It was just after the turn of the new year when he finally thought to search her husband's name, and once he did, he quickly found their address. He booked a flight, told Jane he had an out of town business meeting, and packed a bag. SEA to SFO. In three hours, he was stepping into a clear, bright California morning.

He got a hotel and spent the day walking. He'd been to San Francisco as a little boy, but not since then, and he took in the city with a strange sense of déjà vu, the place a foreign familiar. Certain sights—the red-roofed military buildings of the old Presidio, the pink-pillow dome of the Palace of Fine Arts—sparked in his memory like little firecrackers as soon as he saw them.

By midafternoon he could take his own restlessness no more. He gave a cab driver the address he had noted in his phone, just a few blocks from his hotel. He paid the driver, got out, and stood before the house. It reminded him of her—neat, angular, charming. A four-story wooden Victorian that sat shouldering its neighbors. From the row of mailboxes beside the front door, he gathered that hers was the third-floor apartment, and he looked up, tried to make out any distinguishing features through the windows, but they were opaque with gauzy white drapes, nothing but reflective shadows on the glass.

For a long time he stood in front of the house before walking once around the block. His body was all adrenaline. *I could just leave*, he told himself. *I could go back to the hotel right now.* But he circled the block once more, and then again. It was getting late, and the light was fading. Overhead, the streetlamps came on. Just then, though, her little white car appeared at the end of the block opposite him, the dark shape of her behind the wheel. His stomach seized, and he raised his arm in a wave.

She told him her husband was not home, wouldn't be home until late, but she felt uncomfortable inviting Anders into the house, and so they drove to another neighborhood where she wouldn't bump into anyone she knew. They found an Indian restaurant for dinner. The place was small and overwarm, the walls and ceiling hung in tapestries, the smell of curry thick.

"Why did you find me?" she asked once they were seated.

"I need you to understand something," he began, but she cut him off.

"I'm unhappy here." Her hand was cold when she reached across the table and took his wrist. "I'm so unhappy, and now you've come down here and made it worse." She looked as if she might be sick, her face gray-white and all of the color gone out of her lips. "You should never have come."

They ate without speaking. All around them, Anders heard the sounds of the restaurant as if from inside a tunnel.

"What will we do?" she asked at one point. "What are we going to do?"

At the end of the meal he called a cab to carry him back to the hotel. On the sidewalk, before the cab arrived, she stepped close to him, and he pulled her into a long kiss. When she turned away, Anders watched her walk down the street and get into her car. She would drive home and park in her garage, climb the stairs to her apartment, change her clothes, and get into bed, just like any other night. When her husband came home, he would find her there waiting as always. And he—Anders—would go back to his hotel and call Jane, as he had promised to do, and she would tell him about her day on campus, about her progress with the dissertation chapter she was writing, their conversation no different from those they had most nights. He and Annie were both, he saw, living two lives—one thin and transparent, open for everyone to see, and one shrouded. Here again, he thought, was his father's life tucked inside his own. All those years, when he believed he knew his father's happiness, his worries, he'd been only half right. He'd known half of the man, half of the life his father was living—the half his father wished to have known. Whatever else there was—the truly personal—was unseen, a fragile skeleton just beneath the skin. This is how everyone must live, Anders saw. The inner workings that make a man most human are sewn below the surface, secret, where they can remain safe and unscarred. This is why his father had left and why Annie had made herself invisible online—to preserve the personal. This is why he himself had so long resisted writing to Jane: everything intimate was more easily exposed in writing, the private ghost of every word excruciatingly plain there between the lines.

The next morning, Annie called him from the hotel lobby. She had taken a personal day at work, could she come up to his room? When he opened the door she was there, wearing the red scarf he remembered from the picture of her as a young woman in front of the Winter Palace.

"It's cold out," she said as she unwrapped herself from the layers of scarf and coat and sweater. "The fog is full of ice crystals." She reached for him, and her face against his—her mouth against his mouth—was cold, too, though her skin quickly pinked with the warmth of the room.

"What are we doing?" he asked.

She moved to sit on the edge of the bed. "I've thought of every reason not to do this, but I love you." Her tone was hard, almost defiant. "I don't want to feel like a criminal anymore."

Anders put his face in his hands. He could not stop himself: he began to cry. He thought she might get up and leave right then, disgusted with him and this naked show of need, but she hushed him.

"You're fine," she said. "Go on. We'll be fine."

When he had control of himself again, they sat talking and making plans. For the first time in months, Anders felt free and happy and certain. They would leave their lives for a new one together. They would start over. The worst was behind them, and they would live a long time together, in love. It suddenly seemed wonderfully impossible to either of them that anything but this could be true.

Paris, the Easy Way

T. M. MCNALLY

From *Low Flying Aircraft* (1991)

Sam, 1988

I first learned the importance of air at the Casper Community Pool during my brother's thirteenth birthday party—a big one because now he had finished the eighth grade and was learning to kiss his girlfriend, also our neighbor, Sally Sconzalla. Like my brother, I had a crush on Sally, but what she could do for my brother I was still too underdeveloped to appreciate. I merely liked the way she combed her hair, which was yellow and loose, and I liked the sound of her voice.

At the Casper Community Pool she and my brother were diving from the springboard when I decided to join them. Never before had I been in water so deep. I swam my short, choppy strokes, stopping every five feet to hang onto the wall. I must have been thinking about something. Maybe I thought I was near the wall, maybe I thought the water was shallow. Either way, I took in half the pool, the air washed out of my lungs, and my body caught on—this was not the proper way to float. I couldn't hear anything but the water, and my voice in the water, but I'm sure it was Sally who saw me. I was lifted out of the pool with one arm by a big, tan lifeguard. Later, when Sally wrapped me in her towel and told me I would be all right, this is what I learned. I learned that when our lungs are filled with something they shouldn't be, no one, not even the person we decide to love most in the world, will ever hear us. This was back in Wyoming, during the summer of 1965, where we were all still growing up under a sky the size of history and equally dull.

As a kid watching *Star Trek*, I used to wait for something new to happen: an unfamiliar spaceship, a forceful encounter, things suddenly appearing as soon as the ship's viewscreen was turned on. Now I'm wondering who cleaned the viewscreen, the big windshield they drove behind. I think even space must have debris the way the West has dust.

The windshield wipers on my truck have smeared the dust into mud, and thirty, maybe forty miles ahead, somewhere beyond Trinidad, lightning rips open the sky—long brilliant seams opening for just a moment the possibilities beyond our own atmosphere.

Lightning, gravity, love—I've never properly understood any of it.

I went to college. During the '81 recession, when I couldn't get a job, I did the circuit well enough to break even. For two years I was an overpaid stable manager in Sedona. In my old office, which was really a tack room full of broken-down saddles and loose stirrups, hangs a recent photograph of Sally. She is sitting on a beach in Monaco, her top off, her face angled towards the sea, and on the back she has written "You'd really love it here."

I decided to leave the Boynton Canyon Resort the day after I received Sally's picture, the day old man McClenahan showed up early for his ride. His face had been detailed by the sun, by age and the weather, and I watched the lines shift in his face while he grew angry with me because I hadn't yet grained his mare, Cleo.

"It's climbing," he said, pointing at the sun. "It's climbing. Where's my Cleo!"

I fed his horse, offered him coffee while we waited. Mrs. Mc-Clenahan wouldn't be by to pick him up until noon for lunch and his nap. After his ride, after he'd finished brushing Cleo down, he would ask me to inspect a hoof, trim a frog. Later he'd wander around behind me and talk with the guests or help Gomez with his English. And it was hard to dislike either, the old horse or the old man.

But that morning as we sat in the tack room, drinking coffee and enjoying the morning, the lingering smells of hay and shit and grain dust, the old man grew serious.

"Hey, good buddy," he said.

"Hey," I said.

"When you gonna leave?"

"Leave where, Mac?"

"Leave," he said, nodding toward the door. "When you gonna leave? You know."

"No," I said. "I don't know."

"Cleo, her lungs are about to bust."

"They're fine," I said. "Just a little used up."

"Used up? They're all used up with the heaves. No. Maybe," he said, shaking his head. He began to laugh and looked at the picture of Sally over my desk. "Not like her," he said, laughing. "Not like her, good buddy."

The old man left for his ride, Gomez showed up hungover and late, and I took out a pair of tourists: a husband and wife team from Phoenix, newly married by the looks. They made jokes and giggled while I told them about all the cowboys Rooster had crippled back in his prime. The man kept a sharp lookout for rattlesnakes and occasional mountain lions, and I thought about the old man and his mare, Cleo, combing the countryside next to Highway 89A looking for something vaguely familiar and safe. The old man had kids, he said, only he didn't know where they were, which is why I suppose he told me.

After the incident at the Casper Community Pool, it was decided I would learn to swim as well as I did my chores or homework. My father would drive me into Casper to an indoor pool for weekly lessons, where I would wear black nylon suits and take instruction from people not much older than my brother or Sally. Once, after a lesson, while waiting in a public hallway for my dad, I watched him pull up to the curb. I had been waiting with the others and I left them to meet my dad halfway across the snow and ice. The cold made my hair freeze. My dad waved, slipped and fell. He fell about as gracefully as a horse—scrambling, all legs and panic, trying to pretend that either this hadn't happened or that he did this all the time. I could hear the kids laughing through the still open door. He waved again, this time to the kids behind me, patting at his hip as if feeling for injury.

In the truck he breathed heavily and gripped the steering wheel. "Whew," he said, trying to laugh. "Your old man's not as limber as he used to be."

And I think what I felt then was my embarrassment shift to worry, to a slight tremor of mortality. Hearing my dad call himself old meant he would only get older and, eventually, leave me to myself. In the water, after nearly drowning, I had been frightened, but I was not frightened by death. The fear was too inarticulate to be specific.

"Dad," I said, "you're not an old man!"

And really he wasn't. He was the same age I am now, but when we feel as if we're getting old, there's not much that's going to change that feeling. My father is now fifty-two. He raises some of the finest Morgans in Wyoming and he raises his grandson, Robert, much in the same way he raised me. Only now he really isn't as limber as he used to be. I suppose in truth no one really is.

Why didn't I marry Sally Sconzalla? I guess because my brother already had. My brother was like one of those ensigns or corpsmen who open up every episode of *Star Trek*. The nameless one we've never seen before. The one who beams down with the landing party and gets lost or vaporized by misunderstanding aliens. My brother enlisted in 1970, was beamed down into Cambodia, and disappeared without a trace.

As for the old man, he combed the hillside with his mare while I told the tourists stories. When I returned the tourists to the barn, Gomez took their money and told them to have a nice day. I stood at the corral and watched them leave, walking nervously between the loose horses while I stood behind and admired the man's wife. I watched one horse prepare to kick another. I watched the old man rub down Cleo and lead her into a paddock. Later that afternoon, a large group of realtors from Tucson was scheduled for a ride and cookout: Gomez would meet us at the site with hamburgers and beer, and later he'd take out his guitar to sing love songs from Ethiopia. In the office he sat in my chair, his feet propped on my desk, leafing through a book entitled *Paris, the Easy Way*.

"*Bonjour*," he said. "*Comment ça va?*"

"Fine," I said. I poured coffee and asked about the status of a horse with fistulous withers, so bad the pus still ran after six weeks—a lingering, festering sore caused by an ill-fitting saddle.

"She sure is pretty," Gomez said, rising from the chair and pointing at the picture of Sally. "Pretty like my sister, you know. *Bonita. Tres belle.* Ohh la la."

I drank my coffee, brown and badly burnt, and studied the picture while Gomez loaded up an injection of Combiotic. He pulled down from a shelf the hydrogen peroxide.

"I gonna play darts now," he said, referring to the syringe. "And you gonna feel sad for a while. But you get over it. *Ciao.*"

A month before, Gomez had been Italian; he'd take a green card anywhere. He left while I sat and considered the photograph of Sally. I considered the slow curve of her flank. In the photograph she has a neck like an antelope, and I thought about my father's hayloft where she told me what to do without ever telling me, as if between us someone had strung a fine wire, a telegraph of instruction, of unexpected urgency and regret. Later she left Wyoming to teach at a Catholic school in Dallas, and my brother never came home, which is something I think we each always knew even when we didn't know it. Maybe he was gone too long for any of us to remember clearly. Who knows what we really used to know?

One thing I know is this: if confined, a horse under a sky with lightning is a dangerous thing. It wants only to run because the lightning is too inexplicable, too close to the bone to be considered safe from even a distance. A horse reacts to lightning the way a stud will a mare, and the coupling of horses is not a simple enterprise.

Right now the weather grows temporarily safe. The sky blisters with ions, waiting for rain, and the air is so clear it looks like glass—it's that transparent. The Colorado border smells like rain, like creosote and dust, and I know Sebastian, my own horse in the trailer behind me, is no longer frightened because I, too, am no longer frightened.

We can only know what we once didn't know. At my brother's wedding, I was the best man because his best friend had already been shipped to Asia, and our father thought it would be nice this way. Sally was dressed like an angel, I stood behind my brother, and at the proper time I held out the ring he'd spent six months saving for. It was a pretty gold ring. A wedding ring, he'd explained, and chock-full of meaning.

We stood up against a fence and watched my father work a yearling; my brother, just in from town, took the ring out of the box to show me. The dust from the corral floated all around us, but it never touched the ring. The ring was still too new for dust. "Do you see how it's round?" he said. "That's the meaningful part. The finger is the man and the ring is the woman, and once you're married the two go at it forever, and as long as you wear your ring you can never go at it with anyone else or the whole deal gets all shot to hell."

I found the old man face down in the paddock with a fly on his neck. The horses had circled away from him and he lay in the orange dirt alone. I rolled him over and searched for a pulse. I beat on his chest. I cleared his airway and removed a loose denture. I began to breathe. I beat again on his chest, losing count, searching for his heart because I wasn't sure where it was. I felt his ribs crack beneath my hands and knew I was going to have to breathe into him again—my mouth on his, his lips rough and smelling of garlic and decay and later the whiff of his gut rising up through the throat while I kept breathing into his lungs. I felt them rise while mine collapsed. After a while, I realized he was supposed to be dead, and so I left him in the paddock under the sun with the horses still frightened by the suddenness and smell of death.

By nature, a horse has only three gaits; the others are learned. After work each day Gomez and I would go to the Oak Creek Tavern, order a pitcher and shoot pool. Last summer, though, the local network in Chicago began showing reruns of *Star Trek*—the same reruns I had watched in college, the same episodes I had watched as a kid in Wyoming. So instead of playing 8-ball, I began to reacquaint myself with plots and character traits: who was logical, who was emotional, who was both, which was really all of us. The tavern had a satellite hookup, and watching all these episodes reminded me of the '60s and how hopeful and naive we were all becoming while I was still completely unaware of the world which had created it—Ford Mustang, Simon and Garfunkel, the race for the moon.

I once lived with a woman in Santa Fe. I ran a barn for Lazarus Arabians, where I was instructed by the part-time owners of syndicated studs on the proper music for mares about to foal (Mozart, piped through the stalls with air-conditioning), where I learned to keep my mouth shut and watch people make wise investments. At home it was worse. The woman would paint bad imitations of Georgia O'Keeffe and read D. H. Lawrence, nonstop, reading aloud always the passages which had to do with men and horses and lust until, finally, she asked me to marry her. It was the first time I'd ever been asked, and the next day I gave my notice.

I gave Gomez the blender, my contribution to the barn since I was going to argue with the owner of the Boynton Canyon Resort that, illegal or not, Gomez most deserved the blender. Make him the boss, I would say; the tourists will like the color. They would like the color the way they liked the rocks of Sedona—the red, angry cliffs shaped by the wind into the names of things like Coffee Pot, like Cathedral and Bell.

We sat in the tack room and drank margaritas. Paul Harvey was over, and I advised Gomez to get rid of the horse with bad withers, and to get rid of Cleo, too; sell her quick and send the money to Mrs. McClenahan. "Do it right," I said, "and she'll send you a bottle."

"*Oui*," said Gomez, looking almost lost. "But what about her?" He pointed at the picture of Sally on the wall. Right up there by Will Rogers and a bilingual notice to employees, she really was a fine addition to the wall. It seemed to me she'd do more good on the wall in Boynton Canyon than she would anywhere else.

"I had to kill a horse once," I said. "It ran through a fence and nearly cut off its leg. It wasn't worth the vet bills. The leg would never heal, so I shot it in the head just like the movies. I shot it in the head with a Remington I had to borrow, but the bad part wasn't killing it. The bad part was figuring out what to do next. How do you move a dead horse?"

"Slowly," said Gomez, nodding.

"I put a chain around its neck and drug it out of the corral with a Jeep. I called the foundry, the guy couldn't pick it up for two days. I covered the horse with a ground cloth and put wagon wheels against it—decorations, you know, to please the guests. Four days later it was still there, rising like a balloon—this dead horse covered with wagon wheels and plastic and flies. But what I remember most was wrapping the chain around its neck and pulling it out of the mud with the Jeep. The chain left marks in the neck. When the guy finally showed up he had to pull her on a flatbed with a winch."

After my brother finished basic training, he came home on leave. His hair was short, he wore green clothes, and he spent most of his time with Sally in the big room our father had fixed up just for them. A week later we drove him to the airport where he would catch a plane to Alaska and then pick up a transport going somewhere else. We stood at the gate, my father and Sally and me, and said good-bye. My brother had something special to say to everyone, and he told me to take care of the family, to watch over Dad and the ranch. "We got problems U.T.A.," he said. "But we got you. Take care of Sally," he said. And then he whispered something into Sally's ear, kissed her on the mouth, and walked away up the runway. On the way home, my father pulled over the truck to let me drive, and Sally turned on the radio.

I attended McClenahan's funeral, of course. It was Catholic, long and overcrowded. I saw lawyers and doctors and people who had flown to Sedona from New York and Boston and Chicago in private airplanes. A memorial service was held outdoors beneath the shadow of Bell Rock, a large and brightly colored geological oddity—a source of crystals, of immeasurable energy, swollen with meaning and mystery for the new age.

Mrs. McClenahan was a handsome woman. She stood among these people I would never know and listened to them say nice things about her husband.

"Mac was very fond of you," she said to me.

"I'm sorry," I said.

"He said you always took good care of Cleo. You reminded him of our boys."

But the boys were not present. I had learned one of them was dead, the other in a foreign country. I told Mrs. McClenahan not to worry about Cleo, and she looked at me sadly, as if there were no reason why she ever should. Later that afternoon the body was shipped on a private plane to a cemetery in Illinois.

I think being in space must be like being in water: there is no air. The rain is hard now. It washes over the shell of the truck like a river; it films the windows and the wipers beat at the rain like oars. Denver is still a long way north. I feel the tires skim over flat spots on the road where water stands, and I adjust my speed accordingly.

After I found the old man, after I'd cracked his ribs and breathed into his lungs, I went to the barn and had a drink. I called the ambulance, said they didn't need to rush. I called Mrs. McClenahan.

She arrived before the paramedics. She drove her big car straight past the barn and up to the paddock. Her hair, streaked with gray, glimmered in the light; her face was pale as a woman's breast.

And I watched her go to her husband. She knelt on her heels, cocked in the dirt, and reached for his hand, which must have felt unexpectedly cool. The sun was hot, the hand cool, and by the time the paramedics had arrived, she knew where she wanted him sent. I brought her into the barn, the tack room, where she sat very still in my chair while I poured her a shot of whiskey. She held the cup in her hands and stared at the coffee stains on the cheap porcelain as if trying to identify the shapes.

"Once," she said. "Once before, I thought he was dead. I had to make sure."

"He had a nice ride," I said.

"Yes," she said, nodding, "I'm sure he did."

I watched her watch her drink. The rings on her hands pinched her fingers, grown swollen with age, and I watched the rings pinch her fingers, thinking someday the rings are going to slip loose because that's what life does. It eats away at us until we're empty.

Space may very well be the final frontier, but in what direction should we travel? Right now I'm going home, traveling north, which on a map is not as far away as it seems—a few days' drive up I-25. It's as easy as sending a half-naked picture of yourself through the mail. And while I think about everyone I've ever known and probably damaged, one way or another, this is what I think about most: I think about the old man I couldn't save, the old man lying quietly inside his sealed box, unable to go anywhere but in, inside himself to the core of what he once was. He lies in a grave somewhere in Illinois and he keeps going inside himself, because now when it matters most he can't get out. He can't get out, so he goes in. He goes in, deep inside himself, so deep until he finally discovers that maybe the space around the living is more important than any of us ever thought. Because maybe after a while there really is no place left for us to go.

CONTRIBUTORS

CATHERINE BRADY is the author of *Curled in the Bed of Love*, which won the 2002 Flannery O'Connor Award for Short Fiction. Her story collection *The End of the Class War* was a Book Sense 76 selection, and *The Mechanics of Falling* received the Northern California Book Award for Fiction. Her nonfiction works include *Story Logic and the Craft of Fiction* and *Elizabeth Blackburn and the Story of Telomeres*. She has taught in the MFA in Writing program at the University of San Francisco. Her stories have appeared in such publications as the *Cimarron Review*, *Other Voices*, the *Missouri Review*, the *Kenyon Review*, and *Best American Short Stories 2004*.

PHILIP F. DEAVER (1946–2018) was the author of *Silent Retreats*, which won the 1987 Flannery O'Connor Award, as well as the poetry collection *How Men Pray* and the novel *Forty Martyrs*. His short fiction was published in such literary journals as the *Florida Review*, the *Kenyon Review*, the *New England Review*, and the *Missouri Review*. It was also anthologized in *Prize Stories: The O. Henry Awards*, *Best American Short Stories*, *Best American Catholic Short Stories*, and *Bottom of the Ninth: Great Contemporary Baseball Short Stories*. Deaver taught in the English Department at Rollins College and was permanent writer in residence there. He was also on the fiction faculty in the Spalding University brief residency MFA program.

GREG DOWNS has been the least successful high school varsity basketball coach in Tennessee, the editor of a muckraking weekly newspaper on Chicago's South Side, a karaoke performer profiled in the *Boston Phoe-*

nix, and a reporter on the tail of a fugitive cult leader. A graduate of Yale University, the Iowa Writers' Workshop, and the University of Pennsylvania, he is currently a professor of history at the University of California, Davis. Along with the Flannery O'Connor award–winning *Spit Baths*, he is the author of three books of history and coauthor of the National Park Service's first theme study on Reconstruction, which helped lead to the creation of the first-ever National Park site devoted to Reconstruction at Beaufort, South Carolina. Downs's stories have appeared in such publications as *Glimmer Train, Meridian, Chicago Reader*, and *Sycamore Review*.

AMINA GAUTIER is the author of *At-Risk*, which won the 2010 Flannery O'Connor Award for Short Fiction. She is the author of two other award-winning short story collections, *The Loss of All Lost Things* and *Now We Will Be Happy*. She was the 2018 recipient of the PEN/Malamud Award for Excellence in the Short Story. Her work has appeared in the anthologies *Best African American Fiction* and *New Stories from the South* and in numerous literary journals including the *Antioch Review, North American Review*, the *Iowa Review*, the *Kenyon Review*, and the *Southern Review*.

JACQUELIN GORMAN, Flannery O'Connor Award winner in 2012 for *The Viewing Room*, teaches creative writing at Stevenson University in Baltimore, Maryland. She previously published a memoir, *The Seeing Glass* (1997), and is currently writing a collection of personal essays.

TOM KEALEY is the author of *Thieves I've Known*, which received the 2012 Flannery O'Connor Award for Short Fiction. He is also the author of *The Creative Writing MFA Handbook*. His stories have appeared in *Best American Nonrequired Reading, Glimmer Train, Story Quarterly, Prairie Schooner*, and the *San Francisco Chronicle*. His nonfiction has appeared in *Poets and Writers* and *The Writer*. He received his MFA in creative writing from the University of Massachusetts, Amherst, where he received the Distinguished Teaching Award. Tom has taught creative writing at Stanford University since 2003.

PETER LASALLE, 2006 Flannery O'Connor Award for Short Fiction winner for *Tell Borges If You See Him*, is the author of eight previous books, including novels and short story collections—most recently *Sleeping Mask: Fictions* and *The City at Three P.M.: Writing, Reading, and Travel-*

ing. His fiction and essays have been selected for several award anthologies, including *Best American Short Stories*, *Best American Mystery Stories*, *Best American Fantasy*, *Best American Travel Writing*, *Sports Best Short Stories*, *Best of the West*, and *Prize Stories: The O. Henry Awards*. He lives in Austin, Texas, where he is a member of the creative writing faculty at the University of Texas, and Narragansett, in his native Rhode Island.

KIRSTEN SUNDBERG LUNSTRUM is the author of *What We Do with the Wreckage*, which won the 2017 Flannery O'Connor Award for Short Fiction. She is also the author of two other collections of short fiction, *This Life She's Chosen* and *Swimming with Strangers*. Her short fiction and essays have appeared widely in journals, including *One Story*, the *American Scholar*, *Willow Springs*, and *Southern Humanities Review*. She is also a recipient of a PEN/O. Henry Prize and teaches creative writing and literature.

T. M. MCNALLY is the author of *Low Flying Aircraft*, which won the 1990 Flannery O'Connor Award for Short Fiction. He is the author of six works of fiction. His stories have appeared in *Conjunctions*, *DoubleTake*, and *Prize Stories: The O. Henry Awards*. He teaches in the Department of English at Arizona State University.

GINA OCHSNER is the author of *The Necessary Grace to Fall*, which received the 2001 Flannery O'Connor Award for Short Fiction. Her stories have appeared in such publications as the *Bellingham Review*, *Image*, the *New Yorker*, *Tin House*, *Iron Horse Review*, and the *Kenyon Review*, and they have received numerous awards, including the Ruth Hindman Foundation Prize, the Raymond Carver Prize, and the Chelsea Award for Short Fiction. She is the author of *The Hidden Letters of Velta B*, *The Russian Dreambook of Color and Flight*, and *Pleased to Be Otherwise*, among other books.

LORI OSTLUND's first collection of stories, *The Bigness of the World*, received the 2008 Flannery O'Connor Award for Short Fiction, the California Book Award for First Fiction, and the Edmund White Debut Fiction Award. It was shortlisted for the William Saroyan International Prize for Writing, was a Lambda finalist, and was named a Notable Book by the Short Story Prize. Her stories have appeared in the *Best American Short Stories*, the *PEN/O. Henry Prize Stories*, *ZYZZYVA*, the *Georgia Review*, the *Kenyon Review*, and the *New England Review*, among other publications. In 2009, Lori received a Rona Jaffe Foundation Award. She is the author of the novel *After the Parade* and lives in San Francisco.

MELISSA PRITCHARD is the author of eleven books, including a biography and a collection of essays. Her first short story collection, *Spirit Seizures*, won the 1986 Flannery O'Connor Award for Short Fiction, the Carl Sandburg Award, and the James Phelan Award from the San Francisco Foundation, and it was named a *New York Times* Editor's Choice and Notable Book of the Year. A five-time winner of *Pushcart* and O. Henry Prizes and consistently cited in *Best American Short Stories*, Melissa has also published both fiction and non-fiction in literary journals, anthologies, textbooks, and magazines such as the *Paris Review*, *Ploughshares*, *A Public Space*, *Conjunctions*, *Agni*, *Ecotone*, the *Gettysburg Review*, the *Oprah Magazine*, the *Nation*, the *New York Times*, and the *Chicago Tribune*, among others. She was named the 2016 Marguerite and Lamar Smith Fellow at the Carson McCullers Center for Writers and Musicians in Columbus, Georgia, where she now lives and writes.

HUGH SHEEHY is the author of *The Invisibles*, which won the 2011 Flannery O'Connor Award for Short Fiction. His stories have appeared in such publications as *Five Points*, the *Cincinnati Review*, the *Kenyon Review*, *Glimmer Train*, the *Antioch Review*, *Crazyhorse*, and *Copper Nickel*. He teaches creative writing and literature at Ramapo College of New Jersey.

DAVID WALTON is the author of *Evening Out*, one of the two collections to receive the Flannery O'Connor Award for Short Fiction in the year of its inauguration, 1982. He is also the author of *Ride*, a novel, and another collection of short stories, *Waiting in Line*. He lives in Pittsburgh and is retired from teaching literature and composition at the University of Pittsburgh.

THE FLANNERY O'CONNOR AWARD
FOR SHORT FICTION

DAVID WALTON, *Evening Out*

LEIGH ALLISON WILSON, *From the Bottom Up*

SANDRA THOMPSON, *Close-Ups*

SUSAN NEVILLE, *The Invention of Flight*

MARY HOOD, *How Far She Went*

FRANÇOIS CAMOIN, *Why Men Are Afraid of Women*

MOLLY GILES, *Rough Translations*

DANIEL CURLEY, *Living with Snakes*

PETER MEINKE, *The Piano Tuner*

TONY ARDIZZONE, *The Evening News*

SALVATORE LA PUMA, *The Boys of Bensonhurst*

MELISSA PRITCHARD, *Spirit Seizures*

PHILIP F. DEAVER, *Silent Retreats*

GAIL GALLOWAY ADAMS, *The Purchase of Order*

CAROLE L. GLICKFELD, *Useful Gifts*

ANTONYA NELSON, *The Expendables*

NANCY ZAFRIS, *The People I Know*

DEBRA MONROE, *The Source of Trouble*

ROBERT ABEL, *Ghost Traps*

T. M. MCNALLY, *Low Flying Aircraft*

ALFRED DEPEW, *The Melancholy of Departure*

DENNIS HATHAWAY, *The Consequences of Desire*

RITA CIRESI, *Mother Rocket*

DIANNE NELSON OBERHANSLY, *A Brief History
of Male Nudes in America*

CHRISTOPHER MCILROY, *All My Relations*

ALYCE MILLER, *The Nature of Longing*

CAROL LEE LORENZO, *Nervous Dancer*

C. M. MAYO, *Sky over El Nido*

WENDY BRENNER, *Large Animals in Everyday Life*

PAUL RAWLINS, *No Lie Like Love*

HARVEY GROSSINGER, *The Quarry*

HA JIN, *Under the Red Flag*

ANDY PLATTNER, *Winter Money*

FRANK SOOS, *Unified Field Theory*

MARY CLYDE, *Survival Rates*

KIRSTEN SUNDBERG LUNSTRUM, *What We Do with the Wreckage*

COLETTE SARTOR, *Once Removed*

PATRICK EARL RYAN, *If We Were Electric*

ANNIVERSARY ANTHOLOGIES

TENTH ANNIVERSARY

The Flannery O'Connor Award: Selected Stories,
EDITED BY CHARLES EAST

FIFTEENTH ANNIVERSARY

Listening to the Voices:
Stories from the Flannery O'Connor Award,
EDITED BY CHARLES EAST

THIRTIETH ANNIVERSARY

Stories from the Flannery O'Connor Award:
A 30th Anniversary Anthology: The Early Years,
EDITED BY CHARLES EAST

Stories from the Flannery O'Connor Award:
A 30th Anniversary Anthology: The Recent Years,
EDITED BY NANCY ZAFRIS

THEMATIC ANTHOLOGIES

Hold That Knowledge: Stories about Love
from the Flannery O'Connor Award for Short Fiction,
EDITED BY ETHAN LAUGHMAN

The Slow Release: Stories about Death
from the Flannery O'Connor Award for Short Fiction,
EDITED BY ETHAN LAUGHMAN

Rituals to Observe: Stories about Holidays
from the Flannery O'Connor Award for Short Fiction,
EDITED BY ETHAN LAUGHMAN

Spinning Away from the Center: Stories about
Homesickness and Homecoming
from the Flannery O'Connor Award for Short Fiction,

EDITED BY ETHAN LAUGHMAN

Good and Balanced: Stories about Sports
from the Flannery O'Connor Award for Short Fiction,
EDITED BY ETHAN LAUGHMAN

CPSIA information can be obtained
at www.ICGtesting.com
Printed in the USA
LVHW041650081121
702781LV00016B/2645

9 780820 358697